W9-DDZ-672

## *"Why do you keep running away from me?" John asked.*

Aurora hugged her arms close to her body. "I don't know. I just know I feel all mixed-up inside whenever I'm with you. And that scares me."

"I don't want you to be afraid." He took her hand. "I've done everything I can think of to prove that I've changed, but you keep building walls faster than I can tear them down."

Slowly he brought her hand to his mouth and brushed a kiss across the tender center of her palm. She tried to tug her hand from his grasp, but his fingers tightened just enough to hold her.

"I don't love you anymore," she said.

He turned his head to kiss her wrist. "You want me. Admit it."

"No. I stopped wanting you when I stopped loving you."

His smile was slow, sensuous, and all the more compelling because it was tinged with sadness. "You can tell yourself you've forgotten how good it was for us, but I'll help you remember."

Dear Reader,

This month brings more excitement your way, starting with Emilie Richards's *The Way Back Home*, the sequel to last month's *Runaway*. Rosie Jensen has taken on another name and begun another life, hoping to be safe from her past. But trouble has a way of catching up to people, and only Grady Clayton—a man who has a lot to lose himself if the truth about Rosie is ever revealed—is strong enough both to love her and to keep her safe.

Paula Detmer Riggs returns us to New Mexico's Santa Ysabel pueblo in *A Lasting Promise*, a book that will bring tears amidst the smiles. Maura Seger is back after too long a time with *Painted Lady*, an intriguing mystery set amongst the beauties of Block Island. And Silhouette Desire favorite Naomi Horton makes her second appearance in the line with *In Safekeeping*.

In months to come look for Linda Howard, Barbara Faith, Emilie Richards (with *Fugitive*, a follow-up to her current duo) and more of your favorites to keep the fires burning here at Silhouette Intimate Moments.

Leslie J. Wainger
Senior Editor and Editorial Coordinator

# A Lasting Promise

## PAULA DETMER RIGGS

*Silhouette Intimate Moments*

Published by Silhouette Books New York

**America's Publisher of Contemporary Romance**

**SILHOUETTE BOOKS**
300 East 42nd St., New York, N.Y. 10017

ISBN: 0-373-07344-5

First Silhouette Books printing July 1990

Printed in the U.S.A.

**Books by Paula Detmer Riggs**

Silhouette Intimate Moments

## PAULA DETMER RIGGS

discovers material for her writing in her varied life experiences. During her first five years of marriage to a naval officer, she lived in nineteen different locations on the West Coast, gaining familiarity with places as diverse as San Diego and Seattle. While working at a historical site in San Diego she wrote, directed and narrated fashion shows, and became fascinated with the early history of California.

She writes romances because "I think we all need an escape from the high-tech pressures that face us every day, and I believe in happy endings. Isn't that why we keep trying, in spite of all the roadblocks and disappointments along the way?"

For Lucille and Sam Riggs.
Thank you.

# Prologue

*Santa Ysabel Pueblo, New Mexico*

The night was hot, but John Olvera had no more sweat to cool his blistered skin. He stumbled into the dark shadow of the ruins and slowly sank to his knees.

The gray mist hovering between the crumbling walls beckoned, promising relief from the thirst and heat and pain that had been his constant companions for days now. He fought for consciousness, refusing to give in to the seductive numbness.

In the silence he could hear, as well as feel, the rasping agony of his breathing. His eyes stung with weariness, and his mouth was filled with the dust he could no longer spit out.

The moon was full, the time when his journey must be completed. Beyond the walls of the Ancient Place he could see the pueblo where the elders of the Santa Ysabel People waited with the cleansing water.

He had done all that the ancients had ordained. For fourteen days he had walked grueling miles alone, wearing only the ritual breechcloth and carrying only a knife and a skin bag of water that had lasted less than six days.

Calling on the survival ways of the Old Ones, he had found enough water and killed enough rabbits and lizards to keep himself alive. In the heat of the day when the sun had been merciless over his head, he had rested in the scant shade. And then, too soon, he had wakened to walk through the wild canyons alone, saying the sacred words of the Seeking Way over and over until he had no more voice.

Now he had no more strength. His bare feet were bloody and raw. The burning muscles of his legs would no longer support him. A numbing coldness came over him. But deep inside, his longing was like a burning brand, hurting. Always hurting.

A faint breeze brushed his hot cheek, and he opened his eyes. Above his head the moon was dipping low toward the horizon. In a few hours the People would find his body. But he no longer cared.

He had failed her, and she had left him. Without her, his life had no meaning.

A light shimmering whiter than the moonlight rose against the shadowed wall in front of him. An ethereal form took shape, swaying in front of his weary eyes like the delicate branches of a cottonwood in full flower. She was the spirit called Woman-of-Us-All, the legendary mother of his people.

Her smile was gentle, her eyes wise and soft with compassion. Was she a vision? The creation of a dying man's delirium?

He ran a bruised and dirty hand over his eyes, then blinked. The woman was still there, as divinely beautiful as the legend promised.

Holding out her hand, she spoke to him in a soft voice, using the secret birth name that only he and his mother knew. *Warrior Who Fights Alone, what is it that you seek?*

"To bring my wife back to me," he whispered in the simple language he had all but forgotten.

The vision grew brighter until he was enveloped in light.

*The woman of your heart has a pure and loving soul. She wants only to be loved.*

A trembling began deep inside him, growing stronger with each shuddering breath he took.

"I don't know love." Every word was an agony of sound in the silence.

*You have hardened your heart in order to walk in the world of the white man with pride and dignity. Love cannot flow from a stone, Warrior Who Fights Alone.*

"Tell me, Mother. Tell me what to do."

The vision wavered in front of his eyes like a gossamer veil. *If you truly seek to love the woman of your heart, you must first become a man worthy of being loved.* Woman-of-Us-All smiled at him in benediction, then moved into the fog until she was only a blur.

He swayed, and his body grew heavy. He had tried, but the distance he had yet to go was too difficult to travel.

Out of the blackness of his mind another face formed until he could see each delicate feature. Her smile was radiant, like a summer sunrise. Her eyes, soft as the delicate gray sheen of early dawn, filled him with peace. He knew her face as intimately as he knew his own. For months he had been haunted by her wherever he went.

She seemed clothed in sunshine, her soft hair surrounding her face in a silken frame, her small perfect form enticing him closer.

His tired body longed to bathe in that shining warmth. His arms ached to hold her close until the two of them were no longer separate, but one.

Reaching out his hand, he struggled to say the words of love that would bring her back to him, but the words wouldn't come. Her welcoming smile faltered, and a lone tear slid down her soft cheek.

John cried out, but the light dimmed, and her luminous beauty faded. He had driven her away again. He was alone.

He dropped his head to his chest and stared at the hard stony ground. Behind him stretched a ragged line of bloody footprints. Ahead lay an endless mile, which must be traveled inch by inch.

Woman-of-Us-All had given him the answer he sought.

He would start over.

Somehow he would change the man he had been. Somehow he would learn to give instead of take.

And then he would go to her, the woman of his heart.

Whispering a plea for strength, he dropped his hands to the hot ground and began to crawl.

# Chapter 1

Aurora Davenport rolled the bright green clay into a long tube, then added two bits of red for eyes. "There you go, Miguelito," she told the wide-eyed little boy sitting next to her at the tiny table. *"Es una serpiente."*

Four-year-old Miguel giggled and curled the snake's tail into a menacing coil. Today was his first day at *Los Niños* Preschool, a Headstart day-care center located in one of the poorest sections of Dallas.

*"Es una serpiente cascabel.* Rattlesnake," he corrected in a solemn little voice.

"Aha, so it is." Aurora's soft, slow West Texas drawl was warm with praise, and her smile was bright with satisfaction. When she had first put the block of modeling clay into his hands, Miguel had been too timid to even look at her. But she had patiently guided his small hands until together they had made several fierce-looking snakes.

"This is just about the best darn rattler I've ever seen," she told him as she touched the snake's fat head.

Miguel ducked his head in shy pleasure. *"Gracias, Señorita* Rora."

*"De nada, Miguelito."* Aurora reached out to ruffle his coarse black hair.

Every Friday afternoon in this shabby building smelling of disinfectant and poster paint, Dr. Aurora Davenport, assistant professor of fine arts at Southern Methodist University, became Miss Rora, the Clay Lady.

Nothing interfered with those three hours that she considered the best part of each busy week. She had even juggled her teaching schedule to accommodate *Los Niños*.

"I'm all done, Miss Rora," called another small voice in accented English. "Come see what I made."

Four tables away Francie Gomez beckoned to Aurora with a small grimy hand. Black eyes flashing, the excited little girl bounced up and down in her chair so exuberantly Aurora was afraid the plastic seat would crack.

On the small table in front of Francie was a lumpy orange figure with four legs and a large, misshapen head. Aurora knew immediately that it was supposed to be an elephant. But then Francie always made elephants. Red ones, green ones, purple ones, and now an orange one.

Aurora murmured a few words of encouragement to Miguel, then stood up and brushed the clay from her short denim skirt. In her sandals she stood a scant inch over five feet, and her small body radiated the kind of energy that comes from an innate enthusiasm for life.

Her hair, a red so fiery it was almost copper, added to the air of vitality that had once made her the most popular cheerleader on the SMU varsity squad. Above an almost square chin inclined to stubbornness, her features were fine-boned and dusted with golden freckles that she had once tried to bleach away with lemon juice. Her eyes, a clear gray framed by golden lashes, showed her every thought, something that nearly drove her crazy when she was trying to act professorial.

"Let's all be quiet now, children," she said, raising her voice over the happy dissonance of fifteen shrill, little voices. "Francie has something to show us."

The chattering youngsters scattered, bumping and jostling each other until they found seats. Aurora pulled up a small chair and sat down next to Francie.

She waited until the noise diminished enough to hear herself think, then reached for the bright orange figure in front of her.

"I really do believe it's your very best elephant ever," she said after a moment's somber appraisal.

Francie beamed. "Look for the smile, Miss Rora," she pleaded in her thin, eager voice. "Okay?"

"Okay," Aurora answered solemnly, "but everyone has to be quiet or it won't work."

Several children left their chairs to come closer, and the others sat up straighter. All eyes were on Aurora as she ran her fingertips over Francie's elephant. Even with her eyes closed, she could feel the air of expectancy wrap round her.

"Finding the smile" was her way of encouraging the children to look within a piece of art to find the intangible meaning the artist had put there. The children loved this exaggerated, overly dramatic ritual as much as she did. But while they were having fun, she was also patiently teaching them to use art to express pent-up feelings.

Aurora opened her eyes and gave the waiting little girl an encouraging smile that trapped a wealth of compassion in the soft corners. "Francie, elephant's smile feels sad to us today. Is she unhappy about something?"

Francie's eyes grew solemn, and her mouth drooped. "Uh-huh. My daddy lost his job, 'n' now me'n my brothers and sisters can't have ice cream no more 'til he gets a new one."

Aurora handed Francie the elephant. "I bet you're feeling sad, too, and that's okay. But you know your daddy still loves you, even though he can't give you ice cream right now. Just like you love Elephant."

Francie hugged the lumpy figure and her face brightened. "I forgot."

"I think that's a lot better than ice cream, don't you?"

The little girl's head bobbed up and down. "Uh-huh. Lots."

Aurora tugged gently on Francie's silky ponytail, hoping her smile covered the rush of emotion she could feel on her face. With her black hair and small square chin, Francie made Aurora think of her baby who had died at birth and the child she might have grown into.

Uncrossing her legs, she started to get to her feet, but a little boy with Vietnamese features and a shy smile clutched at her skirt.

"If you please, Miss Rora," he said softly in halting English, "tell story 'bout Clay Boy."

The other children began speaking and shouting at once, and Aurora held up her hand. "Shh. If you want to hear the story, you have to put on your best listening faces."

A hush descended, punctuated by giggles. Aurora pushed her thick bangs away from her face, and let her gaze touch the small faces turned toward her. When everyone had settled down, she pulled Nguyen onto her knee and rested her chin lightly on his dark head.

"Once upon a time," she said in a hushed tone, "when the earth was brand new, there lived a little boy who was always asking questions. 'Why does the sun shine, Mama?' he asked. 'And why do birds sing?'"

"'Because God smiles on them with love and that's the way they smile on us,' Mama answered. Smiles were good, the little boy knew, because when his mama smiled at him, he felt safe and warm and very happy. And so he smiled back.

"But one day, after a hard rain, he went out to play in the mud that his mama called clay. It was fun squeezing the thick wet earth between his fingers. He loved the clay and so he smiled, waiting for the clay to smile back in its own special way, but nothing happened. The clay didn't shine brightly like the sun to show its love. It didn't chirp like the birds or purr like his pet kitten. It didn't do anything.

"Puzzled, the little boy ran to his mother. 'I've tried and tried, but I can't see the clay's smile.'"

"Mama took him by the hand and led him to the muddy puddle where she bade him put his hands on the clay again. 'First, you must put some of the love you carry inside you into the clay,' Mama told the boy with her best smile, 'just like God puts his love into the sun. In that way your love will make the clay smile in return.'

"Mama pressed the boy's hands into the clay. As he waited, the earth grew wonderfully warm under his fingers. 'I feel it,' he shouted, and Mama nodded. 'Now the clay will do whatever you want, and it will be beautiful. That is how the clay smiles for you. Because...'" Aurora paused, holding up her hand like a conductor, and the children shouted in unison, "'...all good things start with love.'"

As the others clapped in boisterous approval, Aurora brushed a gentle hand over Nguyen's shiny hair. "Next time you can tell the story," she told him before giving him a quick hug.

She stood. "Okay, boys and girls," she said, clapping her hands. "Nap time. Let's be just as quick as we can be, so Miss Sofia doesn't scold."

Sofia Pedrorena was the director of *Los Niños* and Aurora's best friend. While Aurora worked with the children alone on Friday afternoons, Sofia took a much needed break and wrote her weekly reports in a cramped cubicle partitioned off from the rest of the room.

Aurora waited until the children were settled on the floor mats, then turned off the overhead lights and stood for a moment at the back of the room, watching. A lump formed in her throat at the thought of having to say goodbye to Francie and the others for the summer.

Although she was looking forward to spending the next three months in Mazatlan working on the textbook she was writing, she would miss her time with the little ones.

A lilting voice calling her name interrupted her sad thoughts and she turned her head to see Sofia watching her from the door to the makeshift office.

"Hey, don't look so sad, *amiga*. They'll still be here in September."

Aurora heard the gently chiding note in Sofia's voice and smiled. "I know, but it's . . . hard."

Sofia's brow wrinkled in sympathy. "I'll make a fresh pot of coffee. You look like you could use a cup before you go."

"Could I ever!"

"Five minutes, then." Sofia ducked back in the office.

The two women had met four years ago on the SMU campus when Aurora had been finishing her doctoral dissertation and Sofia had been working on her master's in primary education.

Newly divorced at twenty-nine, Aurora had been looking for a roommate. Sofia, a few years older, had just left her second husband. The two women had shared a small apartment until two years ago, when Sofia had remarried and Aurora had managed to buy a condominium closer to campus.

Humming softly to herself, Aurora returned the unused clay to the bin, then wiped the tables and neatly arranged the mismatched chairs. By the time she stepped into the office, Sofia had a steaming cup of black coffee waiting.

Aurora stepped over the piles of papers and supplies covering much of the floor space, and flopped into the folding chair next to the cluttered desk.

"Lord, it feels good to sit down in a regular chair," she muttered, arching her back to relieve the stiffness. She took a sip of coffee, then kicked off her leather thongs and wiggled her small, brightly tipped toes.

Sofia raised a thin black eyebrow. "Busy day?"

Aurora ran her hand through her short curls. Her hair tended to friz when the humidity was high, and Dallas was in the midst of an early summer heat spell.

"Finals week is always a madhouse, especially for someone like me who's a little ragged in the paperwork department. Thank goodness I've given my last exam and graded my last paper for this year."

"I'm going to miss you," Sofia said with an exaggerated sigh. "The last time you took time off, I nearly lost my mind, trying to find the damn smile in the clay. You're the only one who knows how to do that particular feat of magic."

Aurora laughed. "I'll send you and the kids lots of postcards so you won't forget me."

"Good idea. I'll explain to the kids that Miss Rora's on the beach, fighting off those rich *turistas gringos*."

"Forget the *turistas*, rich or otherwise," Aurora shot back, brushing bits of orange clay from her sleeve where Francie's small fingers had clutched.

"You're right," Sofia agreed solemnly, her exotic black eyes assuming a wicked look of calculation. "It's better to go for the sexy locals—you know, *muy macho*." She smacked her lips and raised her thin brows. "Believe me, you'll come back a happier woman."

Aurora shook her head. "I'll come back a *dead* woman, if I try to do all the things you keep telling me to do."

"Okay, okay, be stubborn, *amiga*. I lived with you long enough to know you never change your mind once it's made up. But this time I think you'll regret it. A woman who loves life as much as you do shouldn't be living like a nun."

"I'm not," Aurora grumbled. "I'm just . . . particular."

Sofia chuckled. "Yeah, I know. The guy has to be as gorgeous as Tom Cruise, as sexy as Tom Selleck and as perfect as the Pope."

"Oh, lord," Aurora mumbled.

"Him, too."

Aurora laughed and tossed a stuffed parrot at Sofia's head.

Her friend ducked, then shoved aside a stack of folders and rested both elbows on the desktop.

"How come, *amiga*, if you're a potter, you're spending all your time on this book you're writing?" She rested her chin in a cupped palm. "Shouldn't you be, uh, potting some, too?"

Aurora felt a thud in her stomach, but she forced a breezy smile. "I will, as soon as the book is done. But I have to publish soon, or I can kiss my chance at tenure goodbye."

"I thought you promised that gallery downtown some new pieces in the fall."

Aurora's smile faded. "I have time. They still have a few left to sell."

Some she would never give up, like the Brazilian Tapajoz. The perfect replica of the small primitive pot meant too much to her to ever let it go, no matter how much money it might fetch.

"Do you have a title yet?" Sofia persisted. "For this long-awaited tome, I mean?"

*"Pre-Columbian Ceremonial Vessels: Their Origins and Uses."* Aurora grinned, and a small dimple appeared above one corner of her mouth. "Catchy, isn't it?"

"Wonderful." Sofia shook her head, her expression dry.

Aurora stretched out her legs. Years of gymnastics as a girl had given her strong calves and sleek thighs, and her ankles were still trim. She thought about the new bikini already packed in her suitcase and wondered if she would have the nerve to wear it in a place where most of the men were on the prowl, just as Sofia had said. She was too busy for a summer fling, even if she were so inclined. Which, she decided, she wasn't.

"I've finished the research, thank God," she said with a sigh. "All I can do, anyway. I have plenty of pictures and reams of notes. Now I have to put it all together in some kind of readable order."

Much of her information on the more obscure artifacts had been gathered firsthand when she'd been married and living in South America with John Olvera.

Bitterness gathered like acid in her stomach as she thought about her ex-husband. In seven years of marriage they had lived in five different countries. Each change of station had taken him one rung higher in his obsessive drive toward the upper echelons of the foreign service. Their last duty station had been in San Sebastian. As far as she knew, John was still there. After their divorce, she hadn't cared to find out.

Sofia leaned back and rested her feet on a small carton of supplies. "If anyone can make those old pots sound interesting, you can, but it sure seems like a lot of work to me."

Aurora's eyes flashed. "Oh, but it isn't," she exclaimed. Her gray eyes mirrored the vibrant note in her words. "I love writing about those old pots. Some of them go back centuries. Some like . . . like the Santa Ysabel are so old no one knows *when* they were made."

Sofia frowned. "Santa Ysabel? Where have I heard that name before?"

Aurora's good humor disappeared as swiftly as a bubble in a windstorm. "That's the name of the pueblo in New Mexico where I met John."

Sofia's look of puzzlement turned to one of sympathy. "Yeah, that's right. I remember. You were collecting broken pots or something."

Aurora looked down at her small hands. Twelve years ago they had been blistered and sunburned from the long hours of digging in the hard, red New Mexico dirt. The nails that were now well-kept and tipped with clear polish had been broken and caked with grit.

She'd been in the obscure pueblo less than a week when she'd heard the stories about Johnson Olvera, the first of his people to attend an Ivy League university and the first to be recruited by the foreign service.

One hot morning Aurora had been marking potsherds in the shadow of the ruins, when a young man riding a powerful dun-colored mustang had reined up and asked for a drink from her canteen. Even before he'd introduced himself, she'd known who he was.

His face had been a study in copper, angular and harshly formed like the rough majestic mountains of his land, but his eyes were the warmest brown she'd ever seen. Sitting easily in the well-used saddle like his warrior ancestors, his sweat-stained Stetson pushed to the back of his head, he had been the sexiest man she had ever met.

John had flirted with her in a voice that was more Princeton than pueblo, and she had found herself flirting back.

She'd nearly fallen off the rock where she'd been sitting when he had asked her to dinner. She could still see the way his grin had flashed in triumph when she'd blurted out her acceptance. They had been as unsuitable for each other as a hawk and a hummingbird, but that hadn't stopped her from falling in love.

Aurora forced a smile. "Actually, I was in my first year of grad school, working with an archeology team studying the ruins there. We were trying to identify different potters by the distinctive pattern each gouged into the clay. Like painters, each potter has a unique style."

"Forget the pots." Sofia flashed a seductive grin. "I liked the part where he came riding up like some conquering hero to sweep you off your feet." She rolled her eyes. "Dios, what a great story! Why didn't that ever happen to me?"

Aurora laughed, but there was little humor in the musical sound. "If it had, you'd still be divorced. John is all image and no heart."

Sofia sobered. "He really did a number on you, didn't he?"

Aurora sighed. She felt a sad sympathy for the poor love-struck girl she'd been then. Maybe if she hadn't been taught by her minister father to see only the good in people, she might have seen the flaw in John right away.

"I thought he loved me," she said, her well-bred drawl taking on an edge of bitterness. "When I found out he didn't, I thought it was my fault. That I wasn't pretty enough or smart enough or sexy enough. It took me a lot of pain and soul-searching before I realized that John can't love anyone or anything as much as he loves his career. He's like a machine geared for success. Emotions are useless to him. He didn't even cry at his daughter's funeral."

"Has he married again?"

Aurora shrugged. The last time she'd heard from John had been through his attorney. Though not a wealthy man, her ex-husband had offered her a generous divorce settlement, more than enough to see her through graduate school, but she'd refused. Her pride hadn't allowed her to take money from a man who hadn't loved her. It would have felt like charity.

"I expect so," she said, her voice weighted with disinterest. "John is an extremely virile man. I can't imagine him going without a woman for long." Even when they'd been married, women, young and old, married or single, had responded to him in ways that had made her grit her teeth.

Sofia looked interested. "Was he unfaithful?"

Aurora's eyes took on a cynical cast. "Oh, no. An indiscretion would have damaged his career. Every decision he made was based on self-interest. I'm sure that's why he picked me to be his wife—because I knew what fork to use and how to pour tea and make inane conversation with a wide-eyed, innocent look." She grimaced when she remembered the lessons in deportment her genteel mother had instilled into her tomboy daughter, little knowing what disaster those lessons would lead to someday.

She slipped her feet into her sandals and stood, then carried her cup to the small sink in the corner, rinsing it before returning it to the shelf.

"If he *is* married again, I'm sure she has impeccable social credentials," Aurora said, going back to the desk. "John intends to be ambassador of a major country by the time he's fifty."

"And will he succeed?"

Aurora's brief smile was mocking and cold. "Absolutely. Men as self-centered and driven as John always get what they want, no matter who has to pay the price." She grabbed her briefcase and her purse from behind the desk where she had stored them. "Much as I would love to chat about my *dear* ex-husband, I've got to run. I have a million things to do before my plane leaves Monday."

Sofia stood and they hugged.

"I'll call you before I go," Aurora said as she carefully navigated the obstacles in her path.

"Great." Sofia worried her bottom lip with her teeth, looking like a woman trying to make up her mind. Finally she took a deep breath, then said softly, "I didn't mean to pry, *amiga*. But I worry about you sometimes."

Aurora stopped in mid-stride and stared at her. "Why on earth would you do that? I'm doing great. Terrific, in fact."

"Sure, with your career. But your personal life sucks."

Aurora started to speak, but Sofia cut her off. "Don't get all prickly on me. I'm just trying to say that you have so much love to give, and it kills me to see you bottle it up inside the way you do. The only time you allow yourself to let it out is with these kids. But they won't always be here." She drew breath, then added earnestly, "I guess I keep hoping you'll find a nice guy who needs to be loved as much as you need to love someone."

Aurora's face grew warm, and her heart beat unnaturally fast. "Don't include my ex-husband in your list of nice guys," she said as she gave Sofia a goodbye wave. "I wouldn't give John Olvera the time of day."


It sounded like an explosion, and it came from her office.

Aurora quickened her steps until she was nearly running down the wide corridor. She knew the sound of shattering pottery when she heard it.

For insurance purposes the more valuable pieces of her collection of pre-Columbian pots were already stored for the summer in the vault downstairs, but she had asked LuAnn DiMato, her secretary, to pack the copies that she and her students had made so that she could take them with her to Mazatlan.

Please, please, please, don't let it be the Tapajoz Ceremonial, she prayed silently as she wrenched open the door to her office. As soon as she saw LuAnn's white-as-chalk face, she knew that her beloved pot was gone. Smashed to bits, by the sound of it.

"I'm sorry, Dr. Davenport," the young woman whispered in a choked voice. "It . . . it just slipped."

Aurora wanted to scream. Instead she inhaled deeply, letting the air fill her until the pressure in her lungs blocked out the need to lash out.

Slowly releasing the trapped air, she fought the sick, helpless feeling that began to burn inside her. The feeling intensified when she saw the jagged shards littering the floor in front of her desk.

She dropped her things by the door and stepped into the room. In her mind she saw Tapajoz as it had been seconds before—a starkly simple bowl with a wide ruffled mouth and a soft brown patina beneath the thin glaze. It had been the best work she'd ever done.

She bit off a sigh, then returned her gaze to her assistant's shocked face. "Are you okay?" she asked, hoping that her tone was forgiving. "Did you cut yourself?"

"No, no, I'm fine," LuAnn said in a wooden voice. Her eyes pleaded with Aurora to understand.

Aurora forced a light note as she said teasingly, "That's good. Don't tell my students, but I'm lousy in an emergency."

LuAnn's stricken expression relaxed slightly. "I'll just clean this up, and—"

"No!" Aurora interrupted, then winced as her voice came out too fast and too harsh. "That is, uh, don't worry about it. Maintenance will do it."

"But Dr. Davenport—"

She forced a casual note. "No buts, Lu. The semester's over, and we survived. The Tapajoz is gone. No big deal."

LuAnn didn't look convinced. "Are you sure? I'd be happy to pay for it."

"Lu, forget it. Really. It's only a pot, one that I made a long time ago. It wasn't worth more than the price of the clay."

Without waiting for an answer, Aurora crossed to her desk and opened the top drawer to take out a sealed envelope. "This is a thank you for all the hard work you've done for me this semester," she said, handing LuAnn the envelope. Inside was her personal check for one hundred dollars.

"I remember what it's like, trying to work and keep up the grades, so I want you to take a week off and have some fun before you start your summer job." She heard the thinness of her voice, and wondered if LuAnn did, too. Right now she didn't care. She just wanted to be alone.

Pale eyes widening with surprise, LuAnn thanked her, then added softly, "I surely do appreciate this. And…everything else you've done for me this year. All my friends are jealous 'cause I have such a super boss." She started to tear open the envelope, but Aurora stopped her.

"Open it later, okay?"

"Yes ma'am. And thanks again." LuAnn tucked the envelope into the back pocket of her shorts. With one last regretful look at the shattered pot, she grabbed her tote bag from the chair by the desk and made for the door.

"Oh, I almost forgot," she said, turning back. "While you were out, an express letter came for you. I put it on your desk." She eyed the jumble of paper littering the large desktop. "You want me to find it for you?"

"Did it look important?"

LuAnn shrugged. "I don't know. It looked personal, so I didn't open it."

Aurora glanced at the paperwork still to be done and sighed. "Don't worry about it. I'll take care of it along with the rest of this mess. See you in September."

"On the fifteenth, eight o'clock." LuAnn waved, and then was gone.

Aurora stared at the open doorway for a long moment, deliberately allowing the heavy stillness of the huge building to settle around her. The air was thick with the heat of the afternoon sun beating against the walls, and smelled of floor wax and old books. The cabinet shelves looked forlorn without the bright colors of her pots.

"Show Aurora Davenport a pot she's never seen before, and within five minutes she can tell you the date it was made, where, and by whom," the Dean loved to tell VIP visitors when he brought them to see her collection. "She can even make a copy that would pass any test but carbon dating. The woman is amazing."

"Amazing?" she mused aloud. No, not amazing. She had just wanted to be the best. The best potter, the best wife, the best mother.

Her heartbeat faltered, then took off. In the end she hadn't been any of those things.

But that was ancient history. She had made a new life for herself, a better one, because all the choices were hers now.

Setting her jaw, she bent down and picked up a large curving fragment. It still carried the distinctive black stripe of the Tapajoz tribe and felt cool against her palm.

Had it really been five years since she had walked the banks of the Amazon, looking for just the right clay? she wondered with a sigh. Sometimes it seemed like a lifetime.

Aurora smiled, and her smile tasted bitter on her lips. The smile faded, and she knew that her eyes would be shadowed and unforgiving, just as they had been then.

Using her fingertips, she gently wiped the clay dust from the glaze, then ran a thumb over the smooth surface. The clay had been warm from the heat of the blazing equatorial sun when she had dug it from the riverbank. And when she had worked the pale, thick earth, it had been wet and slippery from her tears.

She'd been twenty-eight and waiting for her divorce to become final when she had tried to escape the pain by going off alone to live with the primitve Tapajoz.

She'd had little money, no job prospects and a half-finished doctoral dissertation that needed more effort and concentration than she could give it.

"The woman who walks in sorrow," the chief had called her. And he'd been right.

Night after night, lying alone in her hut, she had stared at the tightly packed palm fronds over her head with only the lonely cries of the night birds and the sound of her own breathing to keep her company.

Her baby was dead, and her marriage was over. Her illusions of love had been in ruins around her. Nothing mattered to her then, not her work, not her life. When she'd felt anything at all it had been hatred—for John and his broken promises.

Numb with grief, she had thought a lot about walking into the jungle alone. She would simply disappear. Her parents would grieve for her, but they had each other. John wouldn't care. He had his precious career.

Then one day, she had dug her fingers into a pile of moist clay and had begun to work. Hour after hour she'd molded the smooth, cool raw material, never resting, not stopping to eat or drink, her body shaking with the pain she had kept inside her for months.

By the time she had finished, she'd made nearly a dozen pots. With each touch of her fingers she had put her grief and her disillusionment into the clay. By the time she'd fallen into an exhausted sleep on that long-ago night she had no longer loved John Olvera.

"Okay, Aurora, no more moping around," she muttered. "Big girls don't cry." She tossed the shard into the trash basket next to the desk. Working quickly she gathered the rest of the pieces until the bottom of the basket was filled.

When she finished, she got slowly to her feet and flexed her tired shoulders. She would take a minute to go through her mail, then call maintenance to help her carry the boxes LuAnn had packed down to her small station wagon.

Humming tonelessly, she began sorting the papers littering the blotter into neat piles. "Now where did Lu put that express envelope?" she muttered. "Oh, here it is."

The hiss of her indrawn breath cut into the lazy summer quiet. Her mouth went dry. She tried to swallow, but there was a knot constricting her throat.

She blinked, but the slashing letters still marched across the envelope. Written in black ink with a wide-nibbed pen, the bold strokes were hard to ignore, like the man who had inscribed them. She dropped the large envelope as though touching it had blistered her fingers, and stared at the return address. *J. Olvera, Chamisa, New Mexico.*

Slowly, her knees bending stiffly, she sank into her chair and gripped the arms so tightly her short nails dug into the leather.

So John was back in the pueblo for one of his duty visits, she thought and then felt a brief, cynical smile touch her lips. How long would he stay this time? A week? Two? Certainly not more than that. A man on his way to the top in the diplomatic corps couldn't afford to take time off. She had learned that the hard way.

When she had gotten pregnant, she had wanted desperately to have her baby in the same hospital in El Paso where she had been born. John had agreed, promising to take a leave of absence two months before she was due so that he could be with her.

But when the time had come, he had been in the middle of important trade negotiations, so reluctantly she had flown to the States alone. John was to follow within a few days, but the negotiations dragged on, and he had postponed his return a second time.

Aurora had been disappointed, but he'd promised to be with her well before her due date. And John always kept his promises.

With her doctor's permission, she had driven to Santa Ysabel to visit John's mother for a few days while she waited.

The first pain had come just as she had turned into the narrow driveway leading to the old adobe ranch house that had been in Morningstar Olvera's family for generations.

There had been no telephone to summon help, and because Mrs. Olvera hadn't known how to drive, no way to get Aurora to the nearest hospital sixty miles away in Gallup.

John's mother had done her best, but the baby, six weeks early and too frail to survive without an incubator for long, had died in Aurora's arms. Her little girl hadn't even opened her eyes to look into her mother's face.

Aurora's chest tightened until she felt as though she were drowning. She forced herself to take a deep breath and then another.

Her hand reached for the envelope, then drew back, the sensitive fingers curling into the small palm. "This is silly," she muttered to her image reflected in the brass shade of the desk lamp. "Read the darn thing and get it over with."

As she heard her own voice, Aurora's generous mouth firmed into the no-nonsense line her first-year art history students had learned to fear.

With hands that trembled, she reached into the opened envelope and pulled out the contents. A soft exclamation of surprise whispered through her parted lips as an eight-by-ten glossy photograph of the famous Santa Ysabel polychrome caught the light.

Called simply the Santa Ysabel by worldwide art experts, the ageless pot was extremely rare. There were only five in existence. Three were in the hands of foreign collectors, locked away in climate-controlled vaults. The remaining two were owned by the People of Santa Ysabel.

Since the loss of the three to outsiders toward the end of the previous century, no one who was not a member of the Santa Ysabel tribe had been permitted access to the pueblo's prized treasures. Countless art experts and archaeologists had tried, but the Tribal Council had turned down all requests.

"My God, it's exquisite," she whispered, her voice carrying a vibrant note of awe. "I can't believe—"

Her voiced faltered as her gaze fastened on the writing at the bottom of the picture. *Once you said you'd give anything in the world to be able to study this. How about two months of your time?* The note was signed with a familiar bold *J*.

The slanting strokes blurred into a heavy black line as the meaning of the words slowly sank in. From the moment she had heard about the beautiful old pot, she had dreamed of touching it. As soon as she had stepped onto Santa Ysabel soil, the longing to feel the clay had become almost an obsession with her. She had yearned to feel its spirit, to learn its secrets, to touch the magic.

Once, when they had been home on leave, John had asked the Tribal Council to grant her permission to see the sacred treasure. But the old men had turned him down flat, explaining that the last white person to see the special pots had stolen three. Not even John's considerable skill at negotiation had convinced the elders to change their minds.

Her finger trembled as she traced the pot's graceful lines. The photograph was cool and slick, but the pot itself would be warm with life and satin-smooth from the hundreds of reverent hands that had stroked it.

The muffled sounds of the campus faded, until she was alone with the Santa Ysabel. No one, nothing else existed. Her heart thumped loudly, and somewhere inside her a pleasurable tension began to spread, as though some powerful force were calling to her.

Deep in her soul she longed to answer that call. What she wouldn't give to be able to feel the life in the clay, its warmth, its very soul.

And she had the time, she thought with rising excitement. Three months of summer vacation. All she had to do was make a few phone calls and—

What's the matter with me? she thought abruptly, coming out of her self-imposed trance. I must be out of my mind.

To see the Santa Ysabel, she would have to go back to the pueblo. To the place where her baby died. But that was the one thing she would never do.

Slowly, inexorably, her hand closed into an angry fist on the paper. "Never," she repeated aloud, staring at her whitening knuckles. "Never."

"Never say never, my love," murmured a deep voice from the doorway. "It'll get you into trouble every time."

It was John.

# Chapter 2

She knew she must have said his name. Or maybe she'd just thought it.

She couldn't seem to move.

He watched her from the doorway with those deep brown eyes that seemed to pick up the color of his surroundings even as they hid his thoughts. His hand was braced casually on the door frame, but the relaxed stance only seemed to emphasize the aura of power and confidence he carried easily on his broad shoulders.

She knew that he was several inches under six feet, but he seemed taller, and his body had a rawhide leanness that hadn't been there five years ago.

Beneath the brim of a plain brown Stetson, his unsmiling, almost stern features carried the stamp of the Spanish aristocrats who had come as conquerors and stayed as husbands and fathers. The pride etched into the angle of his square chin and the sturdy strength reflected in the thick muscles of his legs and arms had come from the men who had fought those arrogant conquerors to the last man.

For an instant she hadn't recognized him, so changed did he seem. His face, toughened in his youth by the hot New Mexico sun, bore new lines. The hollows under his high cheekbones had deepened almost to gauntness. His hair, always clipped short in the approved State Department style, now covered his collar. But his mouth hadn't changed. It still possessed the same sensuous fullness that used to give her such wild, sweet pleasure when he kissed her.

No, she thought in rising dismay. I don't want you here.

John Olvera watched the shock settle like a dark, angry shadow over Aurora's face. Beneath the dusting of freckles over her cheeks, she had gone so white he feared she might faint.

The woman he remembered always had roses in her cheeks and life in her eyes. She'd also had a smile that made his breath catch every time he'd seen it.

Silently he cursed the impulse that had brought him to her without a warning phone call. But he'd been afraid she would refuse to see him.

"Rory, are you all right?" He dropped his hand and stood watching her. "I didn't mean to upset you." He tensed, ready to catch her.

"I'm not upset."

Seeing the trembling of her soft mouth, John took a step forward, then stopped when she flinched. Please, my love, he told her silently. Just take it slow. We have plenty of time.

"Rory?"

"Don't call me that," she said sharply, not bothering to mask the bitterness that rose like a wave inside her. Her mouth was so dry it hurt to speak. "I hate that name."

He remembered the night he had given it to her. She had said that she loved him. "Do you hate the man who gave it to you?"

Somehow she managed a cool smile. "No, I don't hate you. Hating is a waste of energy." But she had tried to hate, hoping that the hating would take away the hurting. It hadn't.

"That's a start, anyway," he said, walking toward her. Instead of the three-piece suit she remembered, he wore a white shirt under an open vest of soft leather trimmed with silver conchs. The sleeves of his shirt had been rolled back to reveal forearms that were thick with hard-edged muscle and roped with tough sinew. Beneath the frayed edges of his jeans, his boots were trail-dusty and worn.

Aurora repressed a need to draw back from him. John had always been single-minded and determined, but this man seemed as tough as the rangy mesquite that dug its roots deep into the rocky land of his birth.

"How did you find me?"

John's face stilled at the rudeness in her tone, but his voice was calm when he answered. "I knew you taught at SMU because of the letters you wrote mother a few years back. You used university stationery. Your office number was on the envelope."

She picked up a pencil, then put it down. Her hands were unsteady. Now that the shock had passed, she was beginning to react. Her heart pounded so ferociously, she was afraid he could hear the beats. And her stomach was hot, as though he had plowed his fist into her.

"I take it you're in the area on annual leave."

"No, I live in Santa Ysabel now." He glanced at the empty chair by the desk. When she didn't ask him to sit down, he shrugged and sat down anyway. Turning sideways, he stretched out his long, muscular legs and crossed them at the ankles. "In fact, I'm head of the Tribal Council."

Her inhaled breath became a gasp. "You're what?"

At the note of wild disbelief in her voice, John felt himself smile inside. No matter what Rory did, she did it full out, without pretense. That had been one of the things he had admired most in her. That and the way she had made him laugh. Right now, however, it felt as though it would be a long time before he laughed again.

"Actually I've been tribal chairman for almost three years now."

Three years? Aurora stared at him, trying to imagine the John Olvera she knew living day after day in the drab, windswept pueblo where life was simple and unpretentious. There were no convenience stores, no restaurants, no medical facilities. Five years ago the plumbing had been primitive and there had been only one phone, at tribal headquarters. Jobs had been nonexistent, and the children often went hungry. As far as she knew, few of the residents had been to college, and none had achieved the kind of success John had.

"You told me you hated the pueblo," she said more abruptly than she intended. "You said anyone with any ambition at all would be a fool to stay there."

He removed the Stetson and dropped it onto the corner of the desk before absently smoothing his glossy black hair the way a man does when he's used to wearing a hat most of the time.

"I was wrong," he said. "I was wrong about a lot of things."

Her disbelief turned to shock. She had never once heard John admit that he'd been wrong. About anything.

"What about your career?" she demanded, leaning forward slightly to make her point the way she did when she dealt with a particularly difficult student. "In a few more years you would have had everything you wanted, or so you said, if I recall correctly."

John settled his wide shoulders more firmly against the back of the chair that now felt too small for his restless body. His gaze flicked over her face, then dropped to the nameplate on the desk.

Slowly he reached out to run a callused finger over the engraved letters of her last name, the name she had taken back after the divorce.

Assistant professor in only three years, he thought with a heavy feeling over his heart. He glanced at the framed diplomas and awards on the wall. She had done just fine without him. Better, in fact.

So why the hell did she need him?

He dropped his hand to his thigh. As he always did when he was troubled, he ran the thumb of his left hand over the twisted silver band around his right wrist.

To those who understood the Seeking Way, the intertwined strands of metal signified a truth learned and a vow made. The shaman had put it there right after he had staggered into the center of the pueblo and collapsed. "I decided I wanted something else."

"I find that hard to believe," she scoffed. She had never known John to change his mind once he'd decided on a course of action.

"And you don't care, either, do you?" His voice was silky.

Guilt stabbed her. John had read her well. She didn't care because she couldn't afford to. Five years weren't nearly long enough to get this man out of her soul.

"No. I don't care," she said with a chill in her voice, "the way you didn't care about me or the baby."

He ran his large brown hand up and down his thigh in a rare nervous gesture. Once she had loved his hands. Square and knotted with muscle, they had been so gentle when they'd reached for her in the night.

Aurora tried to ignore the flood of memories surging past the barriers she had thought so strong. John had made her his so completely she had wanted no other man, even now after so many years had passed since their divorce.

"For what it's worth, I gave you more than I'd ever given anyone," he said after a long, strained moment.

"It wasn't enough," she said, almost tasting the bitterness rising to her throat. "Not nearly enough."

"I know that—now. That's just one of the regrets I have to live with." He raised his head and looked at her. In the sunlight slicing the office, his piercing brown eyes seemed rimmed with fire, like the eyes of a predatory mountain cat at dawn.

When he had made love to her that first time out in the ruins, she had trembled before the hunger in those eyes. But his touch had been slow and gentle, like a man afraid of his own strength.

"So sweet, so tiny and perfect," he had whispered, his fiery gaze banked and smoldering. "Rory. My little Rory with her soul in her eyes."

He had kissed her and petted her, stroking her until she was awash in a sensual fog, every part of her begging him to come closer.

When his hard, masculine body had slid into hers, she had never felt such pleasure, such completeness. She had given herself to him at that moment. Heart, soul and body.

Deep inside her a sadness spread, reminding her that once she had wanted to make a home for this man, to give him children and grow old with him, watching them thrive.

What a fool she had been.

"Regrets, John? You?" The sound she made was too harsh to be called a laugh.

So slowly that it seemed to take forever, his mouth softened into a brooding smile. "Don't you ever have regrets, Rory? Don't you ever think of me, at all? In the middle of the night, maybe, or in the early morning when we used to make love to the sound of the birds waking up?"

His lazy gaze warmed her face, then dipped seductively to the hollow of her throat where her skin was growing hotter and hotter. For an instant she felt as though he'd touched her very gently in that fragile place with one of those strong hands.

"No." Her voice was hoarse, trembling. She swallowed. "No, I don't think of you, John. It took me a long time to stop, but I managed." Pride grew in her as she heard the remoteness in her tone. "I was hoping I'd never see you again."

He didn't respond. Instead he sat perfectly still, watching her in the quiet, reflective way that was such a part of him. But beyond the stoic exterior, she could feel his brilliant mind working. John was a man of logic, not emotion. He might have changed his life-style, but no matter what he claimed, he could never change the man inside.

Finally, just when the silence was almost too tense to bear, he shifted his wide shoulders in what might have been an accepting shrug.

"I hurt you more than I thought, didn't I?" His quiet words seemed edged with sadness.

Something tore inside her. "How could you possibly think you hadn't? When I knew I was losing the baby, I kept thinking you would come, the way you'd promised. And . . . and afterward, when I needed you the most, you walked away and never looked back."

A humorless smile tugged at one corner of his mouth. "I looked back," he said, his voice huskier than usual, "and I didn't like what I saw. I made a lot of mistakes, bad ones, I'll never deny that. And you're the one who suffered." He sat up abruptly. "I'd like to try to make it up to you."

She picked up the pencil again and began worrying it between her fingers. The building was very quiet, and dust motes danced a crazy jig in the light splashing on the picture of Santa Ysabel that lay between them.

"No thanks," she told him coolly. "I don't want anything from you."

"Don't you?"

He leaned forward to pick up the photograph. He tapped the slick paper once with his forefinger before returning it to the blotter where she could see it.

"The Santa Ysabel is waiting for you. You can touch it, study it for as long as you like, take pictures—anything you want. All you have to do is come back with me to the pueblo."

Because she couldn't help herself, she let her gaze drop to the photograph. The Santa Ysabel gleamed softly, its beauty nearly irresistible. She was being offered the chance of a lifetime, of two lifetimes. To study a legend. To find its secrets and reproduce them in her book for the world to enjoy.

She inhaled slowly, exhaled, started to smile inside. Her heart pounded, and renewed excitement flooded her veins.

And then she caught herself. John never did anything without a reason.

"What do you get out of this?" She didn't bother to hide her suspicion.

He brushed a piece of lint from the brim of the Stetson with his left hand. His skin was deeply tanned, showing no sign that he had once worn a wide gold band on his third finger.

"The pueblo needs money. For the school we've started, for housing, for health care." His sigh was impatient. "For a hundred other things. We get some money from the BIA and some from private donations, but it's not nearly enough. I intend to form an artists' studio to reproduce the Santa Ysabel for sale to gift shops in the area."

He glanced toward the books on primitive art lining the shelves. One arrogant black brow lifted a fraction as though acknowledging her expertise. "I've done all I can, but I can't make that happen by myself. I need you."

For a heartbeat Aurora couldn't breathe. He'd said that before—when he'd asked her to marry him.

"No, you don't," she told him, her eyes the color of ashes beneath the golden lashes. "You never needed me."

He seemed stunned by the force of her words. "Is that what you wanted? For me to need you?"

"It doesn't matter what I wanted, John," she replied, her voice weary.

"It matters. It always mattered. I just didn't know how much."

Aurora heard the gritty ring of truth in his voice, and a part of her wanted to believe him. But the part that he'd hurt so terribly refused to care.

"Goodbye, John. I'm sure you'll find the right person for the job. As I recall you were very good at getting what you wanted."

He watched her impassively for a long moment, then smiled with slow sensuality that set her teeth on edge. "I suppose that means we're not going to be friends."

Aurora opened her mouth, then closed it. She blinked and found her voice. "You have to be joking!" she exclaimed. The blood returned to her cheeks in a rush.

"No joke, professor."

Before she could move, his hand reached out to trap hers. She tried to pull away, but his fingers tightened just enough to show her that it was useless to struggle. Years of bucking heavy bales of hay on his mother's horse ranch had given John almost superhuman strength, especially in his wrists and forearms.

Slowly he leaned forward, his gaze holding hers. "You look good, Rory. Single life suits you."

His thumb made lazy circles on the back of her hand, warming the skin until it burned.

"Stop it," she said in a tight, angry voice.

"I see you're not trying to straighten your hair anymore. I like it wild like that. Makes me want to rub my face against it to see if it's as soft as it looks."

Aurora had trouble keeping her lips closed in a disapproving line. Especially when John turned her hand and brushed a kiss on the thin skin covering her wrist.

"Should I take it as a good sign that you're still wearing my favorite perfume?"

"I hadn't noticed," she said in what she hoped was a disinterested tone, but her voice came out oddly rushed.

John's eyes glowed until they were nearly amber. "Chanel, isn't it? Reminds me of the nights when you would come to bed still warm and soft from your bath, and we would make love. Remember, Rory?"

"I asked you not to call me that," she said, trying to wrench free.

"Sorry, my love. Some habits are hard to break."

*My love.* Spoken in his husky baritone, the two words had sounded like a caress.

For an instant, Aurora felt herself begin to soften inside as though the ice that had encased her heart for so long had begun to melt. And then she remembered. His words of love had been as empty as his promises.

"Let me go, John. Or I swear I'll raise such a fuss every security officer on campus will be in here within seconds."

His lopsided grin threw her off-guard. "It might almost be worth it," he said in wry voice, but he let her go.

Aurora resisted the urge to rub her wrist. "What kind of game are you playing?" she demanded, her breath quickening. "What do you want from me?"

"What do you *think* I want?"

Aurora's temper began to simmer. What was with this man? she thought in exasperation. John never did anything without gaining something in return. Never.

And then she remembered the complex trade agreements he'd negotiated in South America. Because he'd had the knack of saying precisely what the man across the table wanted to hear, he'd won more points than he'd lost.

Her cheeks began to burn. He was using sex to entice her to accept his offer of a job, just as he had once used it to entice her to accept his offer of marriage. What arrogance to think that she still wanted him after all these years, she fumed silently.

Leaning forward, she picked up the photograph and glanced down at the aggressive writing. "You're offering me a summer job, isn't that the bottom line?"

John hid his disappointment in a shrug. For an instant, when his hand had taken hers, the stiff line of her mouth had softened, and it had taken all of his considerable self-discipline to keep from leaning across the desk to kiss her.

"If you want to call it that, then yes, part of what I'm offering is a job," he said, dropping into the crisp Princeton accent he had all but abandoned over the past few years. "The council will arrange a place for you to live and a studio in which to work and teach. Right now there are six students lined up who can't wait to learn the things only you have the skills to teach." A brief smile softened the hard corners of his mouth. "There's even a small salary to pay your expenses."

Without seeming to, he searched for the luminous glow of excitement that had been in her eyes when she'd looked at

the Santa Ysabel. But when she looked at him, all he saw
was rejection. He hadn't realized until now how much that
would hurt.

Aurora stood and walked to the window behind her desk.
Her body seemed curiously heavy, and she felt as though she
were moving in slow motion.

The sunlight warmed her cheeks and turned the yellow of
her silk shirt to gold, but suddenly she felt as fragile as those
broken pieces of clay in the bottom of the trash basket.

"Sorry," she said, turning to face him. "I'm not available to accept your offer. I have plans for the summer."

He leaned back and folded his hands over his lean belly.
He was thinner, she noticed, but his shoulders seemed far
more muscular than she remembered. And his thighs bulged
with an extra layer of muscle. She repressed a shiver of sensuous memory.

"Change your plans."

Aurora heard the hard edge of arrogance in his voice, and
she bristled inside. This was the John Olvera she remembered, the man who was obsessed with getting to the top, no
matter what, the man who had put his career before her and
the baby she'd been carrying.

"You're the one who changes plans to suit the moment,
not me, remember?"

He remembered too damn much, he thought, especially
when the light was turning her hair to liquid bronze and
outlining the ripeness of her body beneath the soft material
of her blouse.

John ran his hands down his thighs and tried to ignore the
quickening in his loins, but every breath he took only made
it worse.

He got to his feet and replaced the chair in the exact spot
where it had been before he sat down.

"I remember a lot of things, professor," he said, his tone
flattened by a harshness that hurt her ears. "Probably more
than you think I do. But I'm sure you don't care about that,
either."

Aurora felt herself stiffen. More than his outward appearance had changed. There was a dangerous quality to John now. It was in the hard cast to his eye when he spoke of his new life and in the gritty huskiness of his voice when he spoke of his regret.

"Goodbye, John," she said again.

She crossed her arms over her chest and looked at him, every line of her body demonstrating her disinterest.

He picked up his hat and ran a finger over the narrow leather band. His expression was hooded, his shoulders rigid. And then he raised his head and grinned at her, taking her completely by surprise. Before she could stop herself, she'd taken a quick step backward until her bottom bumped against the sill.

"I'll pick you up at seven," he told her in his slightly raspy voice. "And we'll talk about the Santa Ysabel."

"I'm busy tonight," she said as coldly as she could manage.

"Right, you're having dinner with your husband." His grin grew devilish.

"Ex-husband," she shot back. "And I'm not."

He put on his hat, his hand automatically tugging the brim to just the right angle before he strode toward the door. At the threshold he paused, looking her up and down in a slow, mesmerizing way that made her shiver.

"Don't bother to dress up," he ordered, his eyes warming with a slow heat that touched her like a possessive kiss. "I can't afford fancy these days."

Saluting her with a sideways sweep of two fingers of his left hand, he nodded once, then was gone.

Aurora stood frozen, listening to the sound of his boots slowly fade until silence drew in on her again.

"Damn him," she whispered. "Who does he think he is? There's no way I'm—" Her voice trailed off, and a grin spread over her face. There really *was* no way.

Her home phone was unlisted, and the university never gave out the home addresses of staff members. How could he possibly know where she lived?

He couldn't, she realized as she returned to her desk and sat down. No doubt he was planning to pick her up here, but she would be long gone by seven. And in two days she would be in Mazatlan.

John would never find her.

Smiling to herself, she started to shove the photograph into the envelope, but when her gaze fell again on the Santa Ysabel, she slipped it free, allowing herself one long last look.

Even in a photograph the pot's beauty was indescribable. Her breath caught as she imagined herself touching it. But that would mean opening a door that had been closed for a long time.

"No," she whispered, trying to push the memory of a small, still face out of her mind.

Her eyes filled with tears, and before she could dash them away, a lone teardrop slid down her cheek and onto the photo. Gently she wiped it away, then slid the picture into the envelope and tossed it into the trash.

She would never go back to the pueblo. It would hurt too much.


The small unglazed pot stood on a pedestal in a place of honor in the center of the prestigious gallery. Light from the track fixture above shone softly on the matte black finish, illuminating every perfect line of the simple but elegant pattern etched into the smooth clay.

John stood alone a few feet away, oblivious to the others in the brightly lighted room. He'd seen Aurora's work before, and he'd never doubted her talent. But he'd never seen anything like this. Never.

Beautiful, my love, he thought, his throat tightening. Just like you.

He took a deep breath, trying to ease the pressure in his chest. No, her work was more than beautiful, he realized with a shiver of pride. It was magnificent.

Someone moved behind him. John looked around quickly, his muscles tight with the nearly unbearable tension that had been in him since he'd left Aurora's office over, an hour ago.

A well-dressed couple stood nearby, talking softly as they looked at an oil painting hanging at eye level. The man's hand rested possessively on the swell of the woman's hip, and she nestled against him. A tinkling laugh rang out, and the woman nuzzled the man's neck. He whispered something into her ear and she flushed, her eyes shining as they moved away, laughing together, two obviously happy people.

John glanced down at his work-scarred boots, then expelled the air hurting his lungs. He was alone, just as he'd been all of his life—until he'd married Aurora. Even then he had kept a part of himself locked away from her, the way he had done with everyone from the time he had been a small boy.

A muscle pulled at the side of his jaw, and he forced himself to relax. Without seeming to, he let his curious gaze trail around the bright space. The gallery was small and exclusive, the kind of place where the very rich sipped champagne and ate caviar as they browsed.

Outside the name was spelled out in fancy script. Inside the walls were a soft ivory with accents of gold, and there were fresh flowers everywhere. This was Aurora's world now, as different from his as a crystal goblet from a rusty tin cup.

Returning his gaze to the pot that she had made, he studied the red-and-yellow stripes standing out in stark relief against the ebony background.

The yellow one reminded him of the sun shining through a summer haze right after dawn—fragile, ethereal and yet wonderfully warm as it darted over the clay. But the other stripe was thick and bold and the color of blood. Aurora had drawn it in a rigid, unwavering line that seemed slashed into the clay. For an instant his breath stopped, and he closed his eyes, feeling the dark, violent pain crowd in on him again.

Once, when she'd come home from a day working with a native potter in Peru, she had held up the pot she'd made and told him that every curve she fashioned, ever mark she made in the clay was symbolic.

That pot had been ablaze with color and light. Airy, even. Like Rory herself, with her eyes shining and one of her cheery smiles lighting her small face. She had named that pot "Happiness."

Opening his eyes, he stared at the bloody slash. His heart thudded hard, and his mouth tasted of dust. Before he'd met Aurora, he'd had a vague appreciation of great art. During their marriage she had taught him a lot about pre-Columbian pottery, but he didn't need to be an expert to feel the anger in that vivid swatch of color. And didn't need to understand a lot about symbolism to recognize the despair in the black background.

Aurora had been like that sunny yellow swirl, surrounding him with the kind of warmth and light he had never before known. He had been as unbending as that angry red line, his course set, his pride driving him like a lash.

Leaning forward slightly, he read the elegant hand-lettered card affixed to the polished oak stand. The pot had been made in Brazil a few months after she had filed for divorce. She called it "Dream's End."

He drew a shuddering breath, feeling as though he were being gutted. "No," he said sharply, pushing his hands deeper into his pockets to keep from smashing the damn thing to bits.

A movement at his side drew his gaze. The saleswoman had left her small gilt desk and was smiling up at him, her bright blue eyes discreetly assessing.

Middle-aged but still sleek in beige linen and lizard pumps, she reminded him of the women he'd met in the east, the ones who'd come from old money and impeccable bloodlines. Once he had thought he wanted a woman like that, until he'd met Aurora and fallen for her laughing eyes and innocent smile.

"Lovely, isn't it?" the woman remarked, her tone conveying just the right amount of professional warmth.

"Yes." His voice sounded rusty, and he cleared his throat. "Yes, it's lovely."

"I could see that you were moved by it. Most people are. It makes a very powerful statement."

John removed his hat and held it in front of him, turning it around and around in his hands. "Is the artist very popular?"

"Oh, yes, *very*. I personally believe she'll soon be able to command four figures for a small work like this. That's why this is such a steal at only five hundred dollars."

One side of his mouth made a slight dent in his hard cheek. "Is that all?"

"Yes, sir, that's all."

He nodded. Without seeming to, her eyes took a discreet inventory of his unironed shirt and the jeans that had seen better days. He knew and she knew that he didn't look much like a man who could afford five hundred dollars for a pot.

And he wasn't. Not now. Five hundred dollars would feed his horses for a month during the winter snows. It would also wipe out a big chunk of the reserve in his checking account.

Knowing that he shouldn't, John reached out to trace the bloody gash with his forefinger.

Oh, yeah, John Olvera had been a man with a future, all right, he thought with a stinging bitterness. Everyone knew he was a comer.

So when the ambassador had asked him to delay his departure from San Sebastian a few more weeks to finish up the negotiations, he hadn't even hesitated.

Never mind that his wife had been seven months pregnant and waiting for him at home. Never mind that he'd promised to be with her. Never mind that she'd had her baby alone, with only his mother to help her. Because John Olvera had cared more about success than he had cared about his pregnant wife, the baby had died.

His throat stung with a foul taste, and he swallowed hard. I'm sorry, my love, he thought. More sorry than you can ever know. He closed his eyes on a spasm of remorse.

Rory had been right to divorce him. He hadn't cared enough, not nearly enough. He'd been selfish as hell, and she'd paid the price. Nothing he could ever do would be enough to make it up to her. But God help him, he had to try, no matter how hard she fought him.

Slowly he withdrew his hand and balled it into a fist at his side. He had to get out of this place, away from this damn pot that made him feel sick inside. Away from the memories he could barely stand to face.

A jangle of bracelets reminded him that he wasn't alone. The woman was looking at him intently, her eyes carrying that same look of puzzlement he'd seen before on the faces of other whites when they had tried to fit him into the slot marked "Indian."

"Thank you for your help," he said, with a polite nod to the patiently waiting woman. He started to edge away, but she moved, blocking his path.

"You're most welcome, sir." She glanced toward the pot. "Shall I write it up for you?" she asked, smoothly masking her eagerness with a winning smile.

John started to shake his head, then clenched his teeth. He was wrong. He needed to remember. Every damn day.

"Yes, write it up," he said, his voice husky. His hand shook as he reached for his checkbook.


Juggling her briefcase and purse against her lifted knee, Aurora unlocked the front door of her second-floor condo and threw it open.

A rush of hot air stung her face as she hurried inside and dropped her things onto the small table in the entryway. She closed the door and, without her usual pause to turn on the air-conditioning, hurried down the hall into the spare room that had been converted into a studio.

Taking a quick breath, she grabbed the clay-dappled smock draped over the small electric kiln in the corner, and tugged it over the silk blouse that now clung to her damp skin.

Her movements were jerky as she crossed to the unpainted pine worktable that took up most of the floor space. Easing onto the padded stool, she kicked off her sandals, then slid her feet backward. She straightened her shoulders, taking one slow breath, then another. The bare floor was warm and roughened by fallen bits of clay. The air smelled musty, and the room's temperature was uncomfortable.

She pushed her hands into the thick curls at the nape of her neck and lifted them.

In a little more than an hour John would be knocking on the door to her office, only to find her gone. As soon as he realized that she'd stood him up, his face would get very still. The tiny gold flecks in his eyes would grow brighter, and his brows would tighten into an angry black line. But his anger would stay locked inside, just as it always had. John never lost control. He would never allow himself to be that vulnerable.

Letting the tousled hair fall in the way that showed off the delicate lines of her small, square face, she took a deep, slow breath to steady her galloping nerves. Then, ignoring the stiffness in her fingers, she snatched away the damp cheesecloth covering the moist clay, and dug out a large portion of the slick, wet mass.

Using both hands, she slammed it against the bleached boards, smashing out the air bubbles. Over and over the clay hit the wood, thudding almost as loudly as the raging beat she could hear in her ears. Over and over she threw the clay against the board, trying to drive the memory of his slow smile from her mind. Her arms began to tire.

It had been years since she had thought about him, years since she had stopped mourning for the marriage that had meant so much to her.

After a time, she reached for a small, shallow box sitting on the corner of the worktable. Deftly she adjusted the tension of the thin wire stretching across it until the wire was taut.

Repeatedly, her movements settling into a mindless rhythm, she threw the clay at the wire, slicing it cleanly with the force of a killing blade. Her strong hands worked tirelessly, kneading the heavy earth, packing the tiny granules and pressing out the excess moisture.

Damn him, she heard with every beat. Damn him for making me remember.

When their baby had died, her grief had been wrenching, but she had survived by telling herself that she could still create another kind of life, the kind that lives forever in the beauty of art. She would use the clay to absorb her anguish, to help her heal. She would create a monument to her child in her work, a monument that would never die.

Her fingers gouged into the clay as she remembered that bleak morning when the ambassador had called her parents' house in El Paso, where she and John had been staying after she had been released from the hospital.

She had known without hearing the words that John had been offered the promotion he had wanted so badly. He was to be the new political attaché, the man who would act as the American ambassador's personal liaison to *el presidente* himself. It was a high-profile post, given only to a man who was in line for the position of ambassador someday.

Aurora shivered, remembering how she had started to shake inside at the thought of returning to the house where an empty crib stood waiting for the child who would never sleep there.

Tearfully she had begged him to request a transfer to the State Department in Washington. For a few months, a year at the most, time enough for her to heal.

He had heard her out, but she had sensed an impatience in him and an eagerness to put the loss behind them, as though it had never happened. As though the daughter she had named Dawn Elizabeth hadn't existed.

To her shock, he had refused to give up his post in San Sebastian. "Stateside duty is a dead end at this stage of my career. I thought you understood that," he had told her in voice rough with frustration. "I can't just be good. I have to be the best. And that means taking every opportunity I can force them to give me."

Aurora had searched his face, looking for the understanding she'd needed so desperately, but there'd been only tense, immovable strength in that dark, handsome face. His life had been hard, but John was even harder. He had made his choices out of anger and pride and a fierce determination to succeed. Nothing was more important to him than that. That was when she realized that he loved his career more than he loved her.

Her own pride hadn't allowed her to stay with him after that. She would have felt humiliated every time he touched her.

Two days later he had left without her, taking her dreams with him.

Aurora sat frozen, the sunlight from the window slicing across the clay in her hands. Without her dreams she felt empty deep in the part of her where the flames used to burn so hotly. Now no matter how hard she tried, she could no longer find the life force in the clay that gave her a feeling of oneness with the earth. She could no longer create.

With a cry that seemed torn from her throat, Aurora raised her fist, then brought it crashing down into the middle of the slick clay.

Blinded by tears, she turned away from the table only to freeze at the sound of the doorbell echoing through the house.

Slowly the clock on the mantel in the living room began to bong. It was seven o'clock.

# Chapter 3

The bell shrilled again.

Aurora quickly dashed the tears from her cheeks with the back of her hand. "It can't be," she said, walking slowly to the entry. She counted slowly to three, then lifted her chin and opened the door.

John stood at the edge of her small balcony, looking out over the greenbelt separating her building from the others. Both arms were braced on the railing, and his powerful shoulders blocked out the sun.

At the click of the latch he turned. His dark gaze ran the length of her, taking in the dried bits of clay clinging to the smock. A glimmer of a smile came and went in the warm brown between his thick lashes.

This time he was dressed as she remembered him, in a navy blazer, pale blue shirt and muted tie. His jacket hung open, revealing pleated slacks in just the right shade of tan. His cordovan loafers gleamed.

And yet though the clothing was familiar, there was a primitive quality about him now, a dark and earthy fierceness beneath the sophisticated exterior.

"You don't look as though you're expecting company, professor. Or are you trying to tell me something?" His mesmerizing gaze lingered for just a moment too long on her lips, as though he were trying to read the truth in their soft curve. She felt something give way inside, as though another piece of scar tissue had torn.

For a moment her heart lurched against her chest, reminding her of the years she had lived in blissful ignorance as this man's wife, believing in him, certain that the fire in his eyes was love. Somehow she resisted the urge to shiver.

"I told you I was busy tonight," she said, her voice still thick with tears.

His brows drew together and a look of concern tightened his face. "Is something wrong?"

"Of course not." She rested her hand on her hip and dared him to challenge her. "I know you didn't get this address from one of my letters."

He raised one eyebrow. "You're right. When I discovered you weren't in the phone book, I called Todd Gulbranson and asked him to scare up your home address."

Aurora felt her eyes widen with surprise. "Your college roommate?"

"Yes. He lives in Dallas now. Runs a bank here, knows a lot of the right people," he said in a dry tone. "In fact, I understand he got your address from the university president."

"And Todd passed the information along to you," she concluded, her tone bordering on disgust.

"Along with an invitation to stay with him until my business here is finished." He shoved his hand into his pocket and leaned against the railing. For the first time she noticed that the tailored cut of his trousers only partially concealed the heavy muscle in his thighs.

She frowned. "If your business is with me, it *is* finished," she said, clinging to the doorknob for support. "You'll have to find someone else."

"I don't want anyone else. I want you." He slid his hand from his pocket and stood. He came toward her.

"Stop saying that! I'm not available." Her voice rang with indignation, bringing a pleased grin to his face. She took a tighter grip on the knob, but her damp palm made the brass slippery.

"Aha, temper. We're making progress."

The warmth in her cheeks flared into two angry splotches of red. "John, I don't have time—"

"But I do. All the time in the world. For you, my love." His voice carried a suggestive note that burrowed into her.

"Don't call me that!"

One thick black eyebrow arched. "Just what *can* I call you?"

"Dr. Davenport," she snapped.

He shook his head. "Hmm, I don't think so. Too formal for an ex-wife, especially one as small and pretty as you are." A beguiling grin slashed across his rugged mouth. "We'll compromise. I'll call you Aurora—for now."

He braced his left hand against the stucco and leaned toward her. He had recently shaved, and he smelled of soap. John never wore after-shave or cologne.

"Hold still." His voice deepened, grew husky, more intimate.

"Why?" she demanded, staring at him warily.

Before she could move, his other hand came up to brush across her cheek. At the touch of his hard, warm fingers, she flinched.

"Dried clay," he said, holding up his callused fingers to show her the brown dust. But she couldn't seem to take her gaze from his face.

When he smiled, she could see new creases etched into the weathered skin, reminding her that he was now past forty. There was something else about him that made him look older, something in his eyes that told her he had aged on the inside.

But whatever had occurred in his life to put those deep lines of pain in his face, it had nothing to do with her or the breakup of their marriage. Five years of silence had told her very clearly how little John cared.

"I told you I was working," she said in a stiff, cold voice, scrubbing both cheeks with her palms. Silently she promised herself a cooling bath as soon as she sent him away. No, a cold shower would be better.

John dropped his hand to his neck and rubbed the thick column of muscles as though to ease a tightness there. As soon as he caught her gaze on him, he dropped his hand.

"So you did." He pushed his hand into his pocket again, and the material of his trousers pulled a fraction tighter over his lean hips. "Tell you the truth, I was afraid you had a date. I was all set to throw the guy out of here so that we could be alone."

Aurora stiffened and tried not to notice the slow smile that made his brown eyes crinkle at the sun-weathered corners, just as she tried not to notice the way his well-brushed hair curled over his crisp collar. It had always surprised her that hair so black and thick could also be so soft.

"You would never resort to violence, John," she retorted. "You're too civilized."

He regarded her steadily. "I'll do anything I have to, to get what I want. You of all people should know that."

"What you want or don't want has nothing to do with me," she said coolly, feeling the impact of this man in every part of her.

"Doesn't it?" He raised one eyebrow. "My great-grandfather once tied the woman he wanted to his horse, and took her into the hills until she agreed to leave her tribe and return with him to the pueblo. Maybe that's what I should do with you."

"Don't be ridiculous," she scoffed. "You offered me a job, I turned it down. That's *all* we're talking about here."

"Yeah, but at least you stopped glaring at me for a second or two while you thought about it." He glanced at the gold watch on his wrist. It was one she had given him for his thirtieth birthday. "You need to eat, and so do I. Put on your shoes, and I'll buy you dinner."

She opened her mouth, then shut it again. Without thinking she glanced down at ten tanned toes tipped with fuchsia polish.

Suddenly she felt exposed. Naked.

John knew every inch of her, the only man who did. He had been a patient lover, teaching her slowly to accept his hands and his mouth in every warm and secret place, until she'd cried out in breathless need. And then she had welcomed his hard body inside her until they were no longer two separate people.

Without knowing that she was doing it, Aurora ran her tongue over her bottom lip, then froze at the dark flush that spread along his jaw. His ebony lashes lowered lazily, but not before she'd seen a potent male interest in the dark depths.

She resisted the urge to move backward, like a small bird seeking the safety of her nest. "Goodbye, John. I hope you have a safe trip back to New Mexico."

She started to close the door, but he pressed his big hand over hers on the knob.

"Give me an hour, Rory. Just an hour. We used to have a lot to talk about. Maybe we still do." He wasn't begging, but intuition told her that the half-demand, half-plea in his voice was as close as he had ever come.

Aurora jerked her hand from under his, but she could still feel the warmth of his hard fingers on hers. "As I remember, John, we used to talk mostly about your career." Her soft mouth twisted into a cynical smile. "And since you no longer have one, I doubt that we have anything to say."

His face stilled and his eyes didn't move. Like a hawk, she thought, watching for an exposed target to strike. And yet, there was a new look in his watchful eyes. Something that made her hurt inside. Something lonely and sad. Something he couldn't hide.

Or didn't want to hide.

The thought stunned her. Was John deliberately letting her see a part of himself she'd never seen before? Was he finally revealing more of the man buried underneath the driving ambition? She couldn't seem to breathe.

"Our daughter's people need you, Aurora. Can you really turn them down?"

Aurora went icy cold. Beneath her bare feet the floor seemed to shift, and she locked her knees to keep her legs steady. "That's not fair," she whispered.

At the hurt in her voice, his mouth jerked. "Maybe not, but I can't afford to be fair. This is too important to me."

"Right, important to you, the great John Olvera. Just like the old days." Her voice was dripping with sarcasm, but inside she was in terrible pain. How dare he use his daughter's memory to get what he wanted?

"I was hoping it would be important to you, too. You were always telling me I shouldn't turn my back on my roots." There was a quiet dignity in his voice instead of the remote anger she had expected. And oddly, something that sounded like humility.

Anger drained out of her, leaving her feeling empty. More than anything she wanted to be alone, and yet she couldn't seem to make herself pull away.

"Okay, John. One hour—starting now."

She reheated the quiche she had bought at a gourmet boutique a few days earlier and made enough salad for both of them.

John offered to help, but she refused.

When dinner was ready, she poured steaming coffee into the biggest mug she had in the house and carried it to the table along with the sugar bowl. John liked his coffee boiling hot and sweet.

She sat across from him, trying to ignore the butterflies in her stomach. The hour was nearly half gone.

"Smells good," he said, cupping his big hands around the mug. He sat across from her, his strong legs extended sideways, one arm resting on the small marble-topped table that had never seemed quite so spindly before.

While she had quickly showered and changed into a cool cotton dress, he had removed his jacket and tie and opened his collar. In deference to the heat in the small kitchen he had rolled his sleeves above his elbows. As she picked up her napkin she noticed that he was wearing an odd sort of silver band on his right wrist.

"I'm sorry it's so warm in here," she said in a stilted voice. "I . . . forgot to turn on the air when I got home."

John glanced around the cheery space, a sardonic smile playing over his controlled mouth. "At least you have it to turn on. At my place I have two options. Open the windows and chew on dust all night, or sit in the horse trough. I've done both."

Aurora heard the note of wry humor in his voice and she tried not to smile. But when John chose to be charming, he was hard to resist.

"How's your mother?" she asked, determined to keep to safe topics.

His fingers tightened around the mug until the knuckles were sharply delineated against his copper skin. "She died two years ago September. Heart failure."

Aurora felt a moment of shock. Why hadn't he let her know? And then she realized that she was no longer a member of the Olvera family.

"I'm sorry," she said with quiet sincerity. Without thinking she laid her small hand on his forearm in a gesture of sympathy. At her touch, his arm stiffened as though he were about to throw off her fingers. She recoiled and jerked her hand into her lap.

John ground his teeth. "Aurora—"

She rushed into speech. She wouldn't give him the satisfaction of knowing he'd hurt her. "Your mother was a dear woman. And she tried so hard to...to save the baby. She did save me."

She picked up her fork and began pushing her salad around her plate. "I hope she knew how grateful I was. I told her, but . . ." She shrugged and fell silent, her thoughts full of the dauntless woman who had walked eight miles to the nearest phone to summon help.

John spooned sugar into his cup and began stirring. "She knew. She talked about you a lot."

"Did she?" She reached for her glass of iced tea. For some reason she needed to hold something solid and ordinary in her hand.

"Yes." He took a drink of the scalding coffee in that quick, impatient way he had, then speared her with a dark gaze. "She was hurt that you never visited after you divorced me."

Aurora's hand jerked, and cold drops of tea splashed over her fingers. Hastily she wiped her hand with her napkin.

"I couldn't go back there, John. I just couldn't." She caught her lip between her teeth, then added softly, "But that doesn't mean I didn't care, because I did. I... I wrote every few months in the beginning, but she never answered. I thought she was...was angry with me, so I stopped writing."

A look that might have been sadness crossed his face. "I know. When I came home, she used to make me read your letters to her over and over. She loved showing off the SMU letterhead to her friends. She was very proud of you."

"*You* read—"

"My mother couldn't read or write. She never learned how."

She felt the tug of astonishment on her face. "She never said—"

"She was ashamed." John's shadowed gaze held hers for a long moment, then dropped to the polished marble between them. His forefinger idly traced the meandering pattern in the stone. "A lot of the older people never had the chance to go to the Indian school in Albuquerque, which was all they had years ago. They were needed at home, to help put food on the table so the family would survive. Mother was doing a man's work when she was ten."

Aurora breathed a sigh of sympathy. "Poor Morning-star. She was so proud and so... so independent. It must have been awful, having to ask others to read things to her."

John's mouth twisted. "Don't waste your pity," he said with a bite to his deep voice. "Mother was a strong woman. She had to be."

Stabbed by his harsh tone, Aurora stiffened. "I'm sure she was." Feeling rebuffed, and angry at herself for letting John get to her, she began to eat.

In the living room the clock bonged the half hour. Thirty more minutes, she reminded herself, and he would be gone. She told herself she was glad she would never see him again.

"I thought you were hungry," she said testily when he made no move to pick up his fork.

"I am."

John drank the rest of the coffee in one gulp and began to eat the wedge of quiche lorraine. He'd eaten eggs three times a day every day as a boy, and he hated the very smell of them. No doubt Aurora had forgotten that. Or maybe she no longer cared. Not that he could blame her. He'd given her plenty of reasons to stop caring.

Damn, he thought, watching her small, capable hand push back her tumbled bangs to reveal a tension-furrowed brow. This wasn't the way he'd planned things, at all. By this time she should have agreed to come back with him. That was supposed to be the easy part. He'd been so sure she wouldn't be able to resist the Santa Ysabel.

He'd spent countless hours trying to figure out the best way to approach her, but for the first time in his life, his mind wasn't working clearly. Every time he tried to think things through logically, images of Rory from the past kept intruding.

Sometimes he saw her laughing at something he'd said, her bright hair a halo around her head, her freckles wink-ing at him in the light until he wanted to catch them with his tongue. And sometimes he saw her listening attentively as he talked to her about an embassy problem, her face solemn and concerned and so adorable he usually forgot what he was saying and kissed her.

He had thought it was sex he'd wanted from her. Until he had lost her, he hadn't realized that she had made him happy for the first time in his life. He'd been content then and at peace, even when he'd been working long hours and fighting to get to the top. No matter how hard he'd tried, he hadn't been able to forget.

When he'd eaten all he could, he put down his fork and reached for his cup, only to remember that it was empty.

"Have you thought any more about the Santa Ysabel?" He pushed away his plate and folded his arms on the table.

"No." Her answer was clipped and cold, unlike her usual breezy responses.

"Tell me what you want that I haven't offered, and I'll make it happen. You call the shots. I'll give you whatever you want."

Aurora inhaled slowly, fighting the white-hot anger that flared inside her. "Five years ago I would have given anything to hear those words," she said slowly and distinctly, making every word count. "But today they mean nothing to me. Absolutely nothing."

Slowly she glanced up, months of repressed pain simmering in her eyes, to see John's dark skin pale.

"So because you can't forgive me, good people will continue to be poor, continue to live on the charity of others, even though they want to work." His voice was as sharp as an arrow and just as deadly.

Aurora dropped her fork and threw her crumpled napkin onto her plate. "Don't you ever give up? I said no!" Her voice shook. She pressed her fingers against her lips to stop their trembling.

John bowed his head, and his big shoulders slumped for a brief moment before he straightened them again. "Once you called me a selfish, egotistical bastard. You said I didn't care about people." His voice deepened, grew quiet. "Well, I care now. And I'm trying my damnedest to make things better. Sometimes I just don't know how."

She blinked, then shook her head. She didn't want to remember this man. She didn't want to remember the nights he had called out in a strange guttural language in his sleep as though he were caught in a terrible nightmare. She didn't want to remember how the tiredness would lift from his face whenever she rubbed his big shoulders and nuzzled his neck. She didn't want to remember that she had loved him.

"I'm . . . sorry about your people, but I can't help you." Her voice faltered, but she managed to keep the tears at bay. "You'll have to find someone else."

John leaned forward to pin her with a hard-edged look. "Is this revenge, Aurora?" he asked quietly. "Satisfaction for what I did to you?"

Without answering she stood and carried her plate to the sink. She was shaking so hard inside it was difficult to breathe. Her hands bunched into fists on the counter, and she hung her head.

Behind her she heard the chair bang against the wall, and then John was at her side, his big hand on her shoulder. She shivered, and his fingers tightened convulsively.

"Rory, I'm sorry—"

*"Don't call me that!"* she shouted, wrenching out of his grasp and moving away from him. "I told you not to call me that." Her voice faded into a sob.

"My God, what's wrong?" he said, not daring to move. "Talk to me. Tell me. If it's me, if it's something I've said, I'm sorry. But damn it, this is as hard for me as it is for you."

She heard the raw note in his voice and a part of her was glad. Finally she'd gotten inside that impenetrable shell, where he kept whatever feelings he hadn't managed to bury along with his heritage.

Aurora wrapped her arms around her body and stared at the bright Miro print over the sink. The colors were vivid and full of life, but inside her head she saw only black.

"I do care about my child's people," she told him in a choked tone. "I *do*. But even if I could make myself go back, it wouldn't matter. My hands are like blocks of wood when I touch the clay. I'm no good any more. No good for myself or for them.''

In the thick silence John studied her profile. Her mouth was compressed, and tears shimmered on the long, gold lashes. She was as skittish as a day-old foal. One rash move, one thoughtless word and she would bolt. If that happened she would be lost to him forever, and that was the one thing he couldn't bear. No matter what, he had to keep her talking to him.

"Listen to me, Ro—Aurora," he said softly, keeping his voice low. "Your work is terrific. I've seen it in a gallery downtown. The woman there couldn't say enough good things."

Aurora thought about the abandoned lump of clay drying into a hard, useless dirt clod on her worktable in the other room. Somehow she managed to suppress the urge to laugh hysterically.

"Did you look at the dates on those pieces, John?" Without waiting for an answer she continued her voice as lifeless as the vision inside. "It's been years since I did anything good enough to keep."

"But why? What happened?"

"What do you think happened?" she shot back, her voice quavering. "We got divorced. I stopped believing in love." She thought of the Tapajoz, created during the weeks when her wounds were so fresh, and now a pile of rubbish.

Her eyes flooded with fresh tears, but she dashed them away. "No, that's not true. Somewhere along the way I stopped believing in myself."

John inhaled slowly, as he looked blindly down at his feet. He had more to pay for than he'd thought. Much, much more.

"You can still teach," he said in what he hoped was a reasonable tone. "Come back with me—"

"No! I told you, I never want to see that place again." Her voice shook, and she inhaled hard against the memories that threatened to override her control.

John's brief smile was without humor. "That's what I said—once. But I found out I couldn't run away from who I am."

Stiffly she moved to the window and looked out. The pane was still warm, but outside the sun had dipped behind a building. The expensive landscaping looked lifeless and bleak.

"Well, I know who I am, John," she said, turning toward him. Her small, stubborn chin lifted. "I'm happy with that person. I don't have anything to prove. To you or to anyone."

"Good. Then you won't have any problems taking the job."

She frowned. "Haven't you been listening? *I can't help you.*"

"You can do anything if you want it badly enough."

Want it? She would do *anything* to be able to create again. Anything but return to the place where her baby lay under a pile of stones on her father's land.

Suddenly Aurora felt a stabbing pain in her belly and she nearly gasped aloud. "I've given you my answer," she said in an aloof tone that made John's eyes narrow dangerously. "And your time's up."

John closed his hands into fists to keep from reaching for her. More than anything he wanted to kiss those tears from her lashes and stroke away the tautness from that brave, little chin, but he'd lost the right to touch her in that way years ago.

Swiftly he searched his mind for the right words, praying he hadn't lost all of his persuasive skills, but he was damn rusty. "You used to say that the pueblo was a special place. That you felt a closeness to the earth there and to the people who had lived there. Remember?"

Remember? Aurora thought, staring at the floor. How could she forget? He was talking about the night he asked her to marry him.

The torment inside increased until she could no longer control it. She spun around to face him, tears running unchecked down her face.

"You have no idea what it's like, to want something every day," she flung at him harshly, her eyes blazing, "something that was a part of your soul, your reason for living, and know that you'll never have it again, no matter how much you want it or how hard you try. You don't know!"

"You're wrong," he said in a raw tone. "I do know."

"That's right. I forgot," she said, her voice choking. "Your career." She dashed her tears from her eyes. "You left that voluntarily, didn't you?"

He hesitated, then nodded.

"Well, I didn't choose to stop creating. I've tried and tried and...tried." Her voice rose until it became a sob, and she hugged herself, her small body shaking.

"Oh, baby, don't. Please don't." John hesitated, then reached for her. He wrapped his strong arms around her and held her close, soothing her with a touch so gentle it could have been the wind caressing her.

She fought to contain the tears, not knowing which she was fighting harder, the tears or the nearly irresistible urge to relax against him.

"It's been a long day," she managed to explain in what sounded like a composed voice. "I'm very tired." She used her fingertips to push against his hard midriff.

Reluctantly John dropped his arms, his senses telling him that he would remember her sweetly feminine scent and her softness for a long time. "We'll talk tomorrow."

"No, John. I've given you my answer. I'm not going to change it."

John frowned. "You're upset. I understand, but when you think about it—"

"Please leave," she said in a stilted voice, her expression rigid, her eyes giving no quarter. "Your hour's up."

John dropped his gaze. "I'll go because I said I would, but there's one thing I want you to know before I do. Even when I couldn't love you the way you needed to be loved, I believed in you. I still do."

He grabbed his coat from the back of the chair and slung it over his broad shoulder. "If you haven't heard anything I've said, hear this. You were right when you told me once that there was magic in the land of my ancestors. The pueblo gave me back my life, when I didn't think that was possible. It will do the same for you—if you have the courage to try."

Without another word he turned and walked out of her house.

## Chapter 4

Evening, *señor*. You are back early, no?'' The rotund maid's black eyes sparkled with curiosity as she moved back a step to let John enter. Her name was Maria, and Todd had warned him that the indomitable little woman ran his household with an iron hand.

"I am back early, yes," he said, answering her guileless smile with one of his own that he knew looked phony as hell.

"*Señor* Gulbranson and his guests are in the *sala*, if you would like to join them." She closed the door and indicated the way with an abrupt gesture of her work-worn hand.

John thanked her in Spanish before crossing the gleaming hardwood floor to the open door. At the threshold he paused. The scene was one he'd seen countless times in countless embassies.

The men wore white dinner jackets and starched shirts. Their ladies wore designer finery and glittering jewels. The air smelled of expensive perfume and cigar smoke, and laughter punctuated the buzz of conversation.

John's weary gaze roamed the room until he caught sight of Claire, Todd's glamorous blond wife, a debutante from Philadelphia and one of Dallas's best dressed women.

As though feeling his gaze, Claire glanced his way. Her face immediately brightened into a glittering smile. Excusing herself, she came toward him, her sleek coiffure shining in the light.

"John, darling, you're back early. We didn't expect you until much later, or we would have held dinner."

Tall and slender, she smelled of some exotic flower as she leaned forward to kiss his cheek.

Fleetingly John thought about the delicate scent of violets perfuming Aurora's hair, and the heaviness inside him increased. For the past hour, since walking out of her small condo, he had been sitting alone in his truck in the visitors' lot, fighting the urge to break down her door and haul her off with him the way he had threatened to do.

According to family legend, the beautiful but reluctant Navajo maiden who had spurned his great-grandfather's advances had eventually come to love her captor, but that had been a hundred years ago. This was now, and a man had to offer more than a few horses and skins to win his woman. More than John had ever given to anyone.

"Looks like a great party," he told his hostess with a polite smile. "And you look terrific, just the way the wife of a bank president should look."

Claire beamed, but the light in her blue eyes faded as she studied his taut expression. A small frown puckered her pale brow. "*You* look like a man who could use a drink. What would you like? Todd has everything."

John hesitated. He hadn't had a drink in years, not since that long ago Saturday when the Princeton lacrosse team had won its first game and he'd gotten stinking drunk. The next day, his head splitting and his stomach on fire, he had heard more drunken Indian jokes than he could count. He had vowed never to take another drink, and he hadn't. But tonight it was damn tempting. Too tempting.

"Thanks, but I'll pass." He shoved one hand in his pocket, conscious as always that he'd had to work hard to learn the social graces that these people took for granted.

"At least come in and meet some of our friends. I think you'll like them. They're your kind of people."

*His kind of people.* John resisted the urge to laugh. Todd ran one of the largest banks in Dallas, while most of *his* people didn't even have checking accounts. Claire had decorated her home in museum-quality Chippendale and priceless Bokharas, while his people lived nine or ten to an allotted space where the walls were dried mud and the furniture was handmade or third-hand junk.

As a boy he had hated that life, the only one his parents and their parents before them had known, and so he'd fought his way out by being the best—at school, at sports, at every thing that came his way. Somewhere along the line he'd turned into a man without feeling or compassion. Even having a beautiful, talented wife like Aurora had been like winning another trophy.

Suddenly he felt sick inside, and the noise of the party seemed to pound through his head. He needed fresh air.

Claire's voice interrupted his thoughts, and he jerked his narrowed gaze to her face. "I'm sorry. What did you say?"

"I said, is something wrong? You look like you're ready to whip every guy here." Her tone was teasing, but her gaze was riveted to his face. A half-wary, half-fascinated look had crowded the smile from her face.

John sighed heavily and turned his back on the party. "No, I'm the guy who should be whipped." Before she could say another word, John excused himself and walked away.

A dog howled somewhere in the neighborhood. Just then the clock in the other room began striking the hour. Lying awake in her bed, Aurora silently counted the muffled strokes.

It was midnight.

With a heavy sigh, she flung her arm to the side and kicked aside the sheet covering her bare legs. Around ten she had turned off the air-conditioning and opened the windows.

The temperature outside had fallen into the seventies, but the sheet beneath her was almost as hot as her body. She moved restlessly, trying to relax, but for some reason her skin seemed unusually sensitive, so sensitive that just the pressure of her soft cotton nightie made her nipples ache and her thighs tingle, as though she had been in a deep sleep before awakening suddenly to tiny pinpricks of sensation in her leaden limbs.

She had tried everything—meditation, deep breathing, a glass of wine—but nothing had helped.

At eleven she'd turned on the light and tried to read herself to sleep, but the words had blurred on the page until all she could see was John's face when he had walked out. He had looked stricken—as though he couldn't bear to leave her.

But that must have been a trick of the light or her tear-damp eyes. No matter what she thought she'd seen etched in his tired face, it hadn't been unhappiness. John was too selfish to be unhappy.

"Ridiculous," she muttered, turning onto her side and staring at the shadows on the wall. John hadn't changed. He was still charming and powerful and sexy. He would be a good tribal chairman, using his personal power to get what he wanted from the other members of the council, just as he had tried to use his sex appeal and considerable masculine charisma to get what he wanted from her.

But once he accepted her answer as final, he would find someone else to replicate the Santa Ysabel. John was very result-oriented.

Stretching restlessly Aurora turned onto her back, and a sudden pain stabbed her temple. Her little girl was gone, but there were other little girls and boys on the pueblo who might never have the kind of advantages her child would have had. If her experience could make that happen—

"No," she whispered, her voice a strangled rasp in the silence. "I can't. I just . . . can't."

She had tried over and over until her arms had grown numb and her fingers had bled. Yesterday was the first time she'd been in her studio in months. It hurt too much to see the empty wheel and lifeless pots. Her failures.

If she allowed herself to hope, if she allowed herself to try and then failed again, it would kill her. And yet, how would she live with herself if she refused to do what she could to help Dawn's people?

A sad smile curved her lips as she thought about the small grave in a windswept juniper grove near one of the red mesas. She had left the pueblo right after the funeral and she'd never gone back. Could she make herself face the ghosts? Worse still, could she see John every day without reliving the pain and the anger all over again?

"I believe in you," John had said, and even though she knew he would have said anything to get her to agree to his plan, she couldn't get his words out of her mind.

Could she believe in herself again?

She groaned and buried her head in the pillow. She just didn't know if she had the courage to risk failure one more time.


John slammed his fist into his hot pillow and tried to find a comfortable spot for his aching head. He kicked off the sheet and tucked his hands under his head.

The party had long since ended, and the house had been quiet for hours. His inner sense of time told him it was close to dawn, but he was still wide-awake. His muscles were strung tight with the same tension that drove him to ride Cortes, his mustang stallion, until he was worn out enough to sleep.

He groaned and rubbed his cheek against the pillow, remembering the trusting way Rory had once loved him. She had held nothing back, giving her heart as well as her body. She had been his wife, his lover, his friend. His woman.

John felt a shudder travel through him, and his rough hand clutched the edge of the pillow so hard his tendons strained to the edge of pain. In his mind Aurora's loving eyes still smiled at him, but he knew that the love that had once been there was dead. And he'd killed it.

"Damn," he muttered, sitting up. He turned on the light, squinting as the glare sliced the darkness.

The guest room in the big old home was large and comfortably appointed, but he was as miserable as a prisoner trapped in a narrow cell. More than anything he needed to move, to work off the punishing tension turning his body into sweat-damp knots, but it was far too early to be wandering around Todd's house.

Years ago, when he hadn't been able to sleep, he had reached for Aurora, losing himself in the halo of love she'd created around them.

Groaning softly, he rubbed his belly, trying to erase the sick feeling inside. She'd snuggled so trustingly against him, offering her warmth and her caring without reservation. Like a selfish fool, he'd taken everything she'd offered without questioning what he offered in return.

John turned his head until he could see the small photograph in the leather frame on the nightstand. The glow of the lamp shone softly on the radiant features of his bride.

If he closed his eyes, he could hear the whisper of love in her voice as she'd repeated the customary vows of her people, words that she'd meant with all her heart.

"*. . . to love and to cherish . . .*"

He rubbed the bridge of his nose where the cartilage had mended crookedly after his father's fist had smashed it.

As a kid, watching his mother endure beating after beating because she loved his father, he had seen exactly what love was all about. By the time he was able to say the words, he knew that love meant pain.

"Your father loves us, Johnny," his mother had said when she'd found him crying because he hadn't been able to protect her from the old man's fists. "Some day you'll understand."

But how could he understand when a few minutes later his father had seen his tears and had beaten him unconscious because crying was unmanly, even for a five-year-old?

After that, whenever he had felt any tender emotions at all, he had swiftly stuffed those feelings deep inside someplace where no one would see his shame.

By the time he'd been old enough to stand up to his father and protect his mother, Luis Olvera had been dead, a victim of a stabbing in a bar in Chamisa.

The boy known as Johnny had been nearly ten then, and instead of grief, all he'd felt was relief. His mother had cried during the death ritual, but he'd been dry-eyed and stoic. It had been years before he realized he couldn't cry. He didn't even remember how.

A man didn't cry and he didn't feel. That was how he had survived. John closed his eyes, feeling the pressure behind his lids grow until it became a dull pain.

When Aurora had left him, he'd tried his best to forget her. He'd told himself he didn't need her or any woman in his life on a permanent basis.

But without her laughter and warmth and support, the emptiness that had always been inside him had become unbearable. Challenges that had once consumed him seemed trivial. Nothing had felt good to him anymore. Not his successes, not the admiration of his peers or the approval of his superiors. He had walked through the days and nights like a man suffering from a terminal illness.

When his life had become unbearable, he'd resigned and gone home to a people who held him in contempt for turning his back on his heritage and on them. Facing them as though they'd been a mirror, he'd discovered he didn't like the man he'd become any more than they did.

In desperation he'd turned to the Seeking Way. Somehow he had survived, surprising everyone, even himself. After he'd recovered, he had set about remaking his life. He had rebuilt the fences on the ranch and worked hard to win the forgiveness and respect of the people he had once scorned.

It hadn't been easy. He'd used his savings to buy Cortes and two mares. He was slowly breeding them to reproduce the best qualities of the sturdy, old-fashioned mustangs that had helped his people survive in a hostile land.

Most days he spent alone, with only the hired hands on his ranch for company. When he had the time, he listened to the old people recount the legends he had all but forgotten.

Over the long, lonely months he had won a measure of acceptance, if not affection from most of the members of the tribe. He even had a few friends now, and occasionally he spent time out on the far mesa with his Uncle Spruce's family. But he still had a long way to go before the people he cared about forgot the things he had done to hurt them.

Slowly he turned his head, seeing the silhouette of the pot Rory had called "Dream's End." He went cold inside, thinking about the agony in her eyes when she'd talked about the magic.

With a muttered curse that sounded more like a cry of pain than anger, John turned onto his stomach and buried his face in the pillow. He didn't know how to help her find the magic any more than he knew how to love her.

John's boots made a hollow sound as he entered the silent kitchen in search of the coffee he could smell brewing. Maria looked up from the stove and grinned.

"*Buenos dias, señor.* You want *cafe*, no?"

"*Si, Maria, por favor.*" He switched his gaze to the burly, red-haired man slumped over the table near the large picture window facing the flower-bedecked patio.

Todd Gulbranson was the son of one of the wealthiest men in Texas, but at the moment he needed a shave and his eyes were red-rimmed and watery.

"Looks like I missed some party," John commented with a grin as he pulled out a chair and sat down.

"You always were smarter'n me, John, old buddy." A grimace contorted Todd's pale features as he stared groggily at the fizzing drink in front of him.

Before John could answer, Maria set a steaming cup of coffee on the place mat.

"*Gracias,*" he said with a tired smile. The smell of frying bacon was making his stomach growl. He hadn't eaten since he'd tried to force down Aurora's quiche.

Todd shifted his gaze but not his head. "Way I hear it, old buddy, you got in way too early last night. Sounds like the lady wasn't impressed with your offer." Todd gulped down the seltzer in three quick swallows, then wiped his mouth with the back of his hand.

John sugared his coffee, then took a greedy gulp and waited for the caffeine to hit his system.

"No, and she wasn't much impressed with me, either." John ran a hand through his shower-damp hair. He was bone-tired and depressed as hell.

Todd's bloodshot eyes crinkled at the corners in male sympathy. "You never said what happened to break you two up. Whaddya do, cheat on her?"

John felt his gut tighten. "I never wanted another woman from the moment I saw her. I still don't."

He could tell Todd about the nights he'd awakened in a cold sweat, his body hurting, his dreams filled with her. Or the hours he'd spent trying to figure out a way to win her back. But a man fought some battles alone and in silence.

"What about her? She found another guy?"

The knot in his stomach flared into actual pain at the thought of Aurora taking another man into her bed. "I don't know," he admitted, rubbing his thumb over the twisted silver band encircling his wrist.

She hadn't remarried, but it was very possible that there had been men—lovers—in her life. Rory was too giving, too sensual to live without love for very long. He cursed, first in English and then in the simple, almost primitive language he'd once sworn to forget.

"Whoa, partner," Todd muttered, "I didn't mean to set your temper a-boilin'. I know the lady means a lot to you."

John drained his cup and leaned back, his forearm resting on the shiny table.

"*Buen provecho, señores.* Enjoy your meal." Maria put down plates piled with food in front of them and refilled their cups before padding out of the kitchen.

The two men ate in silence for several minutes before Todd glanced across the table.

"I've looked over the loan application you filed with us last month," he said in a reluctant tone. "For the trust fund you want to set up to pay salaries for that clinic y'all are aiming to build."

John stiffened, but he kept his expression impassive. "You gonna approve it?" He pushed away his food half-eaten.

Todd's gaze dropped to his plate. "My people tell me the pueblo's a lousy risk. No money, no convertible assets. Seems y'all have an ironclad rule against selling off land to raise capital, and if this cottage industry you plan to start fails, you'll have no way of paying off the note."

John drained his cup. "Your people are right. We are a lousy risk." He hesitated, glancing down at his hands. Almost four years of constant hard work had callused his palms, and the sun had turned his skin to leather. These were the hands of a rancher now, not a diplomat.

A poor rancher, he reminded himself. Every cent he made went back into the ranch. Someday, if he could hold out long enough, he would make a decent living selling the mustangs that were enjoying increasing popularity among the rich. But that was a year or so in the future, when the foals he had now were saddle-broken and old enough to sell.

"Can you make it a loan to me personally?" he asked.

Todd cleared his throat. "If it were just me, hell, yes, I'd do it—on a handshake. But I have to answer to the board of directors. What do you have for collateral?" His freckled hand toyed with his cup.

"My stock."

The other man stared at him, his jaw slack. "Are you *loco*, man? If you lose those horses, you're bankrupt."

John thought about the empty place in his bed and in his life. In a way he'd already lost it all. "It wouldn't be the worst thing that ever happened to me."

"You askin'?"

John hesitated. "Not yet. But if I did?"

Todd nodded slowly, but his expression remained troubled. "I think I can push it through for you on that basis, yeah."

The phone rang and Todd winced, holding his head in both hands.

"Maria, get that, will ya?" he bellowed, then winced again.

"*Si, señor,*" she called as she hurried into the kitchen and picked up the receiver.

She spoke quietly, then extended the phone to John. "A woman for you, *señor.*"

He and Todd exchanged glances. "Go for it," Todd muttered, his eyes sympathetic.

John took a deep breath. "Olvera."

"This is Aurora." Her voice was weary-sounding, but there was a thread of determination running through it.

John's heart kicked into a gallop, and his hands began to sweat. "Good morning. You're up early."

"Yes."

He tried not to think about Aurora in the morning, with her eyes still dream-soft and her lips full and wet from his wake-up kiss. His body stirred, and he knew that it was going to be another long and frustrating day.

His hand clenched around the receiver, and he took a deep breath. "Aurora, listen, I understand how you feel about me, but—"

"I don't feel anything for you," she interrupted, a chill in her voice. "But I do care about my daughter's people. So I've decided to accept the job. I'll be there in two days."

She hung up without saying goodbye.

# Chapter 5

This certainly isn't Mazatlan, Aurora thought as she braked her small station wagon to a stop in front of the rock pillar marking the turnoff to John's ranch.

Keeping her hands on the wheel, she allowed herself a moment to rest after her long morning's drive from El Paso where she had stopped overnight with her parents.

Because there were no house numbers on the pueblo living quarters, she had reluctantly agreed to meet John at his ranch so that he could take her to the place where she was to stay. But now that she had arrived, she was having second thoughts. She didn't want to see his house again. She didn't want to see him.

Staring through the windshield, she tried to will away the nervous tension that had been with her since she had turned off the state highway onto the dirt road leading to Santa Ysabel. Nothing moved outside the little yellow car, not even the prickly branches of sagebrush bordering a new-looking barbed-wire fence.

Then directly ahead in the sparse pasture she saw a dun-colored stallion with a black mane and tail galloping to-

ward her along the fence line. Seconds later he thundered
past, his muscles moving with fluid grace beneath the un-
blemished hide that shone from careful brushing.

A thrill ran through her and brought a smile to her face.
The mustang was clearly a champion, one of nature's most
magnificent works of art. He had been bred for stamina and
endurance in a hard land, and his powerful muscles could
carry him for pounding miles over the worst ground without faltering.

She knew without having to think about it that the
spirited animal was John's. In many ways the horse and his
master were alike. Neither would willingly bow to restraint
of any kind.

Biting off a sigh, she put the car into gear and pressed
down on the gas. She had to see John this one time, but after
that she would avoid him as much as possible. She had to
live with her painful memories because she had no choice,
but, thank God, she didn't have to live with the man who'd
given them to her.

As soon as she made the turn, she could see the small,
square ranch house through the windbreak of stunted juni-
pers to the north. There were a few more patches in the ancient adobe walls, and the window frames, while sporting a
new coat of pale blue paint, still sagged. Above the one-
story building the roof displayed a patchwork of old and
new tiles, suggesting a recent repair job.

There were two trucks parked in the wide place in front of
the house, one black and fairly new, the other a rusted pea-
green with mismatched fenders and a gun rack in the rear
window. She hesitated, then pulled behind the newer one
and shut off the engine.

The area around the house had the same wild and empty
look that she remembered. Overhead, the sky was the same
blue, with a few wispy clouds trailing east toward Santa Fe.

But instead of the rickety lean-to that had once sheltered
Morningstar's horses, a large barn had been constructed
behind the house. The wide boards hadn't yet weathered,
and there was a raw look to the land where it stood.

The doors to the loft had been swung inward, and a new-looking rope dangled from a pulley attached to a sturdy frame above the doors. A stack of hay bales stood in front of the barn's big sliding door, which was half open, revealing a dark interior. A man's plaid shirt had been carelessly tossed onto one of the bales. There was no sign of John.

Aurora tilted the hand on the wheel until she could see the face of her watch. It was a few minutes past twelve. No doubt he was in the house having lunch.

Squaring her shoulders she grabbed her keys and purse and stepped from the car. The sooner she got this over with, the better.

Outside, the pungent scent of the scrub piñon stung her nostrils, bringing back a dozen memories, most of them painful now. Through the soles of her sneakers she felt the scorching heat radiating from the dirt, and the glare stung her eyes.

As she approached the front door, she remembered the first time John had brought her here. He'd been quiet and tense and more withdrawn than she had ever seen him. He had treated his mother with the polite indulgence of a dutiful son, but with none of the open affection she'd seen in the other pueblo families.

Later, when Aurora had asked him about the rest of his family, and especially about his father, his eyes had gone cold and hard. His face had become stiff. "He's dead," was all that he would say, all he had ever said. Eventually she had stopped asking.

The front door smelled of fresh paint, but a tentative touch assured her that the rough panel was dry. She knocked loudly, then waited. There was no answer.

Before she could knock again she heard angry male voices coming from behind the house. The words were indistinct, but the deeper voice of the two was John's.

She hesitated, then followed the well-worn path toward the rear. As she rounded the corner of the house, she saw John and another man standing by the open gate to a large corral attached to the barn.

John was bareheaded and his long, thick hair was bound back with a sweat-stained leather thong. His eyes were narrowed against the brightness of the midday sun. He wore only patched jeans and muddy boots. A layer of sweat and grime covered his wide chest, as though he had been working for a long time in the heat.

The man with him stood with his arms akimbo, his head tilted forward like a crazed bull ready to charge. The brim of an old straw hat shadowed his face, but he appeared to be in his mid-twenties, with blunt features and a short, thick neck.

Inside the corral a small brown mare with foam-wet flanks stood with her head down, breathing hard. A boy of about twelve stood next to the little horse, holding the reins. Even from a distance Aurora could see the fear in the boy's eyes as he watched the two men.

She stopped and opened her mouth to call John's name, but his voice cut through the distance between them like the hiss of a steel-tipped lash.

"I'm going to tell you this one time, Ruiz, so you'd better listen. You mistreat one of my horses like this again, and I'll make sure you won't sit a saddle for one hell of a long time."

Ruiz aimed a short, angry kick at a clod of dirt. "Come off it, Olvera. I seen you ride hard—"

"Hard, yes, but I've never ridden a horse into the ground," John cut in, his voice dangerously taut. "You're damn lucky she's not lame."

Ruiz muttered something under his breath, but he seemed unwilling to risk John's wrath by saying the words aloud. Aurora realized she'd stopped breathing and released the trapped air.

John gave Ruiz a long, hard look, then snorted in disgust and turned away. At almost the same moment, Ruiz twisted around and reached into his boot. He came up with a knife and raised it to strike.

"John, look out!" Aurora shouted. "He's got a knife."

John whirled around. She heard him cry out, then saw the blood spurt from a gash in his forearm. Glittering red drops spattered his chest and ran down his arm.

She gasped. Fear and adrenaline shot through her at the same time and with the same force. She had to do something, anything. If his artery were cut, he could bleed to death in minutes.

Frantically she looked around the barnyard but saw nothing to use as a weapon. Except her purse. Clutching the heavy canvas bag tightly, she ran forward. Just as she reached the two struggling men, John closed his fingers around the other man's wrist and slammed it against the corral railing.

Ruiz cried out, and the knife fell to the ground between them. With a violent kick of his boot, John sent it flying under the bottom fence rail.

Hurling obscenities, Ruiz aimed a vicious blow at John's jaw. John's head snapped back, and sweat flew from his face. But before Ruiz could hit him again, John smashed his left into the man's belly.

Aurora's hand went to her own stomach just as Ruiz doubled over. Head hanging, he staggered forward. John grabbed a handful of shirt and jerked Ruiz upright. The straw hat fell between them and was crushed under John's boot.

"You're fired," John spat out, drawing in great gulps of air. He shoved Ruiz backward and released his grip. "Pick up your check at headquarters tomorrow and don't ever come back here again. You got that?"

Ruiz gasped for air. His face twisted. "Yeah, I got it, all right." He coughed, then spit. He glanced sideways, and his black eyes turned ugly. "Man with a mean temper like yours ought not to have an Anglo for his whore. Bruises show too well on that pretty white skin."

John's face grew still. "You got one minute to get out of my sight, or I'll kill you." His voice was as deadly as a rattler's strike.

Ruiz shot John a look of pure hatred, then stumbled toward Aurora. She took a step backward, giving him plenty of room. A few seconds later she heard a truck engine start. The motor raced and tires spun as he backed up and roared down the dirt track.

In a few terse sentences John instructed the boy to walk the mare until she had cooled down. The boy nodded and began to lead the lathered horse around the corral.

John watched for a second, then turned toward Aurora. A terrible anger was still in his eyes, although he seemed to be making an effort to control himself.

"John, you need a doctor." She stared at the gash above his wrist. It was still oozing blood, but it didn't seem as bad as she had feared. "I'll drive you."

John wiped away the blood with his palm. "It's not as deep as it looks. Don't worry about it. I've had worst cuts from barbed wire."

Aurora didn't move. She wasn't sure she could. The silence lengthened, broken only by the strident sound of the mare's breathing and the slow clop of her hooves.

Suddenly she felt faint. She had to sit down. Her legs were stiff as she made her way to the bales and sank down onto the closest one. The hay was scratchy against her bare thighs and smelled of dust and grass.

John hesitated, then walked toward the watering trough six or seven feet away from where she sat. There was an angry red mark on the side of his jaw where Ruiz had struck, and his chest was still spotted with blood.

"You're early," he said, working the old-fashioned pump. A steady stream of water splashed into the half-full stainless-steel basin, splattering drops on his thighs.

"I didn't know there was any set time for me to arrive." Her voice sounded as scratchy as the hay. "You said I could make my own rules."

His gaze searched her face as though he was trying to guess her thoughts. Or tell her something important. "You can," he said finally. "Whatever you want, I'll see that you get it."

"Right now I just want to get out of this heat and settle into my own place."

He stopped pumping to look at her. "You always were a nester. Give you a few weeks and you could make even the worst dump into a home. I was always proud to show it off."

Hurt settled like a sharp stone in the pit of her stomach. Is that all their home had meant to him? Something to show off to his colleagues?

She refused to care. "You'd better use soap on that arm."

At the low note of impatience in her voice, the anger that had gradually been disappearing from his eyes flared again. But he made no comment. Instead he stripped off the leather headband and shoved it into his pocket. Bending stiffly from the waist, he cupped both hands and splashed his face and shoulders until his hair was soaked and his skin glistened.

Slowly he straightened and raked his hair away from his brow. Water ran over the thick muscles of his shoulders and slipped down the ridges of his chest. His jeans were tight, and plastered to his thighs by the dampness. What little the faded denim hid, her memory supplied. John was power-fully male, especially when he'd been aroused.

Heat rushed into her cheeks, making her skin hotter than the sun's rays.

John stood motionless, watching her. She saw awareness in his dusty brown eyes and a barely restrained hunger that made her go weak inside. He'd known exactly what she'd been thinking. She'd never been able to keep her feelings from showing on her face, no matter how hard she'd tried.

Wiping the wetness from his jaw, he strode toward her. As he came closer, she could smell the musky male scent of sweat and hard labor on his damp skin.

For an instant she had an image of John in formal dress, striding into the elegant reception room of the American embassy in San Sebastian, an easy smile flashing suavely as he made witty cocktail conversation in Spanish and English with equal fluency.

Suddenly she didn't know what to say or how to act with this man. When he was around her blood seemed to move faster through her veins, and the skin stretched over her cheekbones seemed to burn. Nothing made sense. He was different, he was the same. She didn't want him, she did.

But that was simply the woman in her reacting to his sheer, hard-driving appeal, she lectured herself firmly. Once he was out of sight she would stop thinking about him.

John sluiced the water from his chest with his good arm, then gave her the kind of lazy one-sided smile that most women found irresistible. She assured herself that she was immune, even though the nervous flutter spreading through her body told her that she was not.

"I'm glad you're here, Aurora," he said. "I...we've been waiting a long time."

"Eight weeks isn't a lot of time to turn out skilled potters," she said, riveting her gaze on a spot a few inches to the left of his eyes.

"Don't worry. I don't expect the impossible. Everyone I've recruited for you has had training of some kind or other. Unfortunately they've learned only white man's art, not ours."

Ours? she thought. What happened to the man who had erased his Native American origins so thoroughly most of his colleagues had thought he was of Spanish descent?

"I didn't thank you for warning me," he continued in a husky tone. He took a step closer, then stopped. Behind him the sun spilled his long shadow onto the ground in front of her. She slid her feet backward until her heels bumped the bale. He was still much too close.

With the sun playing over the hard-packed muscles of his shoulders and arms and the heat of the fistfight still in his eyes, he looked rugged and virile and dangerous.

She pulled a blade of alfalfa from the bale and began twisting it into a knot. "That man was trying to kill you."

John dismissed her words with a shrug. "Probably. But thanks to you, he didn't." Blood ran down his wrist, but he didn't seem to notice.

"Who is he?"

John looked impatient. "His name is Buck Ruiz. His brother, Diego, was the head of the council before me. Diego had been in control for a long time, too long for a lot of us. There were some hard feelings when he lost the last election to me, so when Buck was released from prison last year, I hired him as a favor to his brother." His smile slanted briefly. "Obviously that was a mistake."

"And John Olvera never makes mistakes." The words were out before she could stop them.

The bones in his face shifted, as though he was trying to control himself. "You're wrong, Aurora," he said, biting off his words. "I made the worst mistake of my life when I went back to San Sebastian without you. I'd give everything I have if I could have that choice again."

Aurora's jaw dropped. She crushed the hay stalk in her fingers and stared at him with eyes that grew wider and wider. "I . . . I don't believe you," she said finally.

He stared at her for a moment, then pulled his shirt from the bale behind her. "Then I'll just have to convince you." He wrapped the shirt around his bloody forearm and walked away.

John sat on the edge of his bed and tugged off his boots. One by one he threw them into the corner. His movements were slow and jerky, and his bruised hands were stiff. Now that the danger was passed and the adrenaline was no longer pumping, his arm was beginning to hurt like hell.

On the rare occasions when the anger that was always with him erupted, it was wildly erratic and unpredictable, like a half-tamed animal escaping its cage. Afterward he felt wrung-out and mad at himself for losing control.

Breathing deeply he tried to will his body to relax, but as violent as his rage had been, the hunger that Aurora stirred in him was even more powerful. For an instant when she had looked at him standing by the trough, he'd seen a matching hunger in her eyes.

His chest swelled with hope. If he could make her want him, maybe he could convince her to give him a chance to prove that he'd changed. Damn, he wanted that.

For a silent moment he allowed himself to think about the other women in his life. There had been a lot of them in the lonely months after the divorce—sexy, experienced women with eager smiles and willing bodies. They had slaked his desire, but not one of them had made him feel whole inside the way Rory had.

Closing his eyes, he ran his hand over the thin coverlet beneath him. Unlike this rough material, her skin had been silky and warm, and when she'd been aroused he had felt tiny ripples move under his hand. When they had made love, she had slid her strong potter's hands around his neck to pull him closer until his body had surged into hers.

Never before or since had he known a woman more responsive or more innately sensual. She had been an irresistible blend of uninhibited passion and serene poise that had fascinated him as no other woman had ever done, not even the polished and practiced debutantes he'd met at Princeton who had seemed set on adding an Indian to their long lists of conquests.

He cursed savagely under his breath. He hadn't meant to hurt her. Because he hadn't understood the depth of her suffering, he had misread her reaction to his refusal to give her what she'd asked for. He'd thought she just needed time to get over the baby's death. When he'd left, he had told himself that when she'd finished grieving, she would realize that her place was with her husband.

But he had been wrong. Her grief had made her fragile and easily trampled, like the tiny seedlings that appeared after the first rain. She had trusted him to take care of her. To keep his promises.

He'd done neither.

He hung his head, feeling the sharp bite of regret tear his insides. He'd hurt her so much. Maybe so badly she would never trust him again.

Cursing again, he got to his feet. There wasn't a damn thing he could do about the past. All he could do was try to make these next two months count for something.

He stripped off his jeans and kicked them aside. Pressing his throbbing arm against his belly, he walked into the small bathroom, which he had recently built between the two bedrooms, and turned on the shower. Stepping into the stall, he gasped as the cold water stung his bruised body.

He'd vowed to be patient. He'd told himself a dozen times that it was enough to have her close to him again. But now that she was here, he knew that his need for her was stronger than ever. Stronger than he was sure he could handle.

No, he thought instantly. He had always known how to fight for what he wanted. Somehow he'd find a way to make her trust him again, even if he had to let her see how lost he was without her. Even if he had to let her see who he was inside—for the first time in his life.

The stinging chill began seeping into his skin, making him shiver violently. He leaned against the slick fiberglass and let the water pound against him.

For the first time since he had left home, he was scared. Because if she walked away from him the way he'd once walked away from her, he didn't know how he could stand it.


Aurora rubbed her hands over her wrinkled shorts and stared at the new red tiles dotting the roof. John had patched his roof. Was he now trying to patch up their relationship?

His words hung in the air and refused to fade. A different choice, he'd said. Was he trying to bribe her with the Santa Ysabel into coming back to him?

"No way," she vowed. She didn't care what he wanted or why.

One dose of heartbreak was enough for her. More than enough. She wasn't one for throwing herself into the same burning building over and over again until the fire destroyed her. She would never let John close enough to hurt her again.

Silently confirming that grim resolution with a squaring of her slim shoulders, she picked up her handbag and walked toward the front door. She would wait for John on the stoop.

But as she approached, she saw that the door was ajar. Obviously John intended for her to wait inside.

Her stomach flip-flopped, and the lump returned to her throat. Her palms felt damp, and she wiped first one and then the other on her shorts.

She didn't want to go inside the house, but the heat was beginning to make her light-headed. She could swelter in the car or wait in the front room. There wasn't a third choice.

She waited a few seconds longer, her ear straining for the clatter of boot heels inside, but the small house seemed as silent as a tomb.

Raising her chin, she took a deep breath and pushed open the door. The interior was dim and cool and smelled strongly of wood smoke. She stepped across the threshold, then stopped dead. Her mouth opened in astonishment, and her eyes blinked in disbelief. For an instant she felt as though she were back in San Sebastian, in the cozy little house John had rented for them near the embassy.

Her small rosewood sofa, the one with the tiny cherubs carved into the back, sat in a place of honor in front of the age-blackened fireplace. Next to it was the handmade Moorish table she'd bought in an open-air market in Peru during their first year of marriage. Inlaid with ivory, the little table had been their first piece of furniture, and her favorite.

Her small Victorian chair was there, too, and the needle-point stool that had once supported the tiny slippers of an aristocratic Spanish lady.

How John had teased her about that dainty, little stool! "My gracious lady," he'd called her, before kissing her so hard she'd felt more lusty than gracious.

Aurora walked slowly from piece to piece, the lump in her throat growing larger. The furniture gleamed softly in the dim interior; the pieces had been recently dusted. She sucked in a nervous breath and caught a whiff of lemon-scented polish. Her astonishment grew. Had John been caring for her things all this time?

His things, she corrected, feeling a dull pain beneath her heart. She hadn't wanted anything that would remind her of their marriage.

"They're just things," she whispered, rubbing her fingers over one of the brass fittings on the desk she'd bought him for their fifth anniversary.

They'd gone to an embassy party that night and danced until daybreak. Then they'd gone home to make love with the first rays of a glorious tropical dawn warming their bedroom.

Before she could stop herself, her gaze shifted to the larger of the two bedrooms off the living room. The door was closed, and she could hear the faint sound of water running from some place beyond.

That can't be a shower, she thought, and then realized that that was exactly what it was. Along with his other improvements John must have added a bathroom to the house.

Her breathing faltered as she remembered the times they'd made love in the old-fashioned claw-foot tub in San Sebastian, too eager to wait until they were in bed.

If she closed her eyes, she could feel the slickness of John's skin against hers. And she could hear his laugh caress her when she'd gotten bubble bath on her nose. He'd wiped it away with his fingers before kissing her breathless.

Useless memories, she told herself, but they hurt, nonetheless. Just as it hurt to be in this house.

Slowly she turned her head until she found the curtained entrance to the other bedroom. That had been John's room, the place where she'd delivered their child. She would have died in that room if it hadn't been for John's mother.

Slowly, as though drawn by a power beyond her control, she walked toward the roughly woven curtain. At the threshold she paused, her heart thumping in a slow, steady rhythm like the tolling of a mourning bell. Her hand shook as she pushed aside the dusty drape.

The small room was even shabbier than she remembered. The walls needed paint, and the bed sagged in the middle. Beneath the bare window sat a cheap pine chest. A chair with a broken back served as a nightstand. There were no pictures on the wall to bring pleasure to the eye, no rug to warm the feet on a cold morning. In fact, the rough floor tiles sat directly on the dirt, forming an uneven surface that was treacherous for the unwary.

Her heart slowed until it felt as though it was barely beating, and a heaviness settled over her. Had this room always been so shabby?

"Bad memories?" John's voice came to her from behind, carrying a hint of sympathy.

Aurora's mouth jerked in surprise, and her heart speeded. Turning her head, she saw him standing a few feet away, watching her.

He had showered and his hair was still wet and slicked back from his forehead. He was dressed in clean jeans and a white dress shirt that appeared even whiter against his dark skin. The sleeves were rolled back and a linen handkerchief bound his injured forearm. Blood had already seeped through the cloth to form a ragged circle above his wrist.

Aurora tightened her grip on her purse. Suddenly the small house seemed to close in around her. She took a step back. John didn't move, but his gaze followed her intently.

"Was this room always so...so bare?" she asked, thinking about the colorful touches and special things that might have made it into a place for a little boy to spend his childhood.

His somber gaze shifted to the sad little room behind her, and his big shoulders lifted in a faint shrug. "Looks the way it's always looked. I don't go in there much."

After his return, while his mother had been alive, he had slept on the couch, rather than sleep in the place that was still haunted by his father's memory.

"But surely, when you were little—"

"When I was little, the roof leaked and the window had cardboard in it instead of glass."

She started to put out her hand in an instinctive gesture of comfort, but this time she stopped short of touching him. "I'm sorry," she said, because she didn't know what else to say.

His eyes met hers squarely and a bit defiantly. In her mind she could see this same look on a boyish face, and for the first time she had a hint of the way it must have been for him as a child of poverty in an affluent world. His fierce pride would have made life intolerable for him, then.

John shot a brief glance into the small bedroom, then looked away. "It's not much like the nursery you fixed up, that's for sure."

Aurora didn't want to think about the cheerful little room she'd decorated with such joy. Awkwardly she looked around.

"What do you think of the changes I've made?" he asked when the silence stretched longer.

Intuition told her that he wasn't talking about the house or his profession or any of the things she could see.

Ignoring his question, she asked instead, "What . . . what did you do with the rest of the furniture?"

His gaze shifted briefly, then returned to her face. "Our bed is in the room I use now. I got rid of the other things."

She knew that he meant the nursery furniture. The antique crib, the small yellow chest decorated with butterflies, the big stuffed bear, all the things she had selected with such love and anticipation.

"I see." Her voice was thick, and she cleared her throat, avoiding his gaze. Her fingers twisted the strap of her purse over and over.

He took a careful step forward. "About the baby—"

"No." Her voice was a frantic burst of sound. "I . . . won't talk about the baby."

His mouth went white, and the tawny flecks of his brown eyes dulled. With a quick tug of his big hand, he pulled the curtain closed. "Someday we'll have to talk about her."

Aurora shook her head, and wisps of hair feathered across her cheek. He hesitated, then brushed away the silken strands with one blunt finger. She didn't trust this new tenderness in him. She didn't trust her reaction to it.

She had been prepared for selfishness. Even for seduction. But somehow his patient efforts to be understanding and kind were pushing big holes through her defenses.

"Don't look at me like that," he murmured, his voice a rough plea. "I didn't mean to make you sad."

He came closer. Without thinking, she tilted her head so that she could see the expression on his face. His thumb brushed her lower lip until the tautness relaxed. "Smile for me, Aurora."

She shook her head. She didn't want to smile. She told herself she didn't want to do anything for him.

John accepted her refusal with a fleeting smile of his own. "Someday you'll smile for me again," he said in a soft tone. "And then we'll talk about a lot of things."

What things? she wondered, and then immediately caught herself. She wouldn't allow herself to be curious about this man.

"John, about my apartment . . ."

"It's ready. Everything is ready." But he made no move to leave.

Aurora glanced at the door. "We should go."

"Should we?" His eyebrows drew together, deepening the lines of some past suffering.

"Sweet Rory," he whispered in a voice so low it sounded like a groan. Before she could answer, his mouth brushed hers with a restraint so exquisite she wanted to weep.

She held her breath, unable—or was it unwilling?—to look away. She couldn't seem to move, not even when his hand curled around the nape of her neck. His palm was warm and calloused. His fingers were hard, reminding her of the strength in that hand. But this time his touch was a caress so gentle she wanted to cry for all the times she had reached for him in the dark, only to find his place cold and empty next to her.

"I've missed you," he said in a gruff voice. He tried to smile, but he couldn't seem to manage. His hand tugged her closer. He was going to kiss her again.

No, she thought. No. She had to get away from this place. From him.

"Please don't, John," she whispered, flattening her palm against his chest. His heart was racing. "We don't want this."

"Don't we?" John managed a slow breath. He had felt the shock run through her when he'd kissed her, and then the brief softening of her mouth under his.

Elation shot through him, and he wanted to scoop her into his arms and carry her into their bed—until reality brought him crashing back.

This time he'd taken her by surprise, but that didn't mean she would let him close to her again. He still had a long way to go before she would trust him again.

"Can you try to forgive me?" he asked softly.

Aurora glanced over his strong shoulder at the curtain screening off the sad room. If only he knew how much she wanted to be free of those terrible, haunting memories. If only he knew how hard she'd tried to drive the past from her mind, but the terrible sense of loss was always there inside her, waiting for a word, an image, a familiar scent to trigger it.

John heard the little catch in her breath, and his gut tightened. A tiny line of tension whitened around her mouth, erasing the softness he'd put there with his kiss.

"You were my husband, John," she answered in a small, sad voice that hurt him more than the sharpest rebuke. "I believed in you. I was so sure you would never do anything to hurt me. But you did. No matter what you do now, or even what you say, that will always be between us."

# Chapter 6

Only if you want it to be." The steely control was back in his voice. "Only if you want to hold on to the bitterness."

Aurora challenged him with a look. She was still feeling his warm mouth sliding across hers in a kiss that seemed more like a promise. "I'm not bitter, John. But I'm not a naive twenty-year-old anymore, either. I want more from a relationship than good sex."

"At least you admit it was good," he said in a gritty voice.

For an instant Aurora actually wanted to grin at the intensely masculine look of frustration that crossed his face. And then she remembered how skilled John was at throwing his opponents off-guard.

"Good or bad, it doesn't matter. I'm not going to sleep with you again," she said with a note of finality to her voice. She turned toward the door.

He blocked her way with his body. "What if I told you I've done little else for the past five years but try to figure out how to get you back?"

For an instant she thought he might kiss her again, and her gaze shifted a few more inches to the hard mouth that rarely smiled. Her lashes fluttered down.

For an instant she wanted that stern, masculine mouth on hers, warm and seeking and seductive, and she wanted those big hands on her breast, on her painfully taut nipples, on all of her. Heat rose from the V of her blouse, spreading quickly to her downcast face.

"I wouldn't believe you. You don't need me, John. Any woman would do."

"No, Rory. I've had other women. Some were even prettier, and one or two were even rich enough to *buy* the embassy in San Sebastian. But I've always ended up comparing every woman I've met to you. You won every time." His sudden grin made her blink.

"Thank you very much," she said in a tart tone that bordered on sarcasm. "I'm so pleased you think so."

The fact that he had had other women in his bed didn't surprise her. The fact that she hated the very idea did.

John saw the confusion settle in her eyes, and he told himself that was good. At least she wasn't glaring at him any more.

"C'mon, professor," he muttered. "Let's get out of here."

He stepped back and indicated with a nod of his head that she was to precede him. She could sense him behind her, but she focused her gaze straight ahead.

"I made a few calls these past two days, and we already have orders for about six dozen pots," he said, reaching past her to open the door.

Anxiety made her forget the tangled emotions besetting her. "I hope you didn't give them an early delivery date," she said in a voice that still sounded stiff.

"That's up to you," he said, opening the door for her. John had always had beautiful manners. He told her once that he'd learned them from books, the way he had learned most things about sophisticated mores.

Habit made her smile her thanks, and their gazes locked. For a flutter of heartbeats they shared a memory of times past when they had walked together outside on a day like this one. She had felt so proud of her handsome and brilliant husband. And deeply, happily-ever-after in love. But those days were gone forever.

"All set?" His voice was flat, as though he had read her thoughts.

"Yes."

He reached for the Stetson hanging from a rack by the door, and a swatch of white caught her eye. Blood had nearly soaked the makeshift bandage.

Her stomach jumped wildly, and a metallic taste stung her throat. She'd forgotten about the knife wound in his arm. For a few minutes she'd forgotten about everything but the warmth inside her when he'd kissed her.

"You need to have that stitched," she said, her voice hollow. "A cut like that could easily become infected."

Still holding the hat, he turned his arm so that the blood was no longer visible. "I'll tend to it when I have a chance, but at the moment I can't spare the time. Besides, the nearest clinic is sixty miles from here, in case you've forgotten."

She felt her face grow cold. "I'm not likely to forget that, John."

He flinched. "Sorry. I didn't think." His voice grew tired. "This hasn't been one of your all-time great days, has it?"

She shook her head. "Nor yours." He looked startled at the note of sympathy in her voice.

"I'll manage," he said. He pushed the door wide and waited for her to walk ahead of him.

Aurora shook her head. "First we have to take care of your arm. You need an antiseptic and a tight bandage to stop the bleeding." She spun around, her gaze swinging from the kitchen to the bedroom. "Where's your medicine cabinet?"

"I thought you were in a hurry."

"It's me or the doctor. Take your pick."

He nearly smiled at the mulish look on her face. When she tilted her chin up at him like that and dared him to cross her, he wanted to kiss her so badly he had trouble breathing.

"Stitches or a tight bandage, huh? In that case I pick you."

Aurora knew that he was teasing, but there was something about the way he was looking at her that made her want to curl up in a corner and cover her head so that she wouldn't remember the warmth of his body next to hers in the night.

She cleared her throat and forced a cool note into her voice. "Then tell me where you keep the bandages."

Something shifted in his face, sadness maybe, or determination. She wasn't sure.

With a resigned sigh, he closed the door. "There's a first-aid kit in the kitchen," he told her.

She hung her purse on the doorknob, then led the way into the kitchen. The old oak table with the mended leg still sat in the middle of the oblong space, with the same mismatched chairs pulled up close.

The presence of John's solemn-faced mother was strong in the room where Morningstar had spent so many of her years. Aurora could still see her standing at the old stove, which now bore a few more chips in the enamel.

"Johnny has much to learn about happiness," Morningstar had said the first time she and Aurora had been alone. Her dark eyes had been eloquent with a terrible sadness. "But you will teach him. He needs you like the very air that allows life."

You're wrong, Morningstar, Aurora told her silently. John never needed me, not in any important way. He's never needed anyone but himself.

"Where?" She looked around inquiringly.

"In the cabinet," he said, indicating a crude pine cupboard on the wall by the back door.

"Sit down," she ordered as she opened the cupboard and searched for the kit. She found the small tin box on the bottom shelf and saw that it was fully stocked.

Returning to the table she laid out a roll of gauze, salve and tape. Using the small pair of scissors in the kit, she cut off four large pieces of tape and stuck them on the edge of the table.

John watched in silence, his hat still in his hand.

"You look as though you're about to be staked out naked," she muttered, then stopped in horror when she realized what she had said.

"Sounds interesting," he said. "Do you want to strip me or shall I do it?"

"Just sit down and cooperate," she retorted. But the image of his well-muscled body was firmly implanted in her mind and refused to disappear. He was built for endurance and resiliency, with strong legs and a lean, sinewy torso without an extra ounce of fat anywhere. Even his shoulders were packed with hard, lean muscle.

"Are you going to sit down or are you just going to stand there glaring at me all day?" she said, trying desperately to cover her embarrassment with impatience.

"I'm not glaring. I'm trying to think of a way out of this."

A hard flush darkened his cheekbones, and his eyes glittered like amber as he tossed his hat onto the table, then pulled out a chair and sat down. Without looking at her, he unwrapped the handkerchief and tossed it toward the sink. It missed, falling in a heap to the floor.

Aurora inhaled swiftly, and the heat drained from her face. The slice in his arm was several inches long and oozed blood steadily.

Working as fast as she could, she made a thick pad from the gauze, then squeezed antiseptic from the tube onto the bandage. Tension stretched between them, nearly as oppressive as the midday heat.

Aurora bit her lip, feeling the strength draining from her tired body. She had to struggle to keep her fingers from shaking.

"Where do you keep the clean towels?" she asked, her voice strained.

He jerked his chin toward the metal cabinet that held the sink. "In the top drawer."

She found a piece of faded cotton that looked soft, then held it under the tap. After wringing it nearly dry, she returned to the table. She started to reach for his arm, then hesitated.

"This might hurt," she said tersely.

He shrugged. "Don't worry about it. I won't cry."

Aurora heard the mocking sound in his voice and stiffened. Yes, I know, she thought. You have to feel to be able to cry.

She laid his forearm flat and pressed the damp cloth to the wound. He winced, and his hand clenched. Tiny goose bumps appeared under the soft layer of fine black hair covering his arm.

"Sorry," she murmured as she removed the towel and replaced it with the gauze pad. A trickle of sweat began running down her spine.

"No problem." His voice sounded scratchy.

She glanced up to see a pinched look around his eyes. He sat motionless, his shoulders braced, like a man trying to bear the unbearable.

"Hold this," she ordered, indicating the pad, and he scowled. But he did as she asked. Slowly she wound a strip of gauze around his forearm, pulling it tight so that the pressure would squeeze the edges of the wound together. Her nails ruffled the hairs on his arm and he sucked in.

"I'm trying to be careful," she told him in a thin voice.

He grunted, but kept his gaze focused on his arm. The strong muscles of his neck stood out, as though he was holding himself in check.

"Just get it done," he muttered, not bothering to make his tone civil.

"I'm going as fast as I can." She heard the whisper of hurt in her voice and cringed inside. Even after all the months—years—of hard work she'd put in to forget him, she was still far too susceptible to this man's moods.

John straightened his shoulders, gritting his teeth against the hot flare of pain in his arm. Silently he called himself a fool in three languages, but it didn't help.

He'd promised himself to go slowly with her, to let her get used to him again, but with her here in his house, looking like a rumpled, out-of-sorts angel, he wanted her so badly he was having trouble sitting still. And every time her fingers slid over his skin, he felt the reaction stab him between his legs. He was in agony, and there wasn't a damn thing he could do but sit still and take it.

Aurora saw the sudden glitter in his eyes, and she frowned. Was he feverish? In pain?

"Do you want me to stop for a minute?" she asked, feeling his pulse leap against her fingertips.

"No." His voice was strained, and the color had crept upward to his hairline where it disappeared into the place where an unruly cowlick pushed his thick, springy hair into a natural part.

"Give me your hand," she ordered.

"What?"

"Hold the end of the gauze while I tape."

He did as he was told, watching her without seeming to. He noticed the way she gnawed at her bottom lip as she concentrated, and he saw the tiny drops of moisture above her upper lip. He'd had such a brief taste of those soft lips. Only enough to make him crazy for more.

"Aren't you done yet?" he asked, clenching his fist until his split knuckle began to bleed again. His control was beginning to slip. If she didn't stop soon, he was in trouble.

"In a minute." She sounded harried. She *looked* beautiful, he decided, letting his gaze roam hungrily over her flushed face and down the tawny smoothness of her neck. She was bending over, putting the last piece of tape on the bulky bandage. The two top buttons of her blouse were open, revealing the swell of her small breasts.

He groaned, and she jerked her hands away. Her breathing grew shallow, and a fine film of sweat covered her face.

"That should do it," she said in a hollow tone.

"Thanks," he muttered, not looking at her. His head was bowed, his eyes almost closed. His hair fell into the space between his collar and his muscular neck, and the ends were almost curly. He looked powerfully male. And endearingly vulnerable, all of sudden.

"You're welcome," she said belatedly, jerking her gaze away. Lord, it's hot in here, she thought, tucking the gauze back into the blue-and-white box.

She returned the rest of the supplies to the kit and put it away. Still without looking at him, she washed the salve from her hands, then hurried past him. "I'll wait for you in the car," she threw over her shoulder.

She heard him call her name, but she didn't stop until she was out of the house.

"What'd I do wrong?" John asked the empty room, his shoulders slumping with a sudden weariness. Whatever it was, it had sent her running away from him. Again.

He balled his fists to keep from flinging the damn chair through the window. He couldn't watch every thing he did, every word he said, every accidental brush of his hand, not when he was strung tight as fence wire every time he was close to her.

He swore savagely, then stood, grabbed his hat from the tabletop and tugged it over his brow with an impatient hand. Maybe, just maybe, if he concentrated on the throbbing in his arm instead of the ache in his groin, he might get through the afternoon.

To Aurora the pueblo had always been a study in brown. Brown adobe walls, pale brown grass sprouting in clumps at the edge of the brown land, darker brown rocks lining the bottom of the slow-running creek that bisected the pueblo proper.

The large structures that comprised the living quarters for the majority of the residents had been constructed in ragged, asymmetrical tiers as though following some long-ago whim of the builders. Some of the buildings had two stories, others three or four, with the flat roofs of the front apartments providing access to the second and third tiers. Hand-made ladders of skinned piñon were propped here and there against the thick walls.

John was right, she thought as she followed his truck through the maze of drab buildings. This part of the pueblo was like a complicated rabbit warren where none of the doors to the individual apartments was marked.

The only sign she saw was on Tribal Headquarters, a long, low building fronting the pueblo's only road. The letters were so sun-faded she had to squint to make them out.

John stopped in front of the last door on the ground floor of the newest building. Aurora parked next to his truck and shut off the engine. Dust rose around her in a gritty cloud, and even though the windows were tightly closed, she could taste the acrid dirt.

She rested her hands on the wheel and squinted through the windshield at her home for the next eight weeks. The door looked new and had been painted the same color as the trim on John's house. Bright yellow curtains screened the windows.

The truck door slammed, and John came around the back to open the door of the wagon. "If you give me your keys, I'll get your bags," he said, resting his hand on the top of her open door. From the corner of her eye she saw the ripple of his heavy thigh muscle as he shifted his weight, and for an instant she let herself remember the slide of those hard thighs against hers when he had kissed her.

Her fingers clenched around the tangle of keys, and the sharp teeth of one of them bit into the soft pad of her thumb. "Damn," she muttered under her breath.

"Something wrong?"

Yes, she wanted to shout. You're wrong. You're not cold and hard and selfish, and it scares me.

"No, nothing." She cleared her throat. "Leave . . . leave the big box in the car. It goes to the studio."

"Whatever you say," he said, taking the ring she held out to him. "Go on in. The door's unlocked."

Aurora climbed from the car and looked around. There was a timeless feel to the pueblo, as though the souls of past residents had stayed with the land, lending a serenity to the drab surroundings that she'd never felt anywhere else.

But now, for some reason, the peace that had always filled her when she'd looked out over the ancient place eluded her. She kept seeing John's face when he'd mentioned the baby. His dark eyes had been asking her to understand.

She heard the door of her car slam shut, and she hastily walked toward her apartment. She went inside, leaving the door open behind her. John followed her in, a suitcase in each hand.

"This building has indoor plumbing, thanks to some funds we get from a private benefactor each year, but I'm afraid the money didn't stretch to roof tiles." He glanced toward the ceiling where signs of water damage still showed through the fresh paint. "Pray for a dry summer," he said laconically.

She laughed. "I will. I like mud, but not in my lap."

John felt like shouting in triumph. She had laughed, really laughed, and the sound was like a soothing ointment on the hurting place inside him. Tonight, when he was alone in the bed that she had bought for them, he would allow himself to remember that happy sound.

"The bedroom's through there," he said, inclining his head toward a door to the right.

Aurora looked startled and her gaze slid away from his. "Fine," she said. "Uh, you can put the bags in there."

"Right." He disappeared.

Aurora stood in the middle of the living room and looked around. The walls were sparkling white, and the rooms smelled of paint. There wasn't much furniture, a couch and a matching chair with a couple of tables placed here and there, but the upholstery was a sunny buttercup print she loved on sight.

There was something about the low ceilings and cozy rooms that made her feel safe for the first time in years. And then it occurred to her that she had always felt safe with John. Instantly she dismissed the thought.

Before she could do more than turn in a circle, she heard the sound of bags thudding against the floor, and then he was back. He removed a key from his ring and laid it on the coffee table, along with her car keys, explaining that the key fit the padlock that secured the door.

"The place has only three rooms, but it's the best I could manage. We're short on space." He removed his hat and ran a hand through his hair. His face was lined with weariness, and the quick look he gave her radiated impatience.

"It's darling," she said. "I'll be very comfortable here."

John ran a hand over the swirling pattern on the back of the chair. "Darling? I was just trying for clean," he said, settling his hat over his brow again.

"You did this?"

He nodded. "I had a little trouble picking out the furniture. I knew you liked yellow, but I never knew there were so many different shades. I tried to match the dress you wore to President Salcido's inauguration."

She remembered the dress well. It had been the sheerest of silk, with a dozen buttons in the front. John had taken his time removing it after they'd returned home from the festivities. With each button he'd undone, their eagerness for each other had increased. By the time she'd been standing naked in front of him, neither of them could wait until they reached the bedroom, and they'd made love on the thick rug. She knew intuitively that she'd gotten pregnant that night.

"I'd forgotten," she said. But she knew that she hadn't fooled him. John could always tell when she was trying to hide something.

Her back felt stiff as she walked to the window and looked out. After the bustle of Dallas, the pueblo seemed oppressively quiet.

She heard John cross the room, but she kept her back to him. He was so close she could feel the heat of his body. The thick walls kept the room cool, but she was suddenly warm.

"Storm's coming," he said, looking over her shoulder. "It's the season."

"Yes."

Aurora stared at the darkening sky. Sudden, violent storms were always a danger in this land. Like the savage, often cruel men who had tamed it.

John saw her withdrawing from him, and he cursed silently. For a few minutes when she'd seen the little nest he'd fixed up for her, the strain had dropped from her face and he'd seen joy touch her vibrant features. And then suddenly it was gone again.

The familiar pressure settled behind his eyes. He pushed back his hat with two fingers, then rubbed the bridge of his nose, but it didn't help. Nothing ever helped. He cleared his throat. "I've got things to do. I'll let you settle in by yourself."

"Yes." Still she didn't turn around.

"I'll be at headquarters for an hour or so. After that you can call me from the pay phone outside the office if you need anything. There's a phone at the ranch now."

"Thank you, but I'm sure I'll be fine." Just go, she thought. Leave me alone.

His sigh brushed her neck, and she held her breath. She heard the scrape of a boot heel as he moved away from her. She heard the door open.

"Aurora, look at me." There was a note of command in his voice that told her he wasn't leaving until she did as he ordered.

She turned, exhaling slowly. She was beginning to feel flayed by her own emotions. She waited, her heart pounding in her ears.

He stood in the doorway, the wind plastering his shirt against his thick chest. "I'll be by at eight tomorrow morning to take you to the studio."

A flare of panic took her unaware, and she blinked. No, she thought. No.

"You're busy," she said as calmly as she could. "I can find my way, I'm sure."

The slanted brim of his hat hid the expression in his eyes, but she saw the sudden clenching of his jaw. "Wait for me. I'll take you."

She shook her head. "Really, John, that's not necessary."

"Actually, it is." He shoved his hands into his pockets and glanced up at the black sky. "I gave the council my word I'd be with you whenever you had the Santa Ysabel in your possession. Otherwise I never would have gotten enough votes to swing this for you."

Before she could protest, he turned away from her, closing the door behind him.

John had been gone only a few minutes when there was a knock on the door. Aurora gulped down the rest of the water she'd been drinking, and left the glass on the sink. Had he forgotten something?

But it wasn't John. It was a very beautiful, very pregnant woman with sunny blond hair clipped into a casual style on top of her head.

"Hi," she said, giving Aurora a friendly grin. "I'm Casey Torres." Somehow her crisp white shorts and sleeveless maternity smock managed to look chic and cool at the same time.

Aurora knew that her puzzlement showed on her face, and she tried to wipe it away with a smile. "It's, uh, nice to meet you. I'm Aurora Davenport."

"Yes, I know. I've heard all about you from John." Aurora heard the affection in the woman's low voice when she mentioned John's name. Her smile slipped a notch.

"I . . . do you . . . live here?" Suddenly she felt dowdy and damp next to this woman's sleek elegance.

"Temporarily, yes. Until September, at least. I wanted my baby to be born on his father's land."

Aurora took a moment to let the shock settle into a form she could manage. Was this woman carrying John's child? For an instant she couldn't breathe.

"Uh, is there something I can do for you, Ms. Torres?" Her voice sounded harsh, even to her own ears.

The woman's smile faltered, and she glanced around uneasily. Was she looking for John?

"I have your groceries," she said with a faint look of anxiety.

Aurora gaped at her. "My what?"

"I had to shop anyway, so I volunteered to pick up some staples for you in Chamisa. Didn't John tell you?"

"No." Aurora's voice was thin, and she cleared her throat. "No, he didn't."

Casey shook her head, and a look of exasperation replaced the worry on her face. "Men! And they call us scatterbrained."

"Hey, I heard that," called a deep male voice from the rear of a dusty black Jeep parked on the other side of Aurora's wagon.

The man who appeared carried two grocery bags in each hand and walked with a rangy confidence that reminded her of John. This man was taller, however, and leaner, but with the same copper cast to his skin. And like John's, his features bore the mark of the Spanish conquistadors.

This man could be almost as dangerous as John, she thought. But unlike John, he didn't seem threatening to her. On the contrary, there was something about him that made her trust him implicitly.

"Uh-oh, I think I'm in trouble," Casey said with laughter in her voice, watching him approach.

"Always, *querida*." His autocratic features softened into a beguiling grin as he leaned down to give her a quick kiss. Casey grinned up at him, and Aurora realized that these two were very much in love. Suddenly she felt very foolish and strangely relieved.

"Aurora Davenport, meet my husband, Alex Torres."

Aurora started in recognition. "Not the, uh...um, the—"

"Corporate raider," Casey finished with a grin. "Only he just runs Towers Industries these days."

Aurora tried to assimilate the shock. Alejandro Torres was one of the most famous financial pirates in the country. Or he had been until he dropped out of sight a few years ago. And then suddenly, he'd been back in the news. Something about a feud with another raider, a man who had tried to take over Torres's hugely successful conglomerate. If she remembered correctly, Torres had won, but it had been a bloody fight.

But what was he doing on the pueblo?

"Hello, Aurora Davenport," he said with a slow, sensual grin. His gaze touched her face, and she had the strong feeling he'd taken her measure and approved. She found that she was glad.

"Come on in, please. You're my first guests." She stepped back and held the door wide to let them enter.

"Okay if I take these to the kitchen?" Alex asked, glancing around. "I think the ice cream is melting."

He spoke with a hint of a Latino accent that gave his words an intensely masculine sensuality, yet there was a steely element in his deep voice that told her he was used to being in charge.

"Just put the bags on the counter," she told him, feeling a bit flustered. She hadn't expected a welcoming committee. "I'll, uh, put everything away later."

"No problem. I'll do it for you. Casey has me trained."

No way, Aurora thought as she closed the door and gestured Casey toward the sofa.

"I'm sorry I sounded a little confused," she said, trying to smooth the wrinkles from her shorts. "My brain thinks I should be on a beach in Mexico, and it's having trouble adjusting."

Casey laughed as she settled awkwardly against the plump cushions. "We have plenty of sand for a beach. It's the water we're missing."

"You can't swim anyway, *mi amor*," Alex teased as he walked toward the kitchen. "All you can do these days is float."

Casey laughed, and her hands cradled her swollen belly. "Isn't that what baby whales do?"

"Yeah, but they're not nearly as cute." He laughed at her outraged expression, then disappeared into the kitchen. Seconds later Aurora heard the sound of the refrigerator door opening.

"I hope you don't mind," Casey said, a hint of apology in her lively voice. "Alex needs something to keep him occupied so he won't fuss. You'd think I was the only woman who ever had a baby. Just between you and me, it's driving me crazy."

Aurora laughed, but inside a small kernel of sadness began growing. She had adored being pregnant. And whenever the baby had moved, she'd felt a deep contentment inside.

Covertly she eyed Casey's swelling stomach. Seven months, she thought. Or eight. The baby would be very active, kicking day and night, as though he were eager to leave his warm, dark haven.

"I think you're very lucky," she said in a small voice, perching on the chair opposite Casey.

Casey's expression was suddenly somber. "I'm sorry, Aurora. I didn't think. Talk about a muddled brain."

Aurora looked at her. What was Casey trying to tell her?

As though Casey had heard Aurora's thoughts, she said softly, "I know about your baby. John told me."

Aurora's face flooded with heat. "Did he tell you that she died here because there wasn't any medical care?" She wanted Casey to know what she was risking by living so far from expert medical treatment.

"Yes, he told me," Casey said in a serious voice. "That's why the first thing he did when he took over as chairman was to raise the money to hire a midwife. She's been practicing here for several years now, and the infant mortality rate is way down." Casey glanced toward the kitchen where the sound of cans thudding against the shelves made her smile. "Otherwise, Alex would never have agreed to let me deliver at home. As it is, he's still very uptight about the whole idea." She hesitated, then added, "So is John."

Aurora felt as though she'd taken a punch in the stomach. "What do you mean?"

"He's almost as nervous as Alex about this baby. He doesn't say much, but I can see it in his eyes whenever he looks at me."

Aurora's nails dug into the arm of the chair. A hot spasm of pain shot up her wrist. "Just don't count on him to be here if you need him."

"I hope you're not talking about me." Alex had returned to the living room without Aurora noticing. He was grinning as he settled his long body next to his wife, but his tone had been serious.

Aurora managed a smile and shook her head. "No, I wasn't talking about you. I was just...talking."

"I was just telling Aurora about Susanna," Casey interjected, resting her hand on his knee. Instantly, his big hand covered hers. He was wearing a plain gold wedding band, very much like the one John no longer wore.

"Yeah, well as good as Susanna is," Alex said with a dark frown, "I'd still feel better if my daughter were born in a hospital."

"Your son, you mean," Casey teased. "And I'm not worried."

He looked disgruntled. "I wish the damn clinic was open. John has a hell of lot more patience with government red tape than I do. If it was me, I'd just open the thing and worry about permits later."

"That's because you're not walking the fine line John is," Casey said with a hint of reproach in her soft tone. "His enemies would just love to levy a charge of impropriety against him, especially where tribal funds are concerned. He has to do everything by the book, and that takes time."

"He's not using tribal funds. The money was donated to him personally."

Aurora could guess by whom. Alex Torres was known for his generosity. And his ironclad integrity.

Casey sighed. "As soon as John accepted it, it became communal funds. That was his condition for taking it. You know that."

"Man's too damn stubborn." Aurora heard a note of respect in his deep voice. In spite of the criticism in his words, it was obvious that he thought a lot of John.

Casey glanced at Aurora, a troubled look settling around her eyes before she returned her gaze to her husband's face. "John has to do things his way, and you know it. We only live here part of the year, but this is his home. If Diego wins, John could lose everything."

Alex muttered a curse in Spanish, but Aurora understood the words and flinched.

"Sorry," he told her with a fleeting grin. "Casey's trying to turn me into a gentleman, but I don't think it's going to work."

Aurora acknowledged the apology, then asked almost reluctantly, "What do you mean, John could lose everything?"

Alex scowled and a look of fierce anger settled between his black brows. "Diego Ruiz and some of his *compadres* have gotten up a petition to have John removed as chairman. According to tribal law, if the council decides he's abused the privileges of his office, he could also be stripped of his land and his right to live on the pueblo."

Aurora knew that the laws for each pueblo were different, but this sounded extreme. "Surely that won't happen."

He shrugged. "Tempers are running hot, mostly because John's made a lot of radical changes in a short time. A lot of people are afraid of new things."

Casey added almost gently, "A lot of the older folks remember how John couldn't wait to leave Santa Ysabel, and they don't trust him."

Her face turned pink with indignation. "John is working himself into the ground to help the people here. He's started a school that's won several awards already, and now he's working on creating jobs. All that bozo Diego ever did was talk tough around the stove in the chairman's office and spit tobacco.''

Alex burst out laughing, then dropped a kiss on Casey's nose. "You're just aching for a fight, aren't you?"

Casey looked embarrassed. "Yes. I've kinda gotten used to it. But then living with you, I've had to."

Alex gave her an indulgent look. "Don't worry, *querida*. By the time you're finished giving me a daughter, I'll find something challenging for you to do."

His eyes were very black when he looked up and smiled across at Aurora. "I was told to make my excuses after a reasonable period of time and leave so that my brilliant and very curious wife could check you out, so that's what I'm doing."

Casey punched him, and he laughed. "Easy, *mamacita*. You don't want to get baby all riled up. You know how she keeps you up at night when you do."

"He. And you're the one keeping me up at night."

Aurora could swear Alex blushed, and she was filled with a deep envy. These two were so much in love.

"One hour, *querida*, no more. Otherwise, I'll put you and baby over my shoulder and carry you home."

Casey nodded solemnly. "Whatever you say, Mr. Torres, sir."

He shook his head, then gave Aurora a look of masculine frustration. "Somewhere along the line I lost all control with this woman."

Aurora laughed. "I can see that."

Alex bent over to kiss his wife, his hand gently caressing her belly.

Aurora looked away, a dull pain throbbing inside her. She pressed her flat stomach with a tight fist, but the pain only increased. John had never seen her in the final months of her pregnancy. He hadn't scolded her or worried about her or rubbed the ache from her back the way she somehow knew Alex did for his wife.

Alex told her goodbye and she managed a smile, but after he left, a silence fell. Aurora stared at the straw mat on the floor, thinking about the irony in Alex's words. John had fought hard to leave this place, and now it seemed he was fighting to stay.

Her brain felt sluggish as she tried to cope with the contradictions between past and present. Nothing had made much sense to her since the moment John had walked into her office, changed almost beyond recognition. She was beginning to like the man he'd become, and that was far more distressing than she wanted to admit. Suddenly she had to move or she would go crazy.

"I'll get us something to drink," she told Casey. She leaped to her feet and headed for the kitchen. She opened the refrigerator door and stared at the shelves. She would offer Casey milk, but she couldn't seem to decide what she herself wanted.

Diet soda maybe. Or... or—

Casey touched her shoulder. "Are you all right?" Her voice was soft with sympathy.

Aurora grabbed a half gallon of milk, then closed the refrigerator door and leaned against it. "Honestly I don't know."

Casey cleared her throat, then said softly, "I'm glad you're here, Aurora. Maybe now John will stop driving himself so hard."

"I doubt I have anything to do with that," she said, pushing away from the fridge. As she found glasses and poured the milk, she felt Casey's eyes on her.

"I think everything John's done in the past few years has something to do with you," Casey said, her tone reflecting absolute certainty.

Aurora turned and handed Casey one of the glasses, then said with equal certainty, "You're wrong. It's been five years since our divorce and I hadn't heard one word from him until a few days ago."

"Alex and I had been divorced for six years when I came looking for him because I needed his help to save the company I was running from a hostile takeover. We fell in love all over again. It can happen."

Aurora took a sip of milk. It was still warm and left a bitter aftertaste. "John *never* loved me."

Casey ran a finger around the rim of her glass, and her brow creased in indecision. Finally she nodded to herself. "Did John tell you about the Seeking Way?"

"No, what's that?"

"You've seen that strange-looking band around his wrist?"

Aurora nodded.

"I won't try to pronounce its name because it's just about impossible for an Anglo, but it's a symbol of successfully completing a ritual practiced by the people who once lived in the old ruins. I don't know all the details, but it's some kind of rite of purification. Alex says only men can request it because it's so dangerous."

Aurora found her thoughts tumbling. Was Casey saying that John had undergone some kind of ancient rite? The man who had scorned everything Indian? She voiced her doubts aloud, and Casey nodded.

"Alex said it's done when a man is seeking to change something within himself that has become intolerable. Apparently the, uh, petitioner has fourteen days to walk barefoot and nearly naked from some secret spot out on the far mesa to the ruins. As I understand it, the country is terribly wild out there, and there's almost no water and little food. If the man makes it, he is supposedly cleansed of...well, of his sins, I guess."

Aurora found that she was pressing her lower back against the edge of the counter so hard her legs were becoming numb. She forced her straining muscles to relax. "John walked for fourteen days barefoot? Over this rough ground?"

Casey nodded. "Alex said he was in bad shape when he made it back." She bit her lip, then tried to smile. "Apparently he was delirious for days. Alex said he kept calling your name."

Aurora's heart fluttered, then settled into a fast rhythm.

"I feel like I've been dumped out on that mesa myself," she told Casey in a sad little voice. "Only nothing seems familiar to me. I'm not even sure where I should be going." She caught the quiet sympathy in Casey's eyes and managed a smile. "You like John, don't you?"

Casey nodded. "It was a bad time for me when I had to ask for help from Alex, after he'd made it plain he no longer wanted me in his life. John was a good friend to me when I desperately needed one."

Aurora fumbled behind her for the edge of the counter to steady herself. She didn't know what to say.

Casey's hand pressed her stomach. Her expression grew somber. "Do you still love him?" she asked quietly.

Do I? Aurora thought. Is it possible?

She stared past Casey's troubled eyes toward the sparkling white walls that bore marks of recent patching. The kitchen was tiny, and the appliances were old and mismatched, but everything gleamed with cleanliness.

John had prepared this place for her, and he'd fought to give her access to the Santa Ysabel, perhaps at his own risk. He claimed he was sorry for what he'd done. But he hadn't said he loved her.

That he couldn't change, no matter how many miles he walked. And that was the one thing, the only thing she had ever wanted from him.

"No," she said in a strong, steady voice. "I don't love him. I never will again. It hurts too much."

## Chapter 7

After Casey left, promising to visit again soon, Aurora fixed herself a salad and ate it at the small table without tasting a bite. She was exhausted, and her head was beginning to hurt.

"I need a shower and a nap," she muttered as she washed the dishes and dried them with paper towels she'd found on the counter. She would think about the things Casey had told her later, when she felt better able to cope.

Unbuttoning her blouse with a tired hand, she walked into the small bedroom. There was no closet, only an old armoire placed against the far wall. John had lined her suitcases against the wall and laid her garment bag on the bed.

Aurora reached for the zipper tab, then froze, her slowly widening eyes fixed on the swirl of color under the canvas bag. A quilt had been neatly placed over the mattress like a spread. Not just any quilt, she realized with a start, but *her* quilt, the one she'd made as a teenager for her marriage bed. It had been one of the things she'd left behind.

As her fingertips lightly traced the double-wedding-ring pattern, she fought off a sudden rush of tears. A longing she hadn't felt in years nearly overpowered her, and she sank down on the soft mattress.

A splash of pink caught her eye. A large bouquet of carnations in a canning jar sat on a small chest by the bed. Next to the jar was a note in John's slanting backhand. "Sorry I couldn't give you Baccarat crystal, but what the heck? The jar is signed."

She felt herself smile at the drollery, but her smile faded almost instantly, just as the bright colors of the quilt had faded. As her belief in the man she'd married had faded.

Warm, stinging tears blurred her gaze, and she turned her eyes toward the window where the ruins were framed by the window like a muted halftone painting.

It seemed so long ago when she had last walked beneath those crumbling walls. A lifetime.

The unfamiliar images of the small room faded, and the years collapsed around her until the brightness of early afternoon dimmed into the silver of that moonlit night. She could still see the look of loneliness in John's eyes as he stood silhouetted against the wall....

"For the first time in my life I'm sorry to be leaving this place." His profile was as stark as the outline of the surrounding mesas.

"There's magic here," Aurora whispered softly. The ruins towered above them, the once-square edges blunted by years of rain and wind. Moon shadows scored the blank sides, creating an illusion of movement. "I can feel it the way I feel the life in the clay."

His grin slashed white, but his voice was grim beneath the amusement. "A lot of people here believe this place is haunted by the spirits of the Ancient Ones. As a boy I used to come out here with my friends and listen to the chants of the women who had come to pray to the old gods. We were scared to death that the spirits would actually show up."

"Did they?"

"No."

She felt rather than saw him smile, and a little shiver of pleasure began inside her. At first, when they'd been together at quiet dinners or on long rides together, John had been subdued and his smiles had come slowly, if at all. But lately, his slow smiles had come more and more frequently, making her feel wonderful and warm inside.

"How old were you, then?" she asked, trying to keep her voice steady. She was determined to get through their last evening without crying, but every minute that passed made it more difficult.

"Five or six, I guess. I stopped coming when my old man came home late one night and caught me out of bed. He wore out my only pair of pants and told me I'd be praying harder than the old grandmothers if I ever went wandering again." There was faint amusement in his voice, and something more, something that made her shiver.

His arm moved against her shoulder, pulling her closer. "Cold?"

"Not when I'm with you." Aurora nestled against him, her cheek finding the small hollow in his wide shoulder where it fitted so perfectly.

He dropped a kiss on the top of her head, then rubbed his chin against her temple

"Don't you believe in prayer?" she asked, gazing up into his shadowed face. John rarely spoke of anything but his plans for the future. It was as though his life had begun when he'd left the place where his family had lived for centuries.

"I believe in me."

The moon shone onto his face, etching a hard-bitten pride into every angular line. Something fierce and untamed in his gaze warned her to run, to leave him standing in the ruins of the ancient people whose blood he carried but despised. But she couldn't make herself move.

"I'll miss you," she said in a small, quiet voice.

In the moonlight the hard edges of his smile softened in a sensuous invitation, and Aurora felt a longing burst inside her.

"I'll miss you too, little Rory," he murmured against her hair. Slowly his hand moved to her heated face where a strand of bright hair was trapped against her cheek. His fingers shook as they brushed back the silky curl. "You deserve a man who can see the same beauty you see. I can't."

Smiling softly, she leaned into his hand and thought she felt it tremble. "Everyone can see beauty, even you. If you know where to look."

John cast his gaze over the moonscape around them, his heavy brows a black slash over his brooding eyes. "All I see here is my mother's tears. And the graves of three brothers who weren't strong enough to survive in this place. Nothing more."

Aurora gently smoothed the lines from his brow with a gentle hand. "You're wrong, John. There's courage here and nobility and dignity. Your people have a resilience and strength that made you what you are, even it you don't realize that yet."

His blunt finger traced the curving line of her soft mouth. "You're a dreamer, little one," he said, his features drawn. "I hope no one ever takes that away from you."

Slowly she turned her head and kissed his strong wrist. "Let me show it to you. Let me give you the magic."

His harsh groan cut through her words. His hands pushed into the thick tangle of curls over her ears, his thumbs caressing her temples as his mouth brushed hers.

"You're so lovely," he said in nearly inaudible huskiness. "And inside, inside, you're beautiful, like the anthea blossoms that grow in the shadows of the rocks. I don't want to hurt you."

"You won't."

"I might. I don't know how to be gentle."

She let him see the love in her eyes and in her smile. "I trust you."

On their first few dates he hadn't even kissed her. And then one night his mouth had taken hers with an urgency that had sent wild flurries of newborn pleasure through her small body, keeping her awake and wondering long into the early hours. But he hadn't made love to her.

Smiling softly she leaned into his hand, feeling its strength. "I love you," she said in a nearly soundless whisper.

John's face went still. "No one's ever said that to me before."

His hand slid up and down her bare arm, then moved to the softness of her breast. When she didn't move, he opened his hand and pressed his palm against the tiny, hard nipple.

Heat raced through her veins, arousing a wild need to feel more. She trembled, and his hand stilled. "Do you want me to stop?"

"No, no." The trembling inside her increased until it was a quivering ache.

He inhaled slowly as though it hurt to breathe. When he released the air, it sounded like a sigh of surrender. "I want to make love to you."

She felt a shiver of panic, which quickly dissipated. This was John, the man she loved. He should be the first.

"I want that, too." Her trembling voice was hushed, as though the crumbling walls surrounding them absorbed the sound.

His feet scraped against the hard earth as he moved closer until not even the warm breath of the wind could separate them. Tension radiated from the set of his shoulders and the tautness of his jaw, as though he was holding himself on a tight rein.

"God, you make me crazy wanting you, but I can't offer you more than tonight."

She made herself smile. "I know and I'm not asking for more than that. I can't give you much experience, so—"

John's groan mingled with his kiss, and she relaxed against him, her small hands clinging to his big shoulders.

His fingers were deliberately slow and trembled slightly as he unbuttoned the front of her blouse, letting her get used to the feel of his hands on her breasts. The air felt suddenly cool against skin that had heated at his touch.

Aurora gasped at the wild sensation of pleasure that burned her with the force of a torch. His fingers nudged aside her bra, then lightly stroked the fullness around the tiny nipples.

"Do you like that?" John's voice was raspy but controlled.

"Yes, oh, yes."

Slowly he removed her blouse and her bra and let them fall to the pebbly earth. His eyes shone with a fierce glow that warmed her to the marrow.

"My perfect, sweet Rory." His voice was filled with awe and another emotion that touched her deeply. Aurora closed her eyes, feeling his admiration bathe her bare skin with more brilliance than the sun at midday. She felt no embarrassment, only pride that this intensely masculine man wanted her.

His kiss was gentle, almost restrained. Aurora moaned, wanting more. Instantly his mouth grew hard and hungry. His hands caressed her back, then dipped under the elastic waistband of her shorts to cup her buttocks. His fingers kneaded and stroked her until an exquisite pressure began to build.

Eagerly, guided by some instinct she didn't know she had, she opened her mouth for him, and his tongue lightly touched hers. The fire in her veins burned hotter, and she rubbed against him, reveling in the solid security of his big chest and lean belly.

Love welled inside her until she was trembling with it. This was right all the way. Because she was his, and he was hers. For this moment they were destined to be together, to love.

As though he could no longer control himself, John groaned, then dragged his mouth from hers. Holding her gently, he drew her down to the blanket where they had spread their picnic. The coarse wool was rough against her shoulders. Slowly she let her legs relax.

"You are so beautiful," John whispered, his fingers brushing her ruffled hair away from her brow.

"So are you," she managed, transfixed by the play of moonlight over his strong features.

For an instant a look of what might have been surprise flared in his eyes before his blunt lashes wiped it away. "Men aren't beautiful," he said gruffly, half turning away from her.

"You are."

While she watched, her eyes half closed with pleasure, her breath ragged with short little bursts that matched his, he slipped out of his shirt and tugged off his boots.

His big hands worked the buttons of his jeans, and a shiver shot through her. But before John tugged off his pants, he leaned forward and kissed her, one hand trapping hers above her head, the other slipping beneath the waistband of her shorts. His hand was gently seeking, rubbing her in a slow rhythm that made her cry out. Clinging to his shoulders, she tried to pull him closer.

"Easy, my love. We have until dawn." His voice was labored and thick. Sweat beaded his forehead as he removed the rest of her clothes.

Aurora was lost in sensation, abandoning herself to the pleasure he was creating with his mouth and his hands. She didn't even know when he managed to remove his jeans; she only knew that his skin was warm against hers as he slid one thigh between hers. His arousal pushed against the throbbing moist place between her thighs.

"Rory, is this your first time?" he asked in a voice made harsh by his ragged breathing.

"Yes," she whispered, her voice a sob of need. "Please don't stop."

He groaned and his body arched away from hers. Through the haze of ecstasy surrounding her, she knew that he was holding back, trying not to hurt her.

He pushed slowly inside her, his face twisting with his attempt to be gentle. She felt a sudden stab of pain, and then he was inside her, not moving, but filling her, letting her tight body expand to accommodate him.

Gradually the pain receded until there was only a sweet, urgent need to feel him thrusting against her. She began to move, and with a moan he followed her lead, gradually taking over until she was crying out in pleasure.

Exhilaration and a hot pressure built inside her until she thought she would die of it. She writhed under him, trying to relieve the wonderful pain.

The hoarse sound of his breathing was like a caress that sent her spiraling over the edge into a state of pure bliss. She cried out, a long shuddering cry of ecstasy. He thrust hard one more time, and then he collapsed on top of her.

She rubbed her face against his damp shoulder and let herself drift in the warm haze of euphoria. It might have been hours before he shifted until she was lying in his arms.

"Are you okay, love?" John's voice was rough.

"Mmm." Gradually she felt herself come back into her body, a warm feeling of security cocooning her.

His laugh was gentle. "I guess that's yes."

"Yes, yes, yes. I'm so...happy."

Even in the silver light, she could see the flush touch his skin. "I want you to be happy always, Rory." There was something in his voice that made her twist in his arms until she could see his eyes.

His shadowed brows were lined with the same tension knotting his muscles. "Marry me, Rory. Come to South America with me. Let me make you happy."

She blinked at him in shock, and the smile he gave her was stiff.

"Oh, John, I love you so. I—"

With one finger he stopped the words that began to spill from her. "I want you to think about this carefully." He waved a hand toward the distant pueblo. "This is where I started, but I don't intend to end up here. I know where I'm going and I won't stop until I get there. The life of a diplomat's wife isn't easy. I'll take care of you and protect you, but I can't change the way I am. Not for you, not for anyone. If you want me, you have to take me the way I am."

There was almost a plea in his voice, but not quite. Aurora let the smile inside her bloom on her face.

"I love the way you are, and I know we'll have a wonderful life."

John shut his eyes as though absorbing her words into his soul, then whispered a phrase in his own language. Through the haze of sensation surrounding her Aurora heard the promise in his voice. Or was it a prayer?

Aurora's fingers dug into the quilt, his haunted voice still ringing in her memory. Prayer or promise, it no longer mattered, she thought as she got to her feet and unzipped the garment bag. She would be committing slow emotional suicide if she gave in to him again.

He was too forceful, too determined. Once she was in his bed again, he would demand more and more until she no longer had a will of her own.

She glanced again at the ruins. Because she had loved him twelve years ago, the choices had all been his. But now, because the love was gone, the choices were hers. And no matter what John Olvera wanted, she didn't want him.

It was almost nine when John arrived. Aurora had been awake since six, dressed since seven and pacing since eight. As she opened the door to his abrupt knock, she didn't bother to mask her annoyance.

"Morning," he said, giving her a tired smile. He was hatless and his hair was damp and combed away from his face. He'd nicked his chin with a razor, as though he had shaved in a hurry. "Sorry I'm late."

"No problem," she managed coolly, before turning away to retrieve her tote bag from the corner of the sofa.

"If it's no problem, why are you glaring at me?" he asked as he crossed the threshold and closed the door behind him.

He was wearing another pair of jeans and the same dusty boots. His soft khaki shirt looked new and had been tucked into the low-riding waistband with the neat military precision he'd learned from the marine guards at the embassy.

"I'm not glaring," she threw back at him, her chin lifted. "This time you were only an hour late, not three days. I guess I should be grateful."

Aurora heard the swift intake of his breath and knew that she had hurt him. Guilt overtook her, but she didn't know how to apologize. Actually she didn't know how to act around him at all, and that put her on the defensive, making her feel as vulnerable as a cornered animal whenever he came close.

She started to walk past him, but he grabbed her arm and swung her around to face him. His strong fingers bit into her skin and she winced, but he didn't seem to notice. Anger radiated from the rigid slant of his big shoulders and the set of his jaw. Twin commas of strain bracketed his mouth.

"Cut me some slack here, Aurora," he ordered in a raw tone that shivered her spine. "I'm short on sleep and not much in the mood to spar with you this morning."

Pain shot up her arm and she tried to pull away, but he wouldn't let her go. "You're hurting me," she said stiffly, and a wash of dusky color rose along the rigid muscle at the side of his neck.

He dropped his hand, and some of the anger drained from his face, leaving it pale and gaunt. "Look, I was up all night delivering a foal that lived less than an hour. I guess I'm still mad that I couldn't save him. I didn't meant to take it out on you."

He wanted to take her into the bedroom right now, not to make love but simply to hold her the way he used to when things had begun to pile up on him. Just the feminine scent of her soft skin and the feel of her rounded body cradled next to his had given him strength when his own had flagged.

"If you're ready," he said in a neutral tone, "I'll show you around."

Because Aurora had been so wrapped up in her own problems, she hadn't noticed the dark circles under his eyes, but she saw them now, along with an expression that looked like loneliness in the dark pupils between the thick lazy lashes.

"I'm sorry about your foal," she said, pressing her hands together. "And I'm sorry for what I said just now. I...this is hard for me, John. You've changed so much, I feel like you're a stranger with another man's memories of me. It's...unsettling."

When he focused his watchful gaze on her face, she had a sense of savage energy under strict control. For a moment she felt fear, and then a slow smile slanted across his face. Beneath his dense ebony lashes his eyes were compelling.

Something warm and eager opened inside her, making her want to smile back. The corners of her mouth trembled, then slowly curved upward.

"Apology accepted," he said, moving a step closer. Her stomach somersaulted. She was afraid he was going to kiss her the way he had yesterday, and then was strangely disappointed when he didn't. She gritted her teeth at her own feminine desires that seemed to run amok whenever he was around, no matter how firmly she lectured herself. But as she had told Sofia—was it only a few days ago?—John was an immensely virile man.

"Let's make a deal," he said in a husky voice. "We start here, now, with no past and no future. Just the present. No strings. No expectations. No...promises. Whatever happens, happens." He hesitated, then added softly, "Or doesn't happen."

She fiddled nervously with the wide straps of her tote bag. She didn't know if she wanted to run away from him or bury her face against his shoulder and cry.

John watched her turn away from him again, his hungry gaze taking in the snug fit of her yellow shorts and ruffled top.

He wanted to tell her that he was glad to see her. That for the first time in years he'd gone to bed content because she was back in his life, but she was still skittish. Slow and easy, he told himself. Give her time.

"I'm not sure I . . . understand," she asked, facing him again. "Are you asking for a reconciliation?"

He didn't hesitate. "No," he said firmly. "That implies that we're the same two people we were five years ago. We're not. What we had then is gone."

Something that felt like sadness shot through her, but she made herself dismiss it. "What makes you think we're not the same?"

"You've already said you think I'm . . . different. I would guess that you are, too."

She hesitated. "You're right. I'm a different person now."

He looked away for a moment. When he looked back, the tiredness had returned to his face. "Then it's a deal?" He held out his hand, pleased that he was able to keep it steady.

Aurora glanced down at the hand he held out to her. The twisted silver band was just visible below the cuff of his shirt, a tangible symbol of the changes in him. Suddenly she knew that she had to find out more about the man he'd become.

"Yes, it's a deal," she said, sliding her hand into his. For better or worse she'd given her word. She only hoped she wouldn't regret it.


"Place has been locked up for a few days, so it's probably hot as an oven." John unlocked the door to his office and shoved it open. He stepped back to let Aurora precede him, then snapped on the light and pocketed his keys.

It was past noon and they'd just spent the better part of three hours mapping out short- and long-term goals for the artists' cooperative. Her job was to train the people who would handcraft the pots. He was in charge of developing the necessary administrative personnel to handle sales and accounting.

Because time was short, she had decided to immerse her students in a rigorous hands-on program that would push them to the limit of their commitment. Just meeting the four women and two men who were to be her students and answering their eager questions had made her realize how important this venture was to them and their families. Now she was exhilarated—and exhausted.

John tossed his hat onto the desk, then glanced at the open door to the right. "I'll get us some coffee."

"Fine," she said politely. What she really wanted was a tall glass of ice water, but she doubted that there was a refrigerated cooler in all of the pueblo.

Aurora dropped her bag to the floor and turned around slowly, trying to get a feel of the place where John now worked. Except for the modern telephone console on the corner of the big rolltop desk, the office could have served as a set in an old western movie.

The walls were thick adobe and needed a coat of paint. The ceilings were low, barely a few inches above John's head, and made in the old way with skinned poles supporting closely packed twigs.

She started to smile at the potbellied stove with its lopsided pipe, then froze as her gaze lighted on the big old safe standing in the far corner.

Her mouth went dry, and her stomach leapfrogged. John had told her that the Santa Ysabel was kept in a safe in his office. This safe, with the painting of a grazing buffalo on the front.

She had dreamed of seeing the Santa Ysabel for so long, but John had taught her that a dream could easily turn into a nightmare. What if the Santa Ysabel held no magic for her? What if it was simply another lifeless hunk of clay? She didn't know if she could stand to have another dream shattered.

She heard a step behind her, but she didn't turn to face him. "Who's your friend?" she asked, pointing to a stuffed owl perched on top of the safe. The creature was missing one glass eye, giving it a perpetual wink.

John glanced at the dusty bird. "That's Wise One," he answered with a smile in his voice. "Casey found him at an antique shop in Santa Fe and gave him to me for my birthday. He's supposed to bring good luck."

His birthday had come a few days after Alex and Casey had remarried. Watching his friend come out of his shell and start to smile again had given John the courage to go after Rory. If Alex could win another chance, maybe he could, too.

"And has he brought you luck?"

He could tell that she was intrigued. "I'm not sure yet."

As she turned to face him, John studied her without seeming to. It was so hard to know what she was thinking behind that sunny little face. No, what she was *feeling*.

He felt uncomfortable just thinking about the emotions that she understood so well and he didn't.

"Have a seat," he said, indicating that she should take the chair to the left of the desk. He put the two mugs he carried on a stack of BIA reports and sat in his usual place behind the desk.

"It feels good to sit down," Aurora said with a sigh. "I forgot how the altitude can wear a person out."

She leaned over to blow on the too-hot coffee, and the steam warmed her cheeks. She felt drained.

John raised a questioning brow. "Tired?" He pulled out the bottom drawer and propped his feet on it, crossing his legs at the ankles. He reached for his mug and rested it on his heavy silver belt buckle. His thigh muscles contracted and relaxed in a controlled ripple of power as he rocked his chair gently on two legs.

"A little. It's been a long semester." And an even longer few days.

"Drink your coffee. The caffeine will help." He followed his own advice and took a long swallow.

"Promise?" she asked, staring dubiously at the muddy liquid.

"I don't make promises I can't keep anymore."

Something in his tone made her look up, but his expression was unreadable, just the way she imagined it had been during formal negotiating sessions at the embassy or casual poker parties after hours. She remembered that John had always played his cards close, and he'd invariably won.

"Are you the one who took the picture of the Santa Ysabel you sent me?" she asked, thinking that she should have the negative blown up and displayed in the studio.

"Yeah. I borrowed the camera Alex bought to take pictures of Casey's expanding tummy."

"I like your friends," she said. "Casey has a knack of making you feel comfortable with her immediately."

"She used to be president of a foundry somewhere in Ohio. Alex told me she had worked a miracle there because people trusted her."

Just as people trusted Rory, he realized. Her students had welcomed her with the reticence most Pueblo Indians showed outsiders, but by the time she had finished discussing her ideas with them, all six had been treating her like an old friend.

He raised his mug to his mouth. When he lowered his hand, Aurora reached out to touch the silver band.

"Casey told me about this. She said you almost died." She hesitated, then added, "It must have taken a lot of courage to do what you did."

He glanced down at her hand close to his. It had taken more courage to face her again.

Without answering, he dropped his feet to the floor and turned to look toward the window. He heard a truck start outside. The engine badly needed a tune-up.

"How did you like the studio? Anything else you need?" he asked, shifting in the hard seat. All of a sudden he felt restless as a hawk caught on a high branch in a lightning storm.

"It's perfect," she said. "As soon as I walked in, I felt I belonged there."

No, my love, he thought. You belong with me. You just don't know it yet.

"I was afraid the place might be too small," he said. She'd been like a kid at Christmas, exclaiming over each thing he showed her as though she were unwrapping presents one by one. He had felt himself being entranced all over again.

Aurora shook her head. "Perhaps someday, but right now it's a potter's dream. Plenty of storage, nice big tables and bins. And all those windows for light. I'd love to hold my classes at dawn, just so I could watch the sun come up every morning over the mesa. That has to be glorious." She looked up, her eyes bright, to find him watching her, a strangely arrested look on his face.

"What's wrong?" she asked.

"Nothing." He cleared his throat. "I'm just glad you like the studio. It was the best I could do with the money I was able to scrounge from the building fund. Most of it has to go for the clinic."

"I can't wait to get started," she said, glancing toward the front window. She couldn't see the studio or even the ruins, but she knew that they were there, only a few miles apart. The new and the old, she thought, and it was up to her to blend them, just as John was trying so hard to do.

Casey's words drifted back to her, making her wonder if John had hurt his chances to withstand a recall drive by bringing her here.

Suddenly her anxiety returned in full force. What if she failed?

She gulped down a mouthful of coffee, then grimaced at the bitter taste. John not only liked his coffee scalding hot; he also liked it thick enough to eat through granite. She ran her tongue over her bottom lip in an attempt to wipe away the bitter taste.

"Too strong, huh?" he asked. "I tried to water it down some."

John had never thought watching a woman drink coffee could be so provocative. But then, in his current state of self-imposed celibacy, watching Rory do *anything* was a turn-on for him. He braced his foot on the open drawer and rocked his chair back and forth more forcefully, trying to ease the ache that only she could erase. But the movement only made it worse, and he groaned silently.

He tried to think of the things he had yet to do today. Anything to keep from pulling her into his arms and kissing that soft, almost smiling mouth.

"It's not bad, really," she hedged.

"Would sugar help?" he asked, putting his mug on the desk.

"Sugar's too fattening." Her tongue touched the corner of her mouth, and he inhaled sharply.

"Cream?" The low sensuous note in his voice made her swallow hard.

"Cream has . . . too much cholesterol."

He dropped his feet to the floor with a thud and sat up. The old-fashioned swivel chair squeaked in protest, but he didn't seem to notice.

"A kiss, then."

Before she could answer, he was out of his chair and leaning over her, trapping her with a hand on each armrest. "Kisses aren't fattening, or dangerous to your health."

Yours are, she thought, pressing her spine against the hard slats behind her.

His gaze roamed her face, warm and seductive, but it was his mouth that drew her attention. So hard when he wasn't smiling, she thought, and so soft when he kissed her. She could still feel that warm, sensuous mouth capturing hers with the same fierce mastery John brought to everything he did.

"We're pretending we just met, remember?" she said in a wobbly voice. "People shake hands when they meet."

His grin was slow and provocative. "The first time we met I wanted to kiss you so much I had trouble staying in the saddle. I still want to kiss you."

John saw her tongue run over her lower lip again, and a primitive heat surged into his loins, increasing the ache until it was nearly unbearable. He fought for control, but his sleep-starved brain refused to cooperate. Bone-tired as he was, she still had the power to arouse him, even when she wasn't trying.

"Kiss me, Rory," he ordered in a low intense voice.

She shook her head, feeling herself weaken. She'd never been able to resist him.

His golden-brown gaze swept her face, then moved lower to the ruffled neckline of her white blouse. Her skin began to burn.

"This office is a public place," she proclaimed, and then wondered what was wrong with her voice. She couldn't seem to raise it above a whisper.

"It's only public when there are other people in it."

"We're here," she said inanely, and then blushed when his eyes flashed with humor. He was so close she could see the tension that held the corners of his mouth.

"So we are." His hands gripped her arms and lifted her from the chair and into his arms in one powerful motion. "Welcome to Santa Ysabel, my love. It's been too long." His eyes were lit from within and glowed like a candle on a stormy night.

His hands framed her face, caressing but not controlling. The same sensuous pleasure that he had always excited in her spread through her in a slow crescendo. She wanted to tell him to let her go, but she couldn't seem to open her mouth.

"Kiss me, Rory," he said again. But this time he didn't wait for an answer. His mouth teased hers, warm and tantalizing and soft, and the pads of his fingers began a slow, sensuous massage at the nape of her neck.

His other hand enveloped hers where it rested on his chest. When she didn't pull away, he slid her hand to his shoulder and moved his own hand to the vulnerable hollow of her back.

It was all so familiar—the taste of him on her lips, the crisp, clean smell of his skin, the feel of his broad, warm hand in the place where it fitted so perfectly.

His mouth took hers again. He kissed her over and over, each kiss lasting longer than the one before. Someone moaned, and then she realized the desperate little sound had come from her.

Inside her was a churning emotion that made her feel off-balance, as though her world had suddenly shifted beneath her feet. Tender memories returned to her, blocking out the bad times. Her fingers tangled in his hair. She pressed closer, eager for more. This was John, the only man who had made love to her. Her husband.

A sweet heat spiraled through her and she closed her eyes, surrendering to the wonderful sensations flowing through her in ever strengthening waves. But the feelings shaking her were more than physical. Strangely, as his mouth moved warmly over hers, she felt replenished, as though a part of him was flowing into her like a soothing balm. Some of the deeply buried pain and resentment began to ease.

A sound like a man in deep pain penetrated the soft haze in her brain, and she opened her eyes. When his mouth moved from hers, she was momentarily disoriented, as though she was waking from a deep sleep. Her lashes trembled as she looked up at him, her mouth still warm from his.

"Don't cry, love," he said in a rough whisper. His breathing became ragged as though each breath hurt his chest. His hand shook as his fingers brushed her cheeks. "I won't do anything you don't want."

She wasn't crying. Was she? But she must be, she realized. Her cheeks were wet.

Was she crying for all the times she had wanted him to hold her like this and kiss away the hurt? Or because she was still mourning all that she had lost?

She moved out of his loose embrace, and John let her go, even though every muscle in his body was crying out to hold her so tightly she could never get away from him again.

He searched her face, looking for a hint of caring in her troubled expression. Teardrops as bright as winter stars glistened on her long lashes, and her mouth trembled where her teeth bit into the tender flesh. But beneath the sheen of tears her eyes were still soft with passion, and she was having trouble controlling her breathing.

"I'm not going to apologize for kissing you," he told her with a rasp to his voice. "You got the divorce. I didn't. I still want you, Aurora Davenport Olvera. You might as well get used to that fact.''

Aurora wiped the wetness from her cheeks. The blood still raced in her veins, and her skin felt abnormally warm.

"There's another fact *you* need to remember," she shot back at him in a voice that wasn't quite steady. Because somehow he had gotten past the defenses she had thought impenetrable, she found herself scrambling to make them stronger. "I'm not your wife any more. I don't have to care about what you want. And believe me, John, I don't. Just the way you didn't care what *I* wanted."

Silence stretched between them. Aurora saw the quick pulse beating in his throat, and knew that he was angry. But so was she. Angry at herself for responding to him, and angry that he was making it impossible for her to summon the icy remoteness that she needed to protect herself from him.

She glanced toward the safe where the Santa Ysabel pots waited. "Did you set all this up just to get me to sleep with you again?" she demanded in an indignant tone. "Is this some kind of elaborate seduction plan?"

He leaned against the desk and crossed his arms. "A man would have to want a woman for more than sex to go through that kind of hassle, don't you think?"

Aurora heard the bite of truth in his voice and felt her anger deflate. Of course, he was right. And since he hadn't brought her here because he loved her, she had to believe him when he said he needed her to set up the cottage industry his people needed so badly. But that didn't mean that sleeping with the teacher wouldn't have been a nice bonus for him.

Her jaw tightened. That was John, always looking to maximize his opportunities.

John saw the cynical look narrow her eyes, and the frustration inside him increased. He was still hard from wanting her, and there wasn't one damn thing he could do about it.

"I'll get the pot for you," he said in a controlled voice. "Since that's what *you* want." He turned away from her and walked toward the safe. Without a word he worked the combination, then swung open the door.

There were two shelves in the safe. The top one held neatly piled stacks of paper and ledgers, the second held a small bundle of cash and several leather-wrapped parcels, but it was the two wooden boxes on the bottom of the safe that drew her gaze.

"Which one?" he asked. His voice was without inflection.

She walked with shaky steps to his side. "Either one, I guess. You choose."

John selected the box on the right and carried it to the desk. The quiet in the office seemed to intensify as he opened the lid and stepped back.

The box was lined in sheepskin, which held the contents snugly but not dangerously so. Whoever had designed it had done a masterful job, she thought, taking a slow breath.

John leaned against the desk and crossed his arms. "Take all the time you want."

Aurora sent him an anxious glance, but the anger in his face had disappeared. Instead he watched her with impassive features that gave no hint of his feelings.

"Is it insured?"

He shook his head. "Because both pots are considered irreplaceable, the premiums would have been astronomical. There's no way we can afford to pay them."

Aurora knew he was telling the truth. If the university hadn't paid the premiums on her collection in return for the right to display it on the campus, she would have been hard pressed to pay for even minimal coverage.

"What if I drop it?" she asked with a shaky laugh.

One side of his mouth slanted in a reluctant smile. "Then we're both in trouble."

She took a deep breath. "I'll be careful."

Her hands shook as she lifted the shallow pot from its soft nest. To her surprise the fragile vessel was heavier than it looked. Very gently she set it on the blotter in front of her.

She tried to swallow the excitement clogging her throat, but it only increased until she had trouble speaking.

"It's beyond words," she managed finally. She ran her finger around the lip. The clay had aged to a deep russet, but the yellow glaze was almost as bright as it must have been when the unknown potter had applied it.

Reverently she traced the primitive pattern, her fingertips feather-light on the centuries-old clay. Countless years ago a woman living in the now abandoned dwellings out on the mesa had made this pot to hold the precious water with which the shaman would bless her marriage. Or her child's first cry.

She closed her eyes and pressed both hands against the smooth glaze, letting the life in the clay flow into her. The small sounds of the room faded until she was aware of nothing but the sensory images in her mind. She saw light and felt warmth fill her. Peace enveloped her. She began to smile.

"She was so happy when she made this," she whispered, "so very happy. I can . . . feel it."

Emotion welled inside her, and she was suddenly embarrassed. "I'm sorry," she murmured. "I know you don't believe in . . . in things like that."

John uncrossed his arms and straightened. Months of trying to figure out what went wrong between them had convinced him that Rory was a woman who followed her feelings and called it instinct, while he had always made his decisions based on cold-blooded self-interest and called it logic. No wonder he hadn't understood her.

"I believe that you can feel things most people can't," he said. He hesitated, then added, "I'm willing to learn, if you're willing to teach me."

Aurora felt a moment of surprise. Before, John had always changed the subject whenever she had spoken about the feelings she'd gotten from the old pots.

She searched his face. He looked uneasy but determined, as though he was trying to ease the tension between them. She wanted that, too. Now that he knew she wasn't going to sleep with him, she wanted them to work together to make the studio a success. Otherwise everyone would suffer.

"Give me your hand."

John glanced at the window as though making sure no one was watching. She hid a smile. "You're not doing anything illegal, you know," she said gently.

He reddened but held out his hand. "Now what?"

"First you have to touch it." She took his hand and placed it gently against the clay. His fingers splayed over the rounded contours, and his wrist grew taut with the effort of holding perfectly still.

"Close your eyes and blank your mind," she said softly. "Just try to . . . to feel what's there."

John knew he must look like a damn fool, but he did as he was told. In the darkness behind his closed lids, he saw the pot she'd called "Dream's End." Rory hadn't been happy when she'd thrown that pot. He had a feeling she hadn't been happy for a long time after that. He ground his teeth against the need to beg her to forgive him.

"Can you feel anything?" Her voice carried a hopeful note that sliced him as deeply as Buck's blade.

Everything that yearned to have her back in his life told him to lie. If she thought he understood, she might like him better. She might even lower those damn high barriers a little more. Hell, she might even learn to love him again.

If she thought he understood.

Frustration lanced through him, and he opened his eyes. "No," he said, withdrawing his hand. "I can't feel a thing."

The disappointment in her eyes hurt like hell.

# Chapter 8

John closed the door to the barn and wiped his face with the bandanna he'd pulled from his pocket. He had just given one of the mares a shot of penicillin. After nearly two weeks of fighting the infection she'd developed after she'd lost her foal, Wildflower had begun to eat again. It looked as though she might just make it—if he could pump enough antibiotic into her.

He shoved the damp cloth into his back pocket and walked to the edge of the corral where he could see the ruins in the distance. Beyond the towering walls the sun was a sliver of red on the horizon, and the sky was purple.

Resting his arms on the top of the fence, he watched the day slowly fade. He was almost numb with tiredness, but he couldn't let himself give in to it. Not until he'd had something to eat and put a dent in ranch paperwork that had piled up these last few weeks while he'd spent most of his days with Rory in the studio.

She and the others were using the Santa Ysabel as a model nearly every day. She had measured it meticulously and drawn countless representations from every angle. She had even borrowed Alex's camera and taken roll after roll of film.

Yawning, he rubbed his jaw, letting his shoulders slump and his mind drift. In spite of a rocky beginning, things were turning out pretty good. Better than he'd expected, anyway.

After her initial coldness, Rory had seemed more approachable, more like the warm, receptive woman he remembered.

And she'd let him kiss her.

She'd even kissed him back.

Hadn't she? Or had he wanted to feel her responding so badly he'd only imagined it?

Once, because he'd allowed himself to deal only in tangible results, he would have sworn he had no imagination at all. But now he sometimes thought his imagination was too damn vivid. Especially in the gray time between sleep and waking, when his body urged him to reach for her.

He rested his chin on his fist and looked out over the shadowed land. As a scrawny, half-starved kid he had hated this place, and he'd fought like hell to leave it behind. But out on the mesa, half crazed with thirst and too tired to do more than put one foot in front of the other, he'd sensed an almost mystical connection with the men who'd walked the same path before him. And when he'd closed his eyes, he had seen their faces smiling in encouragement and heard their thoughts urging him on.

He knew now that he'd been hallucinating, just as he'd been hallucinating when he'd seen Woman-of-Us-All and heard her speaking to him out in the ruins.

Even so, he had been irrevocably changed by the experience. For the first time in his life he was proud to be an Indian and proud to be a part of a community that had been in this place long before the first white men had set foot in North America.

He wanted to live the rest of his life on this land. With Rory. And he wanted to raise their children so that they could walk in his world and Rory's with the kind of confidence he'd never had.

He wanted . . .

Hell.

John opened his eyes and stared at the faint glow along the earth's rim where the sun had been. He really was a selfish bastard, thinking only of himself and what he wanted, when he had promised he would think only of Rory and what she wanted.

He muttered a tired curse and headed toward the back door, but before he reached the house Alex's Jeep pulled into the empty space next to his truck. John changed direction as Alex jumped down, and walked to meet him.

*"Hola! amigo. Como esta?"*

John managed a tired smile. "I wish to hell I knew," he answered, shaking Alex's hand.

"That bad, huh?"

John rubbed the throbbing ache in his arm where the gash had become infected. The bandage was soaked through with sweat. At least he hoped it was sweat. "Let's say it's been a long coupla weeks."

"That why you look like you've been dragged through mesquite at a slow gallop?"

John laughed. "C'mon in. I'll buy you a cup of coffee."

"I'm not sure my stomach's up to a cup of that mud you call coffee," Alex muttered as he followed John through the back door into the kitchen.

John lighted the burner under the big metal coffeepot and washed his hands.

Alex dropped his hat on the table and sat down. "How're you doing with the contractor—what's his name, Masterson? Got a start date yet?" he asked.

John took two cups from the cupboard and filled them with coffee. He gave Alex the cup that wasn't cracked.

"Looks like August first, if all goes well. Masterson thinks six weeks of steady work will have the building ready for interior work."

"Got the workers lined up?"

"Yeah, most of them." John settled into a chair and slumped wearily against the hard back. "Some of the men are grumbling because I opened it up to women, but they'll get used to it."

"Need more money?"

"Always," he said with a tired sigh. "But more donations aren't the way. We have to stop thinking of ourselves as charity cases and start making things happen ourselves. That's the only way to get the bureaucracy off our backs."

"Is this a Princeton liberal speaking?" Alex asked with a challenging grin.

John snorted. "Sometimes I forget I was ever part of that scene."

Alex's grin disappeared. "The people signing that recall petition haven't forgotten. Or if they have, Diego reminds them."

John tried to shrug the tiredness from his shoulders, then propped his feet on the empty chair. "Way I hear it, the Ramirez brothers are in Tucson until some time in August. Tribal law says all members of the council have to be present to vote on a recall of any member. *If* we break ground for the clinic on time and *if* I have a doctor lined up to run it, I figure I can swing enough fence sitters my way to win by the time they get back."

Alex took a long swallow before crooking his arm over the back of his chair. "Let me know what I can do."

"Right now you need to make sure Casey takes care of herself. She looked tired the last time I saw her."

"She hasn't been sleeping all that well. Seems my daughter is a night person."

John laughed, but his heart wasn't in it. He tried not to remember the nights that Aurora had prodded him awake so that he could feel the baby kick. He had been interested enough in an abstract sort of way, but Alex seemed almost as intensely involved in Casey's pregnancy as she was.

Lucky man, he thought as he dumped two teaspoons of sugar in his cup, then downed half of it.

"You doin' anything a week from Sunday?" Alex asked.

John ran a tired hand along his jaw, trying to concentrate. "I plan to work the yearlings some, and there's always tack to be mended. Why?"

"I'm putting the roof on the baby's room and I need some help. Casey said to bribe you with a home-cooked meal."

John chuckled. "Sounds good. I'd do about anything for some of Casey's fried chicken."

"If I know Casey, she's trying to fatten you up some. Says you're too skinny. Thinks you need someone to take care of you."

John ran a hand over his belly. "I'll bet she has someone in mind for the job, too."

"My adorable and very perceptive wife has a theory. Want to know what it is?"

John toyed with his cup. "I'm afraid to ask."

Alex chuckled. "Casey is convinced you're trying to win Aurora back." Alex grinned. "That's a direct quote, by the way."

John glanced down at the band on his wrist. "Casey's right," he said quietly. "I want Rory back."

Alex digested that with the impassive calm that had frequently driven his competitors to drink. "And what does the lady want?" he asked finally.

John sighed. "I wish to hell I knew. She's friendly enough, but she has a big 'Do Not Touch' sign hung out whenever I'm around."

"Sounds like you've got a problem."

John grunted. "That's an understatement."

"So what are you doing about it?"

John glanced over Alex's shoulder toward the living room. In the light spilling from the kitchen he could see the chair where Rory had once sat with one knee tucked under her, her finger winding and unwinding a long, silky curl as she read. Her hair was shorter now, and he found that he liked it better that way, especially when the wind blew it around her face in soft little curls.

He drained his cup. "At the moment I'm taking a lot of cold showers." He stood and carried his cup to the sink. After a moment of silence, Alex did the same.

"I'd better get back to Casey. These days I don't like to be away for long." He hesitated, then asked, "Okay if I tell Casey she was right again?"

John managed a tired grin. "Sure. Knowing Casey, she was bound to figure it all out sooner or later anyway."

A fierce look of pride crossed Alex's lean face. "She is amazing, isn't she? Knows people better than anyone I've ever met."

John felt a pang of envy. Alex's wife was one terrific woman, strong enough to keep Alex interested, but soft and feminine, too, in her own way. All the things a woman should be. Like Rory.

Only Rory wasn't waiting for him to come home tonight—or any night.

"You really love her, don't you?"

Alex frowned. "What the hell kind of question is that?" he asked.

"Do you?"

Alex looked down at his boots. "Yeah, I love her, even more than I did before the divorce. Maybe because I had to live without her for so long."

John braced his hands on the counter and looked through the dusty windowpane at the first star. "I didn't love Aurora when we were married."

Alex's head snapped up and he shot John an incredulous look. "Then why the hell did you work so hard to get her back here?"

John bowed his head and looked at the nicks and knife cuts crisscrossing the bleached, water-stained wood between his hands. "Because I felt like I was dying without her," he ground out, half angry at himself for even starting this damn conversation.

"You nearly did, remember? In my book a man doesn't take that kind of chance without a damned strong reason. Sounds to me like you love her."

"I wish I could be so sure about that."

"Give it time, *compadre*. You'll figure it out."

Alex offered his hand and John took it. "I'll see you a week from Sunday."

"Right. I'll be there early."

"Bring a hammer."

Alex walked to the door. At the threshold, he turned and impaled John with a hard glance. "Think what it would be like to live every day of your life without her. If the very idea makes you sick inside, you love her. It's that simple."

Alex opened the screen door and stepped into the darkness. The door slammed behind him, and a moment later John heard the Jeep start. But still he didn't move.

Could it really be that simple? he wondered.

Alex certainly believed that it was. And he respected Alex's judgment more than anyone else he knew.

Could he really live the rest of his life without her? Somehow he had lived without her for over five years. Each day he'd missed her more, until he'd known he couldn't stand it much longer. And then he'd moved a damn big mountain to get her here.

Did that mean he loved her?

*Did it?*

John took a shuddering breath, then slammed his hand down on the counter. Damn it, he still didn't know.

Warm afternoon light poured through the tall windows like a spotlight, illuminating the pot that Aurora had just removed from the kiln. The pot's creator, Ralph Horse Herder, stood at her shoulder, watching her expression with eager eyes. His fellow students waited almost as breathlessly. In a month of steady, intensive work, Ralph's was the first pot that Aurora had considered good enough to be fired.

"Very nice," she murmured, slowly turning the pot so that she could study every inch. "Uniformly smooth surface, good symmetry." Her fingertips traced the zigzagging yellow pattern. "Excellent attention to detail. I like it."

"Do you really think it's good, Dr. Davenport?" Ralph asked, a smile threatening to break over his usually somber features. At twenty-seven he was the oldest of her students, and by far the most talented.

"Yes, I think it's terrific," she assured him. "You have a knack for applying the glaze in just the right thickness so that it appears transparent. And the shape is nearly perfect. C'mon, I'll show you what I mean," she said, leading the students to the far corner of the sun-washed studio where the authentic Santa Ysabel sat in the middle of a sturdy trestle table.

John sat a few feet away, his head bent over a large ledger in front of him. He had diligently kept his promise to the council, staying with her every minute the Santa Ysabel was out of the safe. He had told her he could use the time to attend to tribal business.

She'd been amazed at the things that were the responsibility of the tribal chairman—the school, the midwife and the reams of paperwork involved in governing a community of over a thousand people. John handled all those things and more.

He looked up as she reached his side, a distracted look in his eyes. "Time to quit?" he asked.

His hand raked his thick hair, leaving it in an untidy thatch that looked shiny and soft in the sunshine. She liked it long, she decided, and then noticed that it had grown shaggy in the month she'd been there.

"Just a few minutes more," she told him as she placed Ralph's pot next to the Santa Ysabel. It was past four, the time when she usually called a halt to the day's work.

John nodded and slowly tilted his head forward as though to relieve a tightness in his muscles. The yoke of his blue plaid shirt pulled tight, then relaxed over the powerful spread of his shoulders. He closed his eyes for a moment, then returned to his work.

She hadn't been alone with him since that afternoon in his office. Several times he had invited her for coffee in his office, and once he had offered to take her riding. When she had declined, he hadn't pressed.

She told herself she was glad. But sometimes, catching a glimpse of him from her window or hearing his voice when she was walking past headquarters on her way to visit new friends, she wondered if she was acting like a fool. Other women had affairs with their ex-husbands. Sofia had had several. She claimed it did wonders for the ego to know your ex still wanted you.

Aurora took a deep breath and told herself that her own ego was just fine the way it was.

"Okay, now, when you look at these two pots together, you can see how much alike they are." Using a pencil as a pointer she began to explain the similarities and subtle differences between the two.

Her students listened with rapt attention and occasionally interspersed comments or questions. From the first she had been impressed by their eagerness to improve their already considerable skills.

"By this time next month we should have our first shipment ready for delivery to the three gift shops on top of the list," she concluded before she dismissed everyone for the day.

Still answering questions she walked with them to the front of the studio, where her desk sat under the south window. Perched on the edge, she made notes on the day's work and sketched out informal lesson plans for the next day. Even though it was Saturday, she held classes until noon. The following day was a day off, and she'd been invited to the Torres house for a picnic lunch.

"You need to relax," Casey had proclaimed with her madonna-like grin, when she'd stopped by to extend the invitation. Aurora had agreed. After all, this was supposed to be her vacation, and so far all she'd done was work—and think about John.

By the time she'd finished her notes, her students had departed. She and John were alone. Nibbling on the end of her pen, she studied his stiff back.

In the studio he was all business, available when she needed him, but never interfering. Occasionally, when she'd looked up unexpectedly, she'd found him watching her with a brooding, watchful expression that made her go warm inside. But when their eyes met, he would simply give her a quick half-smile and return his attention to his work.

"Damn it to hell," he muttered, closing the ledger with a loud bang that made her jump.

"Trouble?" she asked, getting up and walking toward him.

His head jerked up, and she realized he'd been concentrating so hard he'd blocked out everything but the problem at hand. He'd done that often in the past.

"You might say that, yes," he told her in a tight voice. "If we want a doctor for the clinic, I need to come up with forty thousand dollars by September."

He hooked his thumbs through his belt loops and rocked his chair back and forth on two legs, his gaze focused on the rough white wall ahead of him. He looked worn out.

"Why forty thousand?" she asked, reaching under the table for the box where the Santa Ysabel was kept.

"Because I've contacted just about every young doctor in the country I could find with Indian blood, trying to get one of them to come here and run the clinic. They've all turned me down, except one, a guy named Greenleaf. He's generously agreed to come—if we pay him the same salary he's been offered by a medical group in San Francisco."

"Nice of him," she muttered as she lifted the pot into its soft nest and closed the lid.

"Yeah, isn't it? But the guy's got great credentials—Stanford, a top-notch residency in family practice, and best of all for our purposes, he's one-quarter Cherokee on his father's side."

He folded his hands behind his head and watched Aurora pull up a chair and sit down. She was wearing shorts again, and when she stretched out her legs, he saw halfway up her thigh. Her skin was tanned, but he noticed a few freckles above her knee.

He remembered that her skin had been as smooth as a colt's nose, and just below her hip, there was a small heart-shaped cluster of freckles that was especially sensitive. Whenever he'd traced it with his tongue, she'd tangled her fingers in his hair and moaned his name.

His body hardened, taunting him. Here he was, forty years old, so tired he had trouble sitting up straight and he was as eager as a stallion whenever Rory was near.

Abruptly he dropped the chair to four legs and leaned forward to rest his elbows on the table. Since his talk with Alex, he'd been trying to take things slow, letting her set the rules, waiting for an invitation to move closer. He didn't dare spook her away by pushing too hard, too fast.

Seeing the lines of frustration settle above the battered bridge of his nose, Aurora asked softly, "So how're you going to get him here?"

He stood up and walked to the window. Shoving his hands in the back pockets of his jeans, he stared out at the stark vista that stretched to the farthest borders of the pueblo.

"I have an idea, and as much as I hate to admit it, Diego is on my side for a change. Even so, it's going to take some heavy-duty horse trading to scare up enough votes to swing the council my way. A lot of the members are still pretty resistant to new ideas."

She blinked. Something in his voice told her that he was picking his words carefully. Too carefully. John never lied, but as a diplomat he'd learned very well how to avoid telling the truth. She had a feeling he was doing that now.

"And what is this 'new idea'?"

He hesitated, then said flatly, "I intend to sell one of the Santa Ysabels."

Aurora gasped. "No! You can't do that. It…it would be like selling the Mona Lisa."

"Not quite," he countered, a hint of humor threading his deep voice. "The Louvre doesn't have two identical masterpieces. We do."

"What about a...a grant? Money from a charitable foundation. You could file a request."

He turned and impaled her with a hard stare. "We've done enough begging."

Aurora frowned. His attitude seemed irrational at best, and selfish at worse. The Santa Ysabel was more than a commodity to be sold to the highest bidder, even in so good a cause.

"What about Alex?" she asked, careful to keep her tone neutral. "Casey...Casey told me that he donated the money for the clinic."

"Alex has already done more than his share. It's time we stand on our feet, find our own strengths. This studio will help, but it's not enough."

Aurora twisted her hands together and stared at his hard profile. Why did he look as though he were ready to put his fist through the nearest wall?

"A loan, then."

"Banks want collateral. We don't have any."

His glance flicked to the box on the table. "You're an expert. You know what a pot this rare is worth."

She knew. She wished she didn't. "If you're talking about money, then yes, you can easily get forty thousand or more, perhaps from a corporation."

His set blank face told her that she wasn't reaching him. But she had to make him understand. "Do you really want to see the Santa Ysabel on display in the executive suite of some...some company?" she asked, coming very close to pleading.

John frowned. "If I can, I'll sell it to a museum here, where people can see it. Does that make you feel better?"

Aurora placed a trembling hand on the polished wood protecting the priceless treasure. It had hurt to lose the Tapajoz, but that pot had been special only to her. Selling the Santa Ysabel would be like bartering away a living, breathing part of these people.

"But what about its history?" she cried. "Or the spiritual meaning it has for your people? How can you put a price tag on that?"

He was quiet for so long she thought he wasn't going to answer her. "We've got plenty of history around here. What we don't have is a doctor and jobs that don't take the people from their ancestral lands, and a long list of things most people take for granted in this country. It's my job to make those things happen."

His job. Always his job.

Aurora sat perfectly still, fighting the feeling of betrayal twisting inside her. In spite of the surface changes, he was still the same man who'd stood dry-eyed and expressionless at the grave of his daughter. Why should she think he would grieve for the loss of an inanimate object, when Dawn's death had barely touched him?

"Dumb me, I was really beginning to think that you'd finally accepted who you are and where you come from," she said in a voice laced with stinging bitterness. "But you haven't changed. There's something missing inside you, John. Nothing touches you."

"That's not true—"

"It *is* true. Your child was dead, *dead*, and you didn't even care!"

For an instant he looked as though she'd slapped him. He turned white and then red. His eyes went blank.

"Think about this, Aurora," he ordered in a flat, cold voice. "If someone had sold one of these pots five years ago, we might have had a doctor here when you needed one. And our child would still be alive."

Setting his jaw, he tucked the ledger under his arm, snatched the box from beneath her hand and walked out.

Aurora was alone in the studio. It was late, nearly eleven. The pueblo was quiet. Because most of the residents rose with the sun, almost everyone went to bed early.

She ran her hands over the smock that covered her, then lifted the damp cloth from the clay.

All of her life, creating beauty had been her passion, her reason for breathing. Without the ability to create, she felt empty and sometimes, on her bad days, like a failure. She'd been able to live with the pain because she'd convinced herself that helping others see the beauty was almost as satisfying.

But deep in her soul she knew that she'd been fooling herself. She needed to work, to create, not stand on the sidelines while her students did what she could not.

John's words came back to her. "The pueblo gave me back my life." He claimed to have started over, for some reasons of his own that she would probably never know.

Could the ancient place give her back the sense of belonging to the earth, to the universal soul, the one thing she prized more than life itself?

It was time she found out.

She took some clay from the bin and began working out the excess moisture. Little by little she let her fingers get used to the smooth, damp earth, searching for the energy within. But she felt clumsy and inept as though she had never worked with clay before.

She clenched her hands, and the slick material slipped between her fingers. The musky scent of damp earth filled the room. Inhaling deeply, she waited for the comforting bouquet to soothe her, but the tangle of feelings knotted inside her remained. Since John had walked out on her, she hadn't been able to get him out of her mind.

Every day she had come to admire him more. He worked the equivalent of two full-time jobs, and yet in spite of the burden he was shouldering, she hadn't heard him complain once.

Even when he was preoccupied, he always seemed to have time for her. During the past month he had frequently brought her small presents. A piece of petrified wood with veins of rich color threading through it. A fragrant sprig of sage to put on her desk. A slab of fry bread he'd cadged from Lucinda Crowe, the pueblo's best cook.

She had sensed that he'd been hoping for an invitation to share the bread with her, but she'd been afraid. Every day she spent near him made her more aware of him as a man. An extremely attractive and desirable man.

She hadn't felt so aware of her body in years. At night she had trouble sleeping because she kept imagining what it would be like if John were lying next to her. She heard his voice in the wind outside, saying the words of love she longed to hear. Every restless movement of her body reminded her of his touch and his kiss.

Sometime in the long weeks she had given up pretending that she didn't want him to make love to her. Several times she had almost weakened and accepted the sensuous invitation that was always there in his eyes no matter what expression was reflected on his hard features.

Now, however, she was glad she had kept him at a distance. His decision to sell a part of his heritage showed her more forcefully than words that he was still as tough and hard on the inside as his body was on the outside.

The clay was smoother now and just moist enough to hold its shape as she kneaded it methodically, turning, kneading, turning again.

She tore off a smaller piece from the lump in front of her and rolled it between her palms. She formed the base and then began layering the graceful curve of the pot itself.

She worked steadily with only the hum of the foot-operated potter's wheel for company. Her concentration was fierce. Whenever thoughts of John came, she pushed them aside. Work was her reality now. Her life.

The words of the story she'd made up for the children suddenly rang clearly in her mind. "Why doesn't the clay smile, Mama?"

She inhaled sharply, nearly choking on the dry air sucked into her throat. She had to create again. She *had* to find the smile. Or she had to walk away from that part of her life forever.

Several hours later her vision blurred, and she had to stop. She was too exhausted to continue.

Inhaling slowly, she stared at the half-formed pot in front of her. Afraid to hope, she ran her fingers over the distinctive curve of the Santa Ysabel.

The shape was perfect, the workmanship was flawless, but there was no life in the clay. No soul. Nothing.

With a choking cry she picked it up and dashed it against the table over and over until it was once more a shapeless lump of clay.

# Chapter 9

Aurora's watch said eight-fifteen. It was Saturday morning, and she had to leave for the studio in five minutes. She could scarcely believe she had been in the pueblo for a month now. On Monday her stay would be half over.

Feeling strangely sad, she wandered to the window, a mug of cold coffee in her hand. Usually she drank half a pot before she began to function in the morning, but today she hadn't been able to manage more than a few sips.

She was worn out, but not merely by lack of sleep. When she'd finally dozed off sometime in the early hours, her dreams had been filled with a disjointed replay of the argument over the Santa Ysabel, but this time the argument had been accompanied by vividly erotic images of John making love to her.

And when she'd awakened at first light, she'd found her nightgown twisted around her waist as though she'd struggled in her sleep to escape.

Suddenly she heard the crunch of tires outside, followed by the sound of an idling motor. A fist hit the door, and she jumped. She set her cup on the coffee table and hurried to the door. Casey had complained about false contractions when they'd last spoken. This could be Alex telling her that he was taking Casey to the hospital.

But it was John on her doorstep.

"Good morning," she said, forcing a smile to cover the nervousness that clawed at her. Whatever he was thinking had turned his eyes to a deep brown that looked almost black.

"Morning."

Silence enveloped them as John looked into her troubled eyes, trying to read her thoughts, but all he saw were the doubts he'd put there.

What the hell? he thought. Might as well give it to her straight. Trying to take his time with her hadn't gotten him anywhere. He was beginning to think nothing would.

"I came by to tell you I can't be at the studio today. I have business in Santa Fe—with the curator of the Native American Museum of Art there."

Aurora uttered an exclamation of protest. "Please don't do this, John. There has to be another way to raise the money."

"Maybe there is, but I've run out of time. If we want Greenleaf, we have to give him an answer before the end of the month." He pushed his hat to the back of his head. "If I can get a decent price for the pot, I'm going to sign an agreement to sell."

"What about the council?"

"I've talked to Diego. Much as he hates to go along with one of my suggestions, he agrees it has to be done. Between the two of us we'll convince the opposition." He gave her a curt nod and turned to go, but Aurora grabbed his arm before he could leave.

"Please listen to me," she pleaded.

His arm tightened until the veins stood out like blue cables, but he didn't jerk away. Instead he turned slowly and looked down at her.

"No more arguing, Rory," he ordered, his voice ragged. "I'm not good at it, and it'll only make the situation between us more strained than it already is."

She dropped her hand. Think of something, she told herself in a growing panic. She hadn't been able to save the baby and she hadn't been able to save the Tapajoz, but somehow she had to keep the Santa Ysabel safe and in the place where it belonged.

She took a deep breath, then plunged ahead. "I have some money saved. About half of what you need. You can have it—"

Fury exploded in his eyes. He grabbed her shoulders, and his fingers dug into her flesh. He pulled her to her toes until her face was only inches from his.

"Don't ever offer me charity again," he ordered in a voice that shook. *"Just . . . don't . . . do . . . it!"*

He released her so abruptly she staggered.

Without another word, he left her, crossing the short distance to the truck with angry strides. He jumped in, slammed the door and spun the wheel, sending gravel flying as the heavy vehicle spun in a wild circle and headed toward the main road.

Aurora lifted her face to the wind and watched the sun turn the jagged hills to gold. In the secluded grove by the trickling stream the air smelled of pine tar and sage. The branches above her head cast lacy shadows on the small grave in front of her.

It had been spring when she'd last stood on this spot. The wildflowers had blanketed the surrounding area with brilliant color. The morning had been warm, and bees had buzzed around the small party of mourners standing next to the hole dug into the pebbly earth.

A deep, slow breath shuddered through her. Raising her gaze to the patch of lavender sky visible through the overhanging limbs, she listened to the land bedding down for the night. She heard the rustle of birds' wings and the whisper of the wind through the leaves.

There were no bees now. And no spring flowers to soften the harsh land.

Her gaze dropped to the small spray of sun-dried pink rosebuds resting on the rounded pile of red rocks. Slowly she bent to place a sprig of sage blossom next to the tiny bouquet.

"I miss you, Dawn Elizabeth," she whispered. "So very much."

Dawn had been such a beautiful baby, a delicate, feminine version of her father. Her hair had been as dark as the night shadows that crept across the sand, and her skin had been tawny, like the streaks of gold in the rocks shimmering below the water in the nearby stream.

Aurora's shaking fingers brushed grit from the top stones, revealing the mottled color beneath the dust, but the grave still looked too forlorn.

She bowed her head, then raised it again as the creak of saddle leather caught her ear.

A dozen yards away John sat astride the stallion she'd seen galloping along the fence line that first day. The spirited horse sidestepped nervously, then arched its strong neck and whinnied. Its ears pricked alertly, and its muscular flanks twitched with an eagerness to move. Only the pressure of John's knees kept the powerful animal from bolting.

Aurora got to her feet, intensely aware of the distant look in John's dark eyes. He looked windblown and weary. His shirt hung open, revealing his dark, muscular chest, and he was wearing chaps over his jeans.

"I forgot how...how lonely it is out here," she said in a thin voice.

"Is this the first time you've been here?" There was no inflection in his voice and no expression on his face.

She nodded, then glanced down at the small nosegay.

"Are the roses from you?"

He nodded once. "I come here sometimes. It's peaceful."

There were no rosebushes at the pueblo; they required too much water. And the nearby village of Chamisa was too poor to support a florist. He must have bought them in Gallup.

Had he made a special trip? she wondered. And then she knew somehow that he had. Sadness sifted through her grief.

A night bird called overhead, and the horse moved restlessly. John glanced upward, his profile starkly outlined against the sky. In the fading light he seemed almost as wild and primitive as the stallion.

"It's getting dark," he said. "Coyotes will be running soon. You'd best not stay here alone."

But Aurora couldn't bear to leave so soon. The place seemed so lonely.

"She looked like you," she said in a wobbly voice. "And me, too. Like . . . like both of us."

His impassive gaze touched her briefly. "I know," he said. "My mother told me."

Tears welled in her eyes, then began to slide down her cheeks. She had held her baby for such a short time, a few minutes really, but she could still remember how the tiny mouth had curved up at the corners as though Dawn had been eager to smile for her mother.

"You told me not to come here alone," she whispered in a trembling voice. "You said to wait until you were home. I should have listened to you. I should have." A sob took her, and she folded her arms across her belly. "I'm so s-sorry."

"Oh baby, don't." John threw one leg over the pommel and slid from the saddle. Cortes pricked his ears, but the trailing rein kept him from bolting.

John reached her in two strides. Without hesitating, he pulled her into his arms. "Poverty killed the baby, Rory." His voice carried a throbbing note of deep conviction. "It happened, and it hurt, but there's no blame in it."

Aurora clung to him and let the sobs come. John whispered words into her hair, gentle, soft-spoken words that made no sense, but comforted nevertheless.

He was strong and sheltering like an oak tree in a wind-storm, a haven she never wanted to leave. His shirt grew damp, then wet, but he didn't seem to mind. His heart pumped steadily, and his breathing was quiet.

Gradually, as the tears ebbed, she felt her strength re-turning. And as awareness returned as well, she realized that she was pressed tightly against John's warm, hard body and that her hands were wound around his strong neck. His thighs felt solid against hers, and his arms kept her safe. She felt closer to him at this moment than she had ever felt dur-ing their marriage. His gentleness, his patience, even his touch made her feel loved and cherished.

But that was an illusion. John hadn't changed. His deci-sion to barter away the Santa Ysabel had proven that.

"I'm...fine now," she murmured. Her cheeks were damp and she swiped them with the back of her hands.

John reached into his back pocket and pulled out a clean, white handkerchief. Ignoring her outstretched hand, he be-gan to wipe the tears from her cheeks. He was wearing gloves, and the scent of sweat and horseflesh trapped in the leather reminded her of the rides they had taken when life had been so much simpler for both of them.

"You would have made a terrific mother," he said, his voice thick. "And I would have tried my damnedest to be a good father."

Suddenly Aurora knew that he was telling the truth. She'd seen him with the children of the pueblo. They trusted him and liked him, especially the little ones. She had seen it in their faces.

She blinked up at him, and her mouth began to tremble. "Thank you for bringing the flowers. I'm glad she hasn't been alone all this time." She bit her lip, then added softly, "I'm sorry for what I said about your not caring."

Taking her hand, he shoved the handkerchief into her palm, then turned away. He hooked his thumbs through his belt loops and bowed his head for a long moment. And then he straightened his shoulders and began to talk. The lack of inflection in his voice made her shiver.

"When I was six, my father took me into Gallup. There was a rodeo there, and I was jumping up and down excited at the thought of seeing all the people and the animals. I'd never been off the pueblo before." He kicked a large dirt clod with the toe of his boot, and it broke into a shower of gravel.

"But we weren't going to the city for fun. My father needed money for whiskey, and I was to get it for him. By begging."

"Dear God," she whispered in horror.

John felt as though he were strangling, but he made himself continue. If there was ever going to be a chance for them, she had to know the kind of ugly memories that had driven him to do things he would always regret.

"I remember one little girl. A dainty little blonde with big blue eyes, maybe eight or nine years old. She had on shiny, white shoes and a pink dress. 'Look at the poor little Indian boy, Mommy,' she said. I still remember how shrill her voice was and how loud."

His voice hardened into a low, angry tone Aurora had never heard before. "I threw the money away, and I never went with him again, no matter how hard he hit me."

John turned to face her. His voice, his expression, his body, all were held under the same rigid control with which he had mastered the stallion. "The bastard died when I was ten. He didn't even give me another chance to kill him."

"Another chance?" she echoed, her own pain temporarily forgotten.

"I tried once. He had a shotgun that he always kept loaded. For coyotes. One night when I couldn't stand to hear my mother scream any more, I went after it." He stopped talking, and Aurora realized that he didn't intend to continue.

"What happened?" she prodded gently.

Hatred flashed in his eyes. She had to fight to keep from taking a step backward. "He caught me before I could pull the trigger."

"And then?"

From the stony expression on his face and the terse quick cadence of his voice, she sensed that he hated to dredge up the past, even after so many years had passed. She was suddenly certain that he had never spoken of these things to anyone before.

"He used a whip on me and by the time I passed out I had stopped caring. I stopped . . . feeling then, Rory. I just went numb inside. It was the only way I could fight him."

Aurora fought the tears. Anger, frustration, desire, even humor, she'd seen them all in his dusty-gold eyes. But never such raw vulnerability. Until now.

"Why didn't you tell me this before?" she asked softly.

He lifted his chin just enough for her to see the tension lying like a wash of color beneath his dark skin.

"I didn't want your pity, and I don't want it now," he told her in a low, gravel-rough voice. "But I couldn't let you go on thinking I don't mourn our baby, because I do—in my own way."

His expression was as impenetrable as the jagged slopes to the east, but his eyes were alive with emotion. He was telling the truth. The midwife and the soon-to-be clinic were John's way of remembering the child he had never seen.

"You didn't want to take my money because of your father and what he made you do." It wasn't a question. She already knew the answer.

His shoulders moved enough to show that she had guessed correctly. "I hate charity. Diego actively solicits it. That's the basic difference between us. If he takes over again—"

He left the words hanging, but Aurora heard the taut frustration threaded through his words.

"I understand," she said soberly. "And I hope you win."

One black eyebrow arched, and she could see cautious interest in his eyes. "Do you? Why?"

She bunched his damp handkerchief in her fist and glanced toward the place where his house had stood for generations. "I'm not sure I can put it into words," she said slowly, struggling to make logical sense of her intuitive feelings. "But seeing you with the young people in the studio and listening to you talk about your goals for your people, it just feels right, somehow." The evening breeze ruffled her hair, and she smiled. "You belong here, John. I hope you never have to leave."

He cleared his throat, and his hand toyed with the ruffled collar of her blouse. "What about you, Rory? Could you be happy here?"

Her heart began to pound. The intense look around his eyes told her that he wasn't simply making idle conversation.

She was suddenly flustered. Somehow he had taken control again. Somehow he was pushing her toward a decision she didn't want to make.

"That's not a question I can answer, John. My life is in Dallas now. I love my students, and mostly I love teaching."

"Mostly?"

The twilight pressed in on her, and she realized that she and John were as alone as any two people could be.

"It's getting late—"

"Rory, I didn't sell the Santa Ysabel. And I won't. You have my word." His voice was quiet but threaded with steel-like determination.

Aurora tried to speak, but her voice was caught behind a lump of knotted emotion in her throat. "Why did you change your mind?" she managed finally.

"Because you asked me not to sell it."

"But this morning—"

"This morning I wasn't thinking straight. Most of the time I'm around you, I'm not thinking straight."

The note of wry humor brought a reluctant smile to her face. John pulled off one glove and touched the corner of her smile with his thumb.

"On the drive to Santa Fe, I started to think about the look in your eyes when you were pleading with me. And I realized I'd seen that look before—when you asked me to request a transfer to the States. I decided if this was that important to you—'' He shrugged. "I'll find the money someplace else."

She looked up into John's face. Outlined against the sunset glow, his features seemed cast in bronze, a dramatic study of fierce strength and restrained power. If she were a painter, she would portray him on a battlefield astride a stallion very like Cortes. He would be in the front, alone, ready to strike the first blow or shed the first drop of blood for his people.

"Thank you," she said softly. "I know how much you're risking by not selling it, but someday I truly believe you'll be glad you didn't."

His face went as still as the air. "Call a truce for tonight, Rory. Stay and watch the sunset with me." She followed his quick glance toward the west. The clouds were washed with gold and seemed to leap out at her from the lavender-and-orange sky.

She inhaled slowly. It would be so easy to love this man, she realized. The sudden realization terrified her. Her throat closed. "I have to go."

John moved so that he was between her and the car. "Why do you keep running away from me, Rory? Haven't I given you everything you want?"

Aurora hugged her arms close to her body. "I don't know why," she said impatiently. "I just know I feel all mixed up inside whenever I'm with you. And that . . . scares me."

John watched the play of expression cross her face. In the glow from the setting sun, she was part woman, part goddess, ethereal, yet so alive it took his breath away.

"I don't want you to be afraid. That's the last thing I want." He took her hand. His thumb lightly brushed the top of her fingers. "I've done everything I can think of to prove that I've changed, but you keep building walls faster than I can tear them down."

Slowly he brought her hand to his mouth and brushed a kiss across the tender center of her palm.

Aurora bit her lip. Her walls weren't all that sturdy, especially when he was touching her. She tried to tug her hand from his grasp, but his fingers tightened just enough to hold her.

"I don't love you anymore," she said, praying that he would let her go.

He ignored her words. "I made a mistake five years ago, Rory. I sold my soul for success and lost you. I know better now."

His fingers curled around hers, and he turned his head to kiss her wrist. His mouth settled on the spot where her pulse fluttered helplessly. Her heartbeat leaped, and he smiled against the erratic throbbing.

"You want me, too. Admit it." His tone was soft, but his body strained with tension. Her own body was growing taut with the need to resist.

"No," she lied, her voice little more than a harsh whisper. "I stopped wanting you when I stopped loving you."

His smile was slow, sensuous and all the more compelling because it was tinged with sadness. "You can tell yourself you've forgotten how good it was for us, but I'll help you remember."

His tongue teased the tender spot below the heel of her hand, and she shivered. His teeth nipped at the place his tongue had sensitized, sending a flare of wild pleasure shooting through her. She tried to jerk away, but his other hand curved around her small waist, inching her closer to him.

She knew she should resist, knew she shouldn't want this, but the sensuous movement of his fingers across her spine was making it impossible to think about anything but the sweet heaviness growing inside her.

The hand holding hers captive slid up her arm, leaving a trail of warm, fluid sensation on the bare skin. His gloved fingers massaged her back, urging her nearer.

She looked at him helplessly, trying to formulate the words to send him away. The waning light slanted across his face, erasing the shadows under the prominent cheekbones and softening the hard line of his mouth.

"Remember, Rory? Remember how you would go wild in my arms?" His mouth settled over hers, hardness accommodating softness in a moist, warm caress.

Caught by surprise, Aurora parted her lips for him, then stiffened as his tongue made one sweet thrust, then another. Slowly he explored her mouth, tasting her, filling her, enticing her. A hot arrow of desire shot through her, making her feel unsteady and disoriented. Closing her eyes, she grabbed his waist to keep her balance. Her fingers dug into the hard slab of muscle above his belt, and he groaned.

His thigh slid between hers, nudging her skirt higher and sending tingling waves along her skin. His mouth lifted, then took hers again, as though he'd been hungry a long time. There was no restraint in him, no holding back. But instead of feeling coerced into surrendering to his powerful male invitation, she felt eager.

A tender, faint response began somewhere in the turmoil inside her. She was aware of a soft note of resistance coming from her throat, but it sounded more like an urgent plea.

"I thought I'd go crazy, seeing you every day and not being able to touch you," he murmured in a voice made rough by the violence of his need.

His fingers tangled in her hair, her head fell back, and his mouth trailed kisses along the curve of her neck. When she didn't push him away John moved his hand downward to trace the ruffled neckline of her thin blouse.

Without taking his gaze from her face, he tugged off the other glove and stuffed it into his back pocket to join its mate. He needed to feel the warmth of her against his palms.

He started at her waist, rediscovering the small-boned fineness that gave her such a deceptively fragile look. He closed his eyes, letting his hands move slowly, caressingly, to her breasts. Even through her blouse he could tell that the nipples were already hard, poking into his palms like tiny pebbles. A wild exhilaration shuddered through him.

He was almost afraid to look at her. But he had to see her reaction. Her eyes were half closed, and her lips were parted. Gently he caressed her breasts, watching her face grow even more beautiful under the passion he was bringing to life inside her.

The emotion that stung his throat felt different from raw need, but he didn't know what it was. He only knew that it made him want to shout and sing at the same time.

John held his breath. She was radiant, her eyebrows and lashes tipped with gold by the setting sun, and her features seemed bathed in a glow that came from within.

His chest was tight with the need to feel those aroused nipples rub his skin. His muscles burned with the throb of a raw male need, pushing blood into the part of him she excited most.

Slowly, one hand gentling her, he tugged the blouse from the waistband of her skirt and began unfastening the tiny buttons that kept him from her.

"John?"

The half whisper, half moan was almost more than he could stand. When her tongue touched the fullness of her lower lip, his own tongue felt hot and swollen in his mouth. And when her lacy, golden lashes fluttered up to allow her to look at him, he felt the reaction all the way to his knees.

"Easy, my love. I just need to see you."

His fingers nudged open the blouse to reveal a wispy scrap of ivory lace and some kind of silky, transparent material that felt slick against his hand. Her nipples looked dark and swollen against the wispy fabric.

John felt her sigh warm his bare chest like the first breath of spring after a punishing winter. God, he needed her to take the endless gray dawns from his life.

An ache worse than any he'd felt before began inside him, but this pain was more than physical. He longed for her so intensely he wasn't sure he could handle the loneliness when he had to let her out of his arms and go home alone.

"Woman of my heart," he murmured, and his desperate need transformed the harsh consonants of his mother tongue into a caress. She was so feminine, so sweet and giving, so alive.

He pulled her to him and buried his face in the soft curve of her neck, fighting for control. He had only meant to kiss her, but now that she was in his arms, her breath warm and sweet on his neck, he wanted her beyond all stopping.

Aurora folded her arms around his neck and pressed her cheek into the hollow of his shoulder. The scent of the wind was trapped in his long hair, mingling with the musky, male scent of his skin to excite her as she'd never been excited before.

She loved the feel of his hand on her skin, and the fire in his eyes. She loved the way his mouth softened just before it touched hers, and she loved the hard, male feel of his body pressed against hers.

Aurora felt pleasure welling within her, shortening her breath until she felt dizzy. He knew just where to stroke, to caress, to rub to make her breasts fill with a pleasurable pressure. His hands were skilled, his fingers gentle. She closed her eyes and let herself flow into the pulsating river carrying her farther and farther from reality.

Sweet heavens, how she wanted him to make love to her!

And then what? prodded an unwelcome voice. Nothing had changed. He wanted her, but he didn't love her. Without love, he would only be using her, just as he had used her before. And if she had a baby...

Suddenly she felt cold to the marrow. She couldn't go through that agony again.

She stiffened and her hands dug into his shoulders. "We have to stop," she said in a choked voice. "I can't...I can't get pregnant again. I just can't. Please, John."

John heard the cry in her voice, but the need for her was like a hot claw inside him. He ground his teeth, struggling against the prowling need to throw her into the saddle in front of him. Five minutes at a hard gallop and she would be in the bed they once shared.

But she was right. He hadn't even thought about a baby. He cursed himself for being a selfish fool. He hadn't thought beyond the moment when he would make her his again.

Even though he knew he would pay for it in another restless night, he let her leave his arms.

"You're right," he said in a husky voice. "When we make love again, everything should be just the way you want it."

He made a mental note to drive into Chamisa first thing in the morning. The little town didn't have much, but it did have a drugstore.

Bending his head so that he could see, he began to redo the buttons he'd opened in such haste. When his knuckles brushed her breasts, she froze. Slowly he withdrew his hands. "You'd better do it."

As she hastily completed what he'd begun, she watched him from the corner of her eye. His strong-boned face closed up until there was nothing written on the hard planes but a tough determination that made her quake inside.

He had let her go this time, but what about next time?

There won't be a next time, she told herself firmly. She wasn't going to let herself be alone with him again.

Without looking at him, she turned away and began tucking the tails of her blouse into her skirt.

"Very tidy," he said when she finished. "But I liked it better the other way."

Aurora didn't have to ask what he meant. "I don't," she said in a tone more sensuous than she intended, and he laughed.

"C'"mon, I'll walk you to your car." John took her hand and tucked it into the crook of his arm as though they were once again walking into an ambassador's tea.

When they reached the car, he released her, but before she could breathe in relief, he rested both his hands on her shoulders.

"Take care. I worry about you out on these roads alone."

He kissed her forehead, then turned her around and opened the car door. Aurora fought a terrible feeling of loss as she slid into the seat and fastened the belt.

"Good night, Rory. Sleep well." He leaned down to brush a kiss over her lips still swollen from his kiss.

"Good night," she murmured. "You, too."

"I'll try," he answered in a dry tone. "But somehow I'm not sure that's possible." He closed the door and stepped back.

Aurora started the engine. Without looking at him again, she made a wide circle and headed back the way she had come. She had never felt so alone.

Aurora's brow creased with worry as she scanned the dusty road ahead. According to the meticulous directions Casey had given her, the Torres house was approximately five miles off the main highway. She'd driven over that on a road that was little more than a cow path in stretches without seeing a sign of life.

"Darn," she muttered, looking for a place to turn around. And then, as the car crested a small hill, she saw a grove of aspens ahead. Nestled between the tall trees was a small stone cottage.

Flowers of every color surrounded the house, giving the place a cheery, welcoming look. Aurora started to smile, and then she saw the familiar black truck parked next to Alex's Jeep.

John was there.

Casey hadn't mentioned that he'd be coming to the picnic.

At least she and John wouldn't be alone, she told herself as she parked in the shade. She took a moment to let her pounding heart settle into a more natural rhythm, then grabbed the apple pie she had baked and started toward the front of the house.

As soon as she rounded the corner, she saw Casey hurrying toward her, moving as fast as her protruding belly would allow. "If you hadn't made it in the next fifteen minutes, I was going to send out a search party. These roads are tricky."

Aurora glanced behind her. Nothing but coarse sand and mesquite stretched toward the horizon. "What road?" she said with a grin. "For the last mile I was sure I was exploring virgin territory."

Casey laughed. "You're here. That's what counts," she said, giving Aurora an awkward hug. They began walking toward the front of the cottage.

Suddenly from some place above her head, Aurora heard the low murmur of male voices, followed by a burst of rich, masculine laughter. A split second later the staccato sound of hammering shattered the quiet.

Shading her eyes, she looked toward the roof. Alex and John were balanced on the steep slope, nailing shingles to sheets of plywood. Neither appeared to have seen her drive up.

As Aurora watched, John stood slowly and leaned backward as though to relieve a kink in his muscles. He was wearing a tight red tank top blotched with sweat and khaki shorts that emphasized the musculature of his bottom. On his feet were heavy work shoes and thick socks instead of the worn boots she was used to seeing. A carpenter's leather belt hung low on his hips like a gunman's holster. His hair was tied at the nape of his neck with a strip of rawhide.

At the sight of him, Aurora felt a sharp, breathless pleasure. He was every woman's dream, strong, sexy, his own man. If things had been different, she would already be sharing his bed.

She transferred her attention to her hostess. "What's going on?" she asked.

Casey tried for a look of innocence. "Alex and John are roofing the nursery. I thought I told you."

"No, actually you didn't," Aurora said drily. "If I remember correctly, you said something about a picnic."

Casey tried to look innocent. "That's exactly what we're having. A picnic lunch." She waved a hand toward a patch of dense shade under the tallest of the trees where a picnic table and benches had been set with colorful china and a cheery centerpiece of dried desert plants.

"It's all ready. Come inside and help me pour the drinks." Casey led the way into the house and Aurora followed. Inside, the living room was cool and filled with sunlight spilling though large windows in one wall.

"This is wonderful, Casey. Absolutely fantastic, all that light and that terrific fireplace. I love it." Aurora turned slowly in a circle, feeling the house reach out to her. "It's ... safe in this place. And welcoming." Her smile wobbled. "You must be very happy here."

Casey's eyes lit up. "We are. And you're right. This is a happy home. Now."

"Now?"

When Casey spoke again, her voice was very quiet. "Alex built this house himself while we were ... apart. He was dealing with a lot of guilt because of a business deal that had ended in a terrible tragedy, and the work was a catharsis for him. I didn't even know where he was then, not until I needed his help."

Aurora saw the shadow of pain touch Casey's face and a feeling of shared grief coursed through her. For years she'd been so sure John was far away, when in fact he'd been only a long day's drive from Dallas.

"John told me that you and Alex are evenly matched."

Casey laughed. "God, I hope so. Alex tends to ride roughshod over anyone who can't hold his own. He doesn't do it deliberately. In fact he tries not to, but he's so forceful he can't help it sometimes." Her expression turned mischievous. "That's one of the reasons I think he and John get along so well. In his own quiet way John gives as good as he gets. Sometimes more—when Alex deserves to be reined in." Casey laughed and Aurora thought it was a happy sound.

She started to follow Casey toward the kitchen when a blur of brown-and-black streaked past her. "What was that?" she exclaimed.

Casey laughed. "*That* was our cat, Butch." She raised her voice and called the cat's name.

A large feline face peered suspiciously around the edge of the sofa. The scruffy animal had only one eye and a torn ear, and his fur stuck up in tufts on the top of his head. In spite of his unprepossessing appearance, however, the gleam in the solitary green eye was pure, arrogant male.

Aurora burst out laughing. "I hope you won't be offended when I tell you that's just got to be the ugliest cat I've ever seen."

Casey sighed. "I know. And I dearly love him." She grinned. "John keeps him for us when we're in New York. He claims Butch is one of the *kachinas* come to life. The one that exasperated mamas threaten their kids with, when they're misbehaving."

Casey ushered Aurora into the kitchen and pointed to a cupboard to the right of the sink. "Glasses are in there," she said as she opened the refrigerator and took out a large glass pitcher of lemonade. From the freezer she took a half-empty bag of ice. She set both in front of Aurora, then said with a grin, "Alex and John must have drunk gallons of ice water already. I just hope I don't run out of ice before the day is over."

Aurora opened the cupboard door and took down four large glasses, which she proceeded to fill with ice. When she noticed the condensation on the pitcher, she immediately thought about the sheen of sweat on John's powerful shoulders. Unbidden, a warm tendril of desire uncurled inside her.

"It has to be like a furnace up on that roof," she murmured, filling the glasses with cold lemonade. John's skin would be hot from the sun and taste salty from sweat.

She picked up a glass and held it against her heated cheek, trying without success to push the tantalizing thought from her mind.

"I should have told you John was going to be here," Casey said quietly, staring down at the salads and fried chicken on the counter in front of her. "But I was afraid you wouldn't come."

"I wouldn't have," Aurora admitted without rancor. Casey was so happy, she wanted everyone else she cared about to feel that same joy. "The more I'm with him, the more I know we can't be together."

Casey turned to look at her. "Why not, for heaven's sake? John sure wants it. Would it be so difficult for you to give him a chance?"

Aurora carefully placed the glass on the counter and wiped her damp hands on a towel. "John doesn't love me. I thought once it was because of me, something I couldn't or didn't give him, but I know now that because of... of some things that happened when he was a boy, he *can't* love me. Or anyone. It's not his fault, but that doesn't change things, either."

Casey's hand went to her back and Aurora knew that the weight of the baby was making it ache. "I think you're wrong," Casey said in a soft, sure voice. "I think John cares so deeply for you he's afraid to face just how much. Alex is like that sometimes, even now, but I know he loves me. He shows me in everything he does."

Aurora bit back a sigh. "I wish you were right, but—"

"I hope that's lunch I smell," a deep voice said from the doorway, causing both women to start at the unexpected interruption. "You've got two hungry *hombres* about to chew on shingles."

John stood on the threshold, one hand on the door frame. When Aurora caught his eye, he straightened and smiled, his gaze traveling slowly from the top of her tousled head to the hem of her short cotton dress.

"Hi," he said, his smile turning into a roguish grin. "That's one great dress. Makes you look nice and cool, like raspberry sherbet." His admiring gaze followed the modest neckline to the faint shadow above her breasts.

The pulse in her throat began to flutter. From the expression that flared in his tired eyes, she knew that he was thinking of last night when his big hand had caressed her bare breasts. She had felt his touch long after she'd turned out the lights and crawled into bed. And now, with only a look, he was making her nipples fill with a heavy sweetness.

"Good morning," she said, her voice scratchy. Somehow she managed a friendly smile. "Shouldn't you, uh, be wearing a hat? You're liable to get sunstroke."

His eyes warmed and crinkled at the corners. "Sounds like you're worrying about me. I missed that." He crossed the short distance between them and gave her a deep, sensuous kiss that made her go hot and cold at the same time.

Before she could blink, he released her, wiped the smear of dirt from her cheek where his hand had rested and picked up the tray of food from the counter.

"I'll wear her down yet," he said to Casey as he walked out.

Aurora stared after him, her eyes wide and unblinking. She heard a soft sound next to her and slowly shifted her gaze to Casey's. Tears stood out on Casey's long lashes, and a mixture of pain and hope shimmered in her kind gray eyes.

"Give him a chance, Aurora," she said urgently. "If you don't, I'm afraid you'll wake up one morning and wish you had. And then, it just might be too late."

# Chapter 10

"Did you hear about Buck Ruiz?" Alex asked. He had just finished his second wedge of apple pie, while Casey was still working on her first. John had eaten two pieces of his own and finished most of Aurora's.

"What's he done now?" John asked, throwing down his napkin. Seated next to him, Aurora felt as well as heard the disgusted sigh that escaped him.

"Got himself arrested for assault in Gallup. Way I hear it, he's headed back to prison for violating his parole."

"At least that's one less problem to worry about." John flexed his shoulders and glanced down at the strawberry on Aurora's plate. "You gonna eat that?"

She shook her head. "I'm stuffed."

His hand brushed her arm as he reached for the fruit. For an hour she'd been trying to ignore the sexy male body close to hers, but every time he moved his leg, she knew it. And every time he reached for something on the table, she had to resist the urge to move away.

Seated so close to his big body, she felt small and vulnerable. She could feel his strong male energy reach out to her whenever she moved. She felt trapped in an electrical force field that was drawing her inexorably toward him.

"How can you eat another bite?" Casey asked incredulously as John crushed the plump berry between his teeth.

John looked wounded. "C'mon, Casey. Hoss, here, claimed you made this especially for me. I didn't want to insult you by leaving any."

Casey laughed and glanced pointedly at the pile of chicken bones on his plate. "There's not much danger of that."

John looked at Aurora, and a look of pure mischief slanted his mouth into a tantalizing half smile. "Remember the night you ate the pig brain because you didn't want to cause an international incident?"

"Pig brain?" Casey looked slightly queasy.

John nodded. "I was the new kid on the block then, and part of my indoctrination was to show the flag at various ceremonies in the surrounding villages. One night we were invited to accompany San Sebastian's minister of internal affairs to a celebration put on by one of the local tribes. In our honor the chief sacrificed his pet pig."

Alex folded his arms across his chest and gave John a disbelieving look. "I smell a put-on."

"True story," John said, raising one palm. When Alex didn't look convinced, John turned to Aurora. "Tell him, Rory."

"It's true, all right," she said, feeling the web John was spinning around her pull tighter. When he was in one of his rare teasing moods, he was irresistible.

"The chief kept looking at her hair. I don't think he'd ever seen hair that color," John said with a glance at her fiery curls. "Finally he sent one of his wives to fetch his personal machete. Before we knew what was happening, he'd sliced off the pig's head and scooped out the brain, which he proceeded to dump on Rory's plate."

Casey shot a look of horror across the table toward Aurora. "What on earth did you do?"

"I ate it," Aurora said, then winced at the memory. "It tasted like sour scrambled eggs."

"That wasn't the worst part—" John began.

"Easy for you to say," Aurora interrupted tartly. "You didn't have heartburn for three days."

John fought a grin. "No, but I had to talk *your* way out of the bargain *you* made."

"What bargain?" Alex asked, his piercing eyes alive with interest.

John sighed dramatically. "By eating the chief's, uh, delicacy, my darling wife was accepting his offer of marriage."

"Oh, no." Casey covered her mouth with her hand, but not before a tinkling giggle escaped.

"Oh, yes," Aurora muttered, ridiculously warmed by the deep note of affection in John's voice. "And John didn't help. He acted like he was going to...to just hand me over."

John saw the smile hovering around her soft mouth and it took all of his control not to answer that sensuous invitation with a kiss.

"That was merely diplomacy, my love," he said, watching the reluctant smile move to her eyes. "I told you I wouldn't have traded you for a dozen beautiful maidens."

Aurora gave him a disgruntled sideways look. "It was the three horses I was worried about."

John burst out laughing. "You had nothing to worry about, believe me."

"Oh, yeah? You should have seen your eyes light up when you saw that palomino stallion."

John looked affronted. "I had to make the chief believe I was really thinking it over. Otherwise he might have used that machete on me and then just carried you off to his hut for a honeymoon. What would you have done, then?"

"Well, I certainly would have gotten rid of the other two wives, that's for sure," she blurted out, and then blushed at the burst of male laughter that greeted her words.

"Whoa," Alex said with a wicked grin. "She's got you there, *amigo*."

John gave Aurora a fond look. "Yeah, I was supposed to be the one who was good with words, but she always managed to win whenever we disagreed."

Casey leaned toward Aurora and said in a conspiratorial tone, "Maybe you could give me some pointers. I'm still trying with this one." She pressed her belly against Alex's side and gave him a lusty kiss. "Not that I'm trying too hard."

Alex pulled her close. "This is getting exciting," he said in a suggestive voice. "Must be the storm. It was storming when you came after me, remember, *mi amor*?"

"How could I forget? You were mad as a hornet because I couldn't turn around and drive away."

Alex kissed her. "I didn't stay mad long. How could I when I kept thinking about kissing you?" His black eyes were lit with a fierce inner fire that Aurora knew was love.

Casey saw it, too, and a loving smile broke over her face. "You made up for lost time," she said, taking one of his hands and pressing it to her belly.

Aurora felt a small tremor run through her body, but she managed to keep her smile in place. John took her hand and entwined his fingers with hers before resting both hands on his thigh.

Grateful for the silent gesture of understanding, she let her fingers respond to the steady pressure of his. Their eyes met and held, and she felt the closeness they had shared for a moment last night encompass her again.

"Damn," Alex said suddenly, cocking his head. "Was that thunder?"

John released Aurora's hand and slid his arm around her waist. But even as he pulled her close, he cast a worried look at the sky. "Probably. I don't like the look of those clouds."

Aurora was shocked to see the thunderheads that had piled up above them as they'd been eating.

Alex sighed and stood. "I should have asked Grandfather Horse Herder for a weather prayer." He helped Casey pull herself up from the bench, then dropped an arm over her shoulder and kissed her temple. "Walk me to the ladder, *mamacita*," he said with a grin.

"Gladly, *papacita*," Casey answered, her expression smugly serene. As Aurora watched them walk toward the side of the house, she was acutely conscious of John's hand pressed snugly against her side. Though their bodies were inches apart, she felt as though he were touching every part of her.

"Who's Grandfather Horse Herder? Is he any relation to Ralph?" she asked, feeling John's forearm move against her spine.

"His father," John explained. "And he's also our shaman."

"Really? I didn't know you still had one."

John moved closer, until his thigh was brushing hers. The curly black hair covering his skin felt soft and fluffy against her leg. "As far as I can tell from tribal records, we've never been without one, even when the Spanish priests were here. If you'd like, I'll introduce you to Grandfather. He knows a lot more about the Santa Ysabels than anyone. In fact he sometimes uses one in the blessing ceremonies he still performs."

"I'd like to meet him."

John grinned. "I'll see to it. And when you meet him, put in a good word for me. He's a member of the council and firmly in Diego's camp. He thinks I'm ruining the young people by introducing radical ways to the pueblo."

"Are you?"

"If you call quality education and jobs radical, then I guess I am."

Suddenly he bent toward her and gave her a hungry kiss that left her wide-eyed and longing for more.

"Hold that thought, my love," he ordered in a husky voice. He swung his legs over the bench and stood. Before she could answer he turned and jogged away from her.

The first drops hit the dust ground with a soft plopping noise. In less than ten minutes the light sprinkle had turned into a deluge.

Under the thick canopy of aspen limbs Aurora sat next to Casey on one of the benches. They had been watching the men work for the past several hours.

On the roof John and Alex were nailing the last row of shingles to the ridge pole. It was nearly five, and the two men had worked all afternoon without a break in order to beat the storm.

"They're going to make it," Casey said in a voice full of relief.

Aurora hugged the yellow slicker she'd borrowed from Casey more snugly around her and watched the men fit another shingle into place. There were only a few more to go.

"I don't know why they couldn't have stopped when the lightning started," she muttered, sending another nervous glance toward the swollen black clouds that looked close enough to touch.

Casey gave her a sympathetic look. "That would be admitting defeat, and Alex and John would rather die than do that."

Aurora's eyes rounded in horror as her gaze flew to the roof where the wind was driving the rain sideways into the two men. "Don't even think that," she said, her voice catching.

"Sorry," the other woman said quickly, lightly touching Aurora's arm. "That was just a figure of speech."

"I know," Aurora said with an embarrassed sigh. "The first day I arrived John was nearly killed by that man, Buck Ruiz, Alex was talking about. Since then I keep seeing him dead. I've had these nightmares...."

Casey wiped drops of moisture from her brow. The canopy over their head kept them relatively dry, but an occasional drop fell from the leaves. "Does John know about that?"

Aurora shook her head and looked down at her hands. "He's been going out to Dawn's grave. Taking flowers." The words were out before she'd known she was going to say them.

"And that surprises you?"

The wind blew her bangs into her eyes, and she impatiently brushed them away. "Yes. No." She sighed. "I don't know what to think any more. John has changed so much."

Casey's smile was warm with understanding. "When I first met him, I thought he was the kindest man I'd ever seen. And one of the sexiest."

Aurora felt a razor-sharp emotion slice through her. It took her a moment to realize that it was jealousy.

As though reading her thoughts, Casey chuckled softly. "I also knew that he wasn't available, even though he mentioned that he wasn't married."

Aurora watched the rain dripping from the leaves overhead. The relatively dry circle where they sat was getting smaller. "I'm sure he's had affairs," she said. Was that her voice that sounded so stilted?

"I don't think so, Aurora. If he has, Alex doesn't know about them." Casey paused, as though letting Aurora absorb that fact, then added, "John said something to me one night I've never forgotten. He told me that every man longs to love and be loved. He was talking about Alex at the time, but I had the strong feeling he was also talking about himself."

Aurora stared at her friend. "John said that?"

"Yes, and he also said that more than anything a man wanted to belong to one special person. I think that person is you."

Aurora bit her lip. Is that what he truly wanted? To belong to her? She started to smile inside, then remembered that belonging didn't necessarily require love.

She stared at the rain beating the dust to mud beyond the sheltered circle. Since she'd learned more of the life John had led as a child, she'd found herself filtering the past through a lens with a sharper focus. Things she hadn't understood were clear now—his almost obsessive drive to succeed, his determination to leave the "poor little Indian boy" behind, his inability to break through his self-imposed emotional numbness in order to love her or anyone.

No wonder he hadn't understood her need to come home to heal, she thought, staring at the snug, cheerful home Alex had built to heal himself. John's home had been a hell, a place of hurting instead of healing, a place to escape from.

Slowly she raised her gaze to the roof. John had taken the bandanna from his pocket and tied it around his brow to keep the rain from dripping into his eyes, and his shirt was plastered to his broad back like a second skin. He was down on his haunches, working steadily, his back muscles moving with the hammer blows he was striking.

As she watched, he glanced at the sky and said something to Alex that made the other man nod his head.

"They're done," Casey exclaimed, clutching Aurora's arm. "They're coming down."

Aurora narrowed her eyes against the wind and watched anxiously as the men began making their way down the sloping roof toward the sturdy wooden ladder propped against the edge. Water beaded on the pebbly shingles and ran in shiny rivulets toward the eavestrough.

"Thank goodness," Aurora muttered, her gaze riveted on John's soaked shorts and shirt. "They're going to need something warm—" Aurora broke off in horror as Alex's booted feet suddenly shot out from under him. He landed on his back and began sliding rapidly toward the edge.

Hearing Alex's hoarse shout, John whipped around and lunged toward Alex's outstretched hand. Miraculously he managed to grab Alex's wrist, but the momentum of Alex's heavy body jerked John sideways and he lost his footing.

"Oh, no. No!" Aurora shouted into the wind, her nails digging into her palms. Somehow John had kept his grip on Alex's wrist, but gravity was against them, pulling them both toward a certain fall.

A split second before the struggling men went over the edge, John managed to hook his right arm around a vent pipe. Alex's wildly swinging foot kicked the ladder, and it fell to the ground with a jarring crash.

"Hang on, John, please hang on," Aurora pleaded, staring at John's straining biceps. His teeth were clenched and his feet were braced against the sloping roof as, inch by inch, with just the power in his right arm and shoulder, he pulled Alex to safety.

"We have to get them off the roof," Aurora shouted into the wind. Ducking her head against the driving rain, slipping and sliding in the mud, she ran toward the fallen ladder. Casey followed at a more careful pace, picking her way through the slick places, her hands protecting her belly.

The ladder was fifteen feet long and slippery. Aurora had trouble getting a secure grip. Muttering a few choice words, she ripped open the slicker and hastily ran her hands down her hips to dry her hands. As she tried again, mud squished over the thin soles of her sandals, making her footing precarious.

"Rory, what in God's name do you think you're doing?" came a harsh shout from above.

Aurora looked up to see John leaning over the edge, a frown on his face. "Getting you down," she yelled impatiently, pushing back her dripping bangs.

"You can't lift that ladder," he shouted over the noise of the storm. "It's too heavy for you."

"I'll manage," she shouted back.

"The hell you will!"

She took an impatient breath. "Do you want to stay up there until someone bigger comes along?"

Rain dripped down his face and into his mouth. He swallowed and wiped his jaw. "We'll get down—"

"Stop arguing and grab this thing when I get it up to you."

The ladder was heavier than she expected and unwieldy, but she managed to raise it far enough for John to catch the end and pull it toward the roof.

She settled the ladder securely at the bottom, then held one side to keep it steady. Casey, ignoring the rain that pelted her face, held the other side.

Alex climbed down first, and Casey launched herself at him. "You idiot," she said, half laughing, half crying. "Promise me you won't do anything like that again."

Alex kissed her soundly, then scowled at her dripping face. "You shouldn't be out here in this rain, *querida*."

"Now that you're safe, I feel fine."

Alex encircled her with a strong arm, then hastily glanced upward. John was nearly down.

Aurora narrowed her gaze against the stinging rain and watched him manage the last rungs. Both calves were bleeding where the coarse shingles had abraded the skin, and he favored his right arm as he moved.

As soon as John stepped off the last rung, Alex stuck out his hand. "I owe you one, *compadre*," he said with a quick look at the deep gouge where the ladder had crashed to the hard earth.

"Forget it," John said, then winced as he shook Alex's hand.

"You okay?" Alex asked.

"Other than being half drowned, yeah, I'm okay."

"I hear you. Let's get inside." Alex scooped Casey into his arms and hurried toward the house.

Aurora and John were alone.

"I told you I'd be back," he said, removing the bandanna and wiping his dripping face. "Miss me?"

Aurora didn't feel the rain beating on her head or the wind pushing at her back. In fact, she was beginning to feel very strange. When she'd seen first Alex and then John sliding toward a bad fall, she'd been terrified. And furious, because she felt so helpless. Now she couldn't seem to stop shaking.

"You hurt your arm," she said, touching his shoulder.

John covered her hand with his. His palm was damp and cold. "A little horse liniment and I'll be good as new," he said with a dismissive shrug that ended in an almost comic wince.

Aurora took a shaky breath. Why did she feel like hitting him and kissing him at the same time?

"Hey, don't look so upset," John ordered with a tired grin. "Nothing happened."

Something gave way inside her, and a wave of anger rolled over her. "Nothing happened? *Nothing happened?* Lord save me from macho men." She felt the blood pound through her head. He could have been badly hurt and he was talking about horse liniment. The shaking turned into a shudder.

"Rory—"

"Don't Rory me," she shouted, pulling her hand from under his and balling it into a fist. "I'm furious with you, do you hear me, John Olvera? Furious. You knew better than to stay on that roof when it was raining this hard. You could have been struck by lightning or...or you could have gone over the edge. There are rocks down here. You could have hit your head—"

She had a sudden vision of John lying in the mud, his steady brown eyes staring sightlessly at the sky. No, she thought frantically, not him, too. Not John.

She glanced around wildly, looking for her bright yellow car. "I was stupid to come back. I have to get out of here. I have to go home."

"What you have to do is talk to me." John attempted to take her hand again, but she jerked it away.

"I don't want to talk. I want to *leave*," she shouted. She turned to walk away, but John grabbed her waist and spun her around. His arm pinned her against his wet body, and she knew it would be useless to struggle. Even with one arm, John was far too strong for her.

"What did I do wrong this time?" he asked in barely leashed frustration. "Why are you yelling at me?"

"Because I don't want you to die, too." Her face crumpled, and she started to cry.

"Oh baby, don't—" Before he could finish, lightning split the sky. Thunder cracked directly overhead.

He muttered a ripe expletive that carried an edge of frustration. "C'mon, let's get the hell out of this rain," he shouted. He released her long enough to grab her hand, and they ran toward the house.

Inside, Aurora kicked off her sandals and John took off his soaked shoes and socks. Casey was ready with towels.

Aurora pressed the soft cloth to her face, wiping away the tears as well as the rain. She had overreacted, but she couldn't seem to help herself. Standing in the rain, praying that he would get down safely, she'd stopped kidding herself. She had fallen in love with him all over again.

Casey handed John a large black towel. "Thank you," she said, holding onto his shoulders to brace herself as she went on tiptoe to kiss him on the cheek.

"*De nada,*" he said, giving her pregnant body an awkward one-armed hug. "Couldn't let Hoss end up in hospital when you need him most."

Casey wiped the tears from her lashes. "Alex put out some dry clothes for you in the bedroom. He's in the bathroom, showering."

John wiped the rain from his face, then turned to Aurora. "You okay?" he asked in a low, deep voice.

She summoned a smile. "Yes, fine. You go ahead and get into some dry clothes."

He tossed the towel to his shoulder and gave her a penetrating look. "You sure you're okay? I don't want to come back in here and find out you've decided to take off for Texas."

Aurora heard the gravelly note of warning in his voice, and she bristled. "And if I did?"

"You can't run away, Rory. Not this time."

"I'm not—"

"Yes, you are. But wherever you go this time, I'll follow you. I'm not letting you go again."


"Ransom's Wash must be flooded again. Franco isn't here," John said as Aurora parked his truck in the usual spot in front of the ranch house. It was almost seven-thirty and the air smelled of wet sage and drenched earth.

By the time the rain had abated enough for them to leave, John's shoulder was sore and his arm was so stiff he couldn't drive. Aurora volunteered to see him home.

At John's insistence she drove his truck because the four-wheel drive made it easier to navigate the flooded spots on the bad roads. Even though she had vowed never to be alone with him again, the only sensible plan was for her to drive John to his place, then keep the truck and pick him up in the morning. If he was able to drive, they would retrieve her car then.

"Is that bad?" Aurora asked, turning off the engine. "That he's not here, I mean?"

John sat up, grimacing as the movement jarred his sore shoulder. "You might say that. Now I have to do his work and mine, too."

Aurora frowned. "John, be sensible. You can barely lift your arm. You can't work."

John gave her a tired smile. "Tell that to my hungry stock."

"John—"

"Don't fight me, Rory. Kiss me."

Before she could argue he slid toward her and hooked his good arm around her shoulder, pulling her close.

"Your shoulder—"

"Is just fine. Kiss me."

His mouth hovered over hers, waiting, demanding.

Slowly, knowing that she was stalling, she reached out to trace the uncompromising line of his upper lip. Even when he smiled, it never softened. Only when he kissed her.

His teeth nipped her finger, and she felt her resistance melting. It was cozy in the cab, and John's body was warm and solid. In the silence she became aware of the quickening of his breath and the tension vibrating in the big body so close to hers.

Because he was more muscular in the thighs and broader in the torso than Alex, the clothes he'd borrowed clung to him tightly, emphasizing the power and strength in those work-hardened muscles.

Her own clothes had been protected by the slicker, but her sandals had been soaked, and she'd borrowed a pair of Casey's sneakers that suddenly felt too tight for her feet.

A shiver raced up her spine. She was still trying to accept the fact that she loved him.

But that didn't mean he loved her.

Still, he'd changed so much. Was it possible...?

"I need to touch you," she whispered, raising her hand to his cheek.

He looked startled, then pleased. "Sounds good to me," he said in a low, sensuous tone that jerked her pulse into a faster rhythm. "Start anywhere you like."

Aurora cleared her throat and tried to concentrate. But she knew that they were both thinking about the times when she'd touched every part of him. "No, I mean I need to touch you **the** way I touch the clay."

Instantly the seductive gleam in his eye faded. "Why?"

"If you don't want me to..." She left her words hanging. If he shut himself away from her now, the tiny ray of hope she was trying to nurture would be doused forever.

His frown deepened, and his eyes grew wary, but his words were calm. "I told you, love. Whatever you want from me, you can have." He withdrew his arm from her shoulder and leaned back against the seat. Aurora moved until she could rest both hands against his face.

She could feel tension snake through him until his muscles were rigid. She knew it was costing him dearly to submit, but he didn't pull away.

She closed her eyes and inhaled deeply, letting her mind empty. Sensations came, faint at first, but as she concentrated, they grew stronger. Her breathing slowed, became quiet.

He smelled of coffee. His skin was raspy and warm against her fingertips as they lightly traced the jutting line of his cheekbones.

She recognized the mark of generations of rugged, powerful men. Men of the wind and the sky and the land. Conquerors. Warriors. Peacemakers.

Silent, strong men who did what had to be done for their women and children. Men who could kill. Or plant new life in the bodies of their women.

With a feather-light touch she traced the hard curve of his jaw. There, in the sudden tightening of the muscles, she felt his personality—forceful, turbulent, compelling, like a raging river buried underground. But she'd always known that part of him.

She needed to know the man who went out of his way to bring delicate pink roses to the child he'd never known. The man who would risk failure and ostracism because she had asked him to keep the Santa Ysabel safe. The man she wanted to love her.

Slowly she moved her fingers to the network of lines next to his eyes. Gently she brushed his closed lids with her thumbs, feeling the thick lashes quiver under her touch.

She inhaled swiftly, sensing an emotion she didn't recognize. Slowly it took shape. Anguish. Deep and soul-felt. And a terrible longing, so violent it hurt to feel it.

For her?

Shaken, she dropped her hands and opened her eyes. Not a single muscle in his face moved, but she knew that he waited. Finally, when she didn't speak, he said in a low, almost hoarse voice, "Now you know how much I want you."

With his left hand he reached over and opened the door, wincing as the movement jarred his shoulder.

Aurora watched stiffly as he climbed from the cab and slammed the door. He hesitated, then leaned through the door to order gruffly, "Be careful in the low spots."

Without waiting for an answer he turned and walked rapidly toward the barn. She watched him awkwardly push one of the big doors to the side and disappear inside.

John opened the small door built into the waist-high wall that formed the lower half of the box stall, and tossed in a generous measure of hay. Wildflower nickered and shifted her feet, her iron shoes making a pleasant sound on the sawdust-strewn floor.

"How's it goin' girl? Feelin' better today, are you?" The mare moved a step closer and lowered her head so that John could rub the dark blaze under her black forelock.

Wildflower snorted and shied sideways, her ears pricking as though she sensed danger. "Whoa, girl."

"I didn't mean to scare her."

John spun around to see Aurora standing a few feet away. Something painful swelled in his chest. "What's wrong? Truck won't start?" he asked, bracing himself to accept one more problem.

Curiosity gripped her as she walked down the wide aisle between stalls. She counted six mares and two foals. All looked sleek and well cared for. The sweet smell of hay and the pungent odor of horse dung scented the cool air; the barn was very clean.

"Nothing's wrong. I'm going to help you with your chores." Her approach was greeted by a stamping of hooves and a ragged chorus of whinnies and snorts, which she ignored.

John raised his eyebrows. "You are?"

"Yes," she said in a clear voice that betrayed none of the turmoil inside her. "Only you'll have to tell me what to do."

For weeks he had helped her whenever she'd needed him. And today he had helped Alex and Casey. It was time someone helped him. Tomorrow she would worry about the unresolved feelings tormenting her.

"Rory, I'm tired, it's getting dark. You need to get back to the pueblo while you can still see the road."

Aurora felt her face warming. Could he tell that she was worried about him? Or that she thought he was working too hard and shouldering too many burdens? Could he tell that she loved him?

"If you want me to leave, you'll have to throw me out," she countered, planting a small fist on her hip.

"I will?" John rested his back against the steel bars forming the top part of the stall, and watched her.

"Uh-huh, and stop looking at me like I'm crazy."

John studied the stubborn line of her small chin. She looked cute as a day-old foal with her face washed clean of makeup and her hair pushed back from her face in soft, disheveled curls.

It made him feel good inside just having her near, but try as he might, he couldn't read her, and that made him nervous. He couldn't afford to make any more mistakes with her.

Keep it light, he told himself.

He pushed away from the stall and took a quick look over his shoulder. "Hear that, Flower?" The horse lifted her head from the fresh hay and looked at him with curious eyes. "The lady says she's not leaving. You think I can throw her out with one arm?"

Aurora found herself smiling at the rueful note of humor in his voice. "Do you want my help or not?" she asked, glancing pointedly at the hand he held stiffly splayed against his midriff.

He raised one black eyebrow. "If I say no, are you going to start yelling at me the way you did this afternoon?"

"Yes."

His face assumed a resigned expression, but the light in his eyes was as welcoming as the first rays of sun on a dark morning. "Then I want your help."

"I'm not kidding, Rory. You are *not* driving back to the pueblo in the rain." By the time she and John had finished feeding and watering the horses in the barn and done the same for Cortes, who was housed in a separate shed, and the yearlings in the corral, another storm had moved in, almost as ferocious as the last one.

"Well, I can't stay here," she said in a strained voice. Just thinking about sharing the same quarters with John was doing strange things to her equilibrium.

"Then I'll drive you. You're not going alone."

Aurora gripped the rough edge of the barn door and stared at the sheeting rain. There was only a sliver of moonlight, and the night was inky black beyond the slanting drops.

The unpaved road leading back to her apartment would be a quagmire. Even with four-wheel drive it would be a struggle to keep the heavy truck on the road. Tired as John was, and without the use of both hands, he couldn't manage easily.

"All right," she said with a resigned sigh. "I'll stay."

## *Chapter 11*

Aurora finished rolling up the sleeves of the shirt John had lent her and tugged the tails another inch lower on her thighs. Her hair was still damp from the shower, and her body was warm and pink from the hot water.

It was nearly ten. While she'd been showering, John had gone to the barn for one last check on Wildflower, who was in foal again.

Aurora snapped off the bathroom light and walked into John's bedroom. Rain beat against the window panes, and the wind blew through the trees outside. From the dresser came the steady tick of an old-fashioned alarm clock. The heat of the morning was still trapped in the thick walls, and the room was pleasantly warm.

When she reached the bed, she sank down on the soft mattress and folded her hands in her lap. Maybe if she looked calm, she would feel calm, she told herself one more time.

"You're sleeping in here," John had told her when he'd handed her the shirt. When she'd started to protest, his tired face had tightened. "No strings, Rory. Nothing will happen you don't want to happen. I'll bunk down in the other room.''

And he would. When he had told her he wouldn't make her a promise he couldn't keep, she hadn't believed him. But she did now. The man he had become would always keep his promises.

Still she was beginning to have second thoughts about staying. All during the supper John had made for them she had fought a dozen different emotions pulling her in all directions.

It was almost as though time had rolled back and they were newlyweds again, talking in spurts, then falling into short, tense silences that first one and then the other rushed to fill.

By the time the meal was over, she had been so tense her muscles ached. The back of her neck was still so tight she was beginning to get a headache.

She raised a slender but strong hand to the nape of her neck and tried to rub away the tightness. For the first time in her life she didn't know what she wanted, and not knowing was slowly tearing her apart.

''Rory?''

She looked up to find John standing at the open door, a large brown bottle in his hand. When she'd insisted on cleaning up the kitchen after dinner, he'd taken his shower and changed into a clean pair of jeans that had seen far better days. He must have removed his shirt and boots after he'd returned from the barn, because his feet and his chest were bare.

Ever since that first night out on the ruins, she had loved looking at his body. Without seeming to, she reacquainted herself with the curved muscles of his shoulders and the flat planes of his spreading chest. The polished copper of his skin was smooth and stretched over his hard torso without showing the smallest ripple of fat. His belly was flat, and his navel rode just above the button fly. She felt a tiny flutter of reaction when she noticed that the top button was open.

"Sleepy?" he asked, his voice almost gruff. His eyes had a lazy cast, as though he was having trouble keeping them open. His hair was disheveled and made her want to smooth it into a glossy thickness against his neck.

"No, not sleepy. Tired. How about you?" Her hands groped for the coverlet.

"I'm more sore than tired." He held out the bottle. "Liniment. Would you mind?"

"No." Her voice came out raspy, and she cleared her throat. "I don't mind."

He smiled, but she noticed how severe the planes of his face could be, and how tightly the copper skin stretched over them. John would never be a man who smiled naturally.

She stood abruptly, and the shirttails brushed like a gentle hand against her bare thighs.

He strode toward her, his expression shadowed in the dim light. "Where do you want me?"

Hastily she looked around. The bed was the only place where he could sit comfortably. His bed now. The bed where their child had been conceived.

"Uh, right here I guess," she said, gesturing toward the place she had just vacated.

John was beginning to think he'd made a mistake asking for her help. She looked so damn desirable standing there in her bare feet, his last clean shirt hiked more than halfway up her smooth thighs, that he was having trouble keeping his mind on his aching shoulder.

"Rub it in good," he ordered as he handed her the bottle.

"I know how to apply liniment, John." She sounded testy, and he hid a smile. For such a small person, she could more than hold her own with a man. With him, anyway, and that had always surprised him. For some reason he didn't understand, Rory had been the only woman in his life he had ever allowed to put a curb on him.

"Sorry."

He tried to ignore the way the light shone through the shirt to outline the soft, lush curves of her small body. She was wearing panties but no bra. With every breath she took, her breasts lifted and pushed against the thin blue material until their shape was clearly outlined.

He knew he should look away, but he couldn't. Not even to save his soul from the eternal damnation the Spanish priests had once used as a constant threat to control his people.

Desire hit him like a swift punch below the belt, and his body began to react. Frustrated and angry at his lack of control, he reached past her to jerk back the spread.

Wincing at the pain in his arm, he sat down and pulled one of the pillows onto his lap. Pretending to use it as a cushion for his sore arm, he stared at the wall and tried to ignore the way his body was getting hard, just being in the same room with her. He was too sore to make love to her properly, but that didn't mean he wasn't slowly going crazy with wanting her.

Aurora uncapped the bottle. A pungent odor wafted past her nostrils, and she wrinkled her nose in disgust. "What is this stuff?"

"Deep heat. It's great for sore muscles."

"In horses, maybe, but it smells awfully strong to me." She placed the cap next to the lamp. Her gaze slid away, then returned like a homing dove to the small photograph in a worn leather frame propped against the base of the lamp. It was a picture of her in her wedding dress.

She had burned her wedding pictures. And then cried herself to sleep.

John watched the play of expressions over her face. A dull pain began in his heart and he realized he was holding his breath.

"It's my favorite picture of you," he said with a quiet intensity that brought a look of surprise to her smoky eyes.

"Why did you keep it?"

John's gaze rested thoughtfully on the radiant face in the small frame. Rory was no longer the young and wide-eyed virgin he'd taken as his wife. He'd been fond of that adorable girl, and he'd worried about her and protected her from the rougher parts of the life they'd led.

He shifted his gaze to Aurora. The woman she was now needed no protection. She was strong and resilient and brave, probably a hell of a lot braver than he was.

He sighed and made himself tell the truth. "You were always my candle in the dark, Rory. You still are. When I'm with you, I don't think about the bad times."

He glanced down at his rough hands as though it was easier to tell her these things without looking at her. "Everywhere you look, you see the good instead of the bad. You even saw beauty in this place, where all I saw was my mother's pain." When he looked up again a look of longing as savage as any rage filled his eyes. "When you loved me, I didn't see the ugliness any more."

"Oh, John," she said helplessly. She had never seen herself as he saw her, never really understood that he could need her love with the same intensity as she needed his.

A single tear quivered on her golden lashes, catching the light. John felt the deep burn of frustration begin inside him. Sharing his feelings with her had been difficult enough, but somehow wounding her with them was worse. He didn't know what the hell he was supposed to do.

He muttered a harsh curse under his breath and stood. The pillow fell to the floor, but he didn't notice. He had to get out of here. But when she bit her lip and looked up at him, he groaned. "Don't cry," he muttered through a tight jaw.

"I'm not crying," she said, and then sniffed.

"Then what's this?" He brushed a lean, brown finger across her lashes and held it up for her to see the drop of moisture collected there.

"Leftover rain?" she murmured in a voice made low and sultry by the tension knotting her vocal cords. All of her was tense, even the hand she raised to transfer the tear from his finger to hers. John's hand flattened against hers. Larger, stronger. Warm and possessive. Their fingers entwined, and John tugged her closer.

His mouth was only inches from hers. His hard, beautiful, rarely relaxed mouth.

Anticipation shivered through her, but instead of kissing her, he brushed the back of his hand across her cheek. The tender gesture from such a virile man was rare, and infinitely sweet.

His fingers brushed Aurora's scalp, and she leaned against him. His hand stilled. His eyes, warm brown fire within a dark frame, sought and held hers. His expression grew tortured, then tightened into a look of raw need.

He said her name so tenderly she began melting inside. Of her own volition, she tipped her head back and parted her lips.

John recognized the invitation and the ache in his loins increased, as the pain in his shoulder was forgotten. His hand flattened against her cheek, and his mouth came down on hers.

As fresh and life-giving as the rainwashed air outside, his breath filled her mouth, mingling with hers until she couldn't tell whether he was breathing for her or she was breathing for him.

Desire moved through her in a fluid spiral, heady and exciting. She started to smile, but the instant her lips moved against his, he deepened the kiss.

His hand cupped her head, and one knee slipped between her legs, rubbing her bare thighs. He dropped his hand to her waist and pulled her against him.

"My sweet Rory. So many times I've wanted you here with me. I can hardly believe—" His voice was ragged and filled with a rough yearning that made her want to curl up next to him and rub her face against his strong, smooth chest.

Instead she rested her hand on the warm spot over his heart, just as she had done countless times in the past when she had no words to tell him how she felt.

"I'm here, now," she whispered, only half aware of the words she was saying.

"So you are." His voice was a low rumble that held amusement and another more fervent emotion that nudged her heartbeat into a faster rhythm. A shivery feeling invaded the pit of her stomach, pushing outward until her skin tingled. It was still there, the mystical craving to be one with this man. To be his woman. To be the echoing beat of his heart.

She wound her arms around his neck and kissed him, eager for the taste of his mouth and the feel of his hands. No other man could ever make her feel like John. No other man could ever make her tremble and shake with just a look. No other man would make her feel such a sense of rightness deep inside.

John saw the passion settle on her like a gentle sigh and something burst inside him, spilling a brilliant warmth into the cold, black well deep within, where no light had reached for years.

When she rubbed against him again, a groan he couldn't quite master escaped his lips, and a shudder rode the length of his hurting body. "Don't move, Rory. Please don't move."

His loins filled with heat and his body throbbed. In a haze of need he closed his eyes and thought about easing the ache in the moist, sweet essence of her. But he wanted more than release. He wanted, no, he *needed*, the joining that would give them a new start. But only if that was what she wanted, too. Otherwise the very act would be a violation.

A shiver of response ran over her small body, and it was all he could do to stand perfectly still. Otherwise the little control he had left would be lost.

"Tell me you want me, Rory," he ordered, holding his voice under the same rigid control. His arms bulged with restraint, and the heavy sinews stood out in dark relief under his skin.

She tried to swallow past the fluttering in her dry throat. How easy it would be if he just took her, seducing her with his hands and his mouth until she had no more will to resist, the way he'd done the first time. And she realized with a burst of tenderness, how wrong.

John had been honest with her. No games. No tricks. He'd even opened the gates to the hell of his childhood so that she could understand him. But he wouldn't force her, not even with the subtle coercion of seduction.

If she shared the lovemaking, she had to share the responsibility for her feelings when it was over. She couldn't blame John if she felt pain or remorse or anger, later.

Slowly she slid her hands up his powerful arms to his shoulders and then to his neck. Because she loved him, she would take what he had to give. Tomorrow she would sort out her feelings. Tomorrow she would deal with... tomorrow.

"Make love to me, John," she whispered. "I want you."

She pulled his head down until she could reach his mouth. The kiss she gave him left him hard and shaken and aching to feel her soft, responsive body under him, welcoming him, loving him.

She saw a vivid emotion come into his eyes, driving out the shadows and lighting a golden flame in the dark pupils. A look of wonder was there, and longing, and something even more potent.

"I'll take care of you," he said in a husky voice. "Protect you." He glanced toward the drawer of the night table, silently thanking the impulse that had led him to plan ahead, just in case.

"My darling John," she whispered. "I've missed you so much."

He looked at her for what seemed like forever and then he smiled, erasing much of the tiredness lining his face.

"Let's take this off," he said, unbuttoning the shirt that still held the crisp scent of starch.

Quick flutters of anticipation followed the path of his fingers, until her body was quivering with eagerness. His hands added to the shivery feeling as they slid the shirt from her shoulders, then did the same with the wisp of silken panties.

John looked down and his mouth went dry when he saw her naked breasts. They were fuller than he remembered, and the nipples were a deeper shade of brown. "My beautiful lady," he whispered, rubbing first one tiny nipple then the other with his thumb.

Aurora inhaled, loving the feeling of fiery urgency his hands evoked. Eagerly she ran both palms over his wide, smooth chest, then slowly traced the angular planes with her nails.

John groaned and gently eased her backward onto the cool, crisp sheets. They smelled of soap and sunshine and John.

A helpless whimper escaped her throat, and his hands moved over her body, exciting her in the special ways that only he knew.

The rain beat against the roof, and the darkness beyond the light blocked out the rest of the world until there was only John's kiss inflaming her, John's touch caressing her, John's husky whisper praising her until she knew that she was beautiful and feminine and desirable.

But that wasn't enough. She needed to be closer, to be a part of him and he, a part of her. She needed to give herself to him in the same elemental way that she longed to be taken.

The longing built inside her, erupting in a moan. She arched her back, trying to get closer to him.

"Easy, love," he murmured, his hand making slow, sweet circles over the small mound between her legs. "Let me make it good for you." His mouth was warm and moist on her breast, his breath an exquisite whisper against her skin. The moist place between his hand warmed and quickened, becoming ready to welcome him.

She pushed her hands into the thick hair that lay like the inky shadow of midnight against her skin. A sense of elation spread through her as she bunched the damp, soft thatch in her fist. Beneath her, through the skin that was sensitized from his touch, she felt his restraint, his raw male power, his savage need.

"Yes, oh, yes. John."

Her nails raked his scalp, and he raised his head from her breast.

She was so beautiful, his Rory, with the passion turning her eyes to the stormy gray of a summer evening.

He took her mouth without restraint, his control gone. She was his hope, his peace. His salvation. He would pour all the feelings he couldn't put into words into this moment. He would drive the bad memories from her mind until all she knew was the man he was now.

He pressed her against the pillow, the force of his kiss taking her breath. His chest crushed hers, his skin smooth and damp with the slickness of his desire.

Aurora reveled in the heaviness of masculine sinew and muscle on her breasts and her belly. She moved against him, and hard tremors ran through him, shaking both of them.

He froze, then rolled away to rid himself of his jeans.

When he touched her again, his hands shook and he had to fight to wait, to hold back the savage urge to thrust into her silken body. His hard, callused fingers stroked the satin warmth of her skin; his mouth took hers over and over, sampling the rich taste of her lips and her tongue.

"My love, I want you so much," he murmured against the sensuous curve of her breast. His mouth slid lower. He tasted all of her, wetting her skin until she moaned and tossed beneath him.

She reached for him, her nails raking his back. She moaned his name over and over, until it burned into him like a sweet litany that he would hear in the quiet moments when he felt the most alone.

His hand slid up her satin-smooth inner thigh to the hot, welcoming center of her. Over and over his fingers dipped into the slick wetness, until she was quivering and mindless with need for him.

Aurora gasped as his thighs slid between hers. She held her breath, anticipating the glorious feel of his body thrusting into her.

"Oh baby, I want you so much. Too much."

His arousal surged against her belly, hard and hot and swollen. Aurora opened her eyes. His face was flushed, his eyes burning, his teeth bared in an agony of need. "I don't want to hurt you."

"You won't," she whispered on a choked breath. "Now, John, now."

She arched against him, her need matching his. Wrapped in a delicious haze of pleasure she was dimly aware of the things he did to protect her, and then he parted her legs and settled over her. He cried out, but his words were smothered against her breast as he slowly sank into her.

Aurora's hands clutched at the sheet as she arched upward, her body opening and stretching to welcome him. Ecstasy bubbled up inside her, filling her to the point of a sweet pain.

A terrible tremor shook his body as he slowly thrust deeper, making himself wait. Her body was almost as tight as it had been that first time on the ruins.

Aurora felt his caution, but she knew only a wild need to get closer. She arched against him, her hands twining around his strong neck.

Through half-closed lids John saw the savage sensuality that he'd always sensed in her. He uttered an incoherent plea as he drove into her in one powerful thrust. He filled her, hot and strong, and she cried out, her pleasure bursting into a golden shower inside her. She shuddered in mindless ecstasy, calling his name.

Elation shot through him, and he held himself still inside her, feeling the small, sweet movements of her release. He wanted to stay this way forever, joined to her in the bond that survives even death.

Another small tremor shook her, and he moved against her, trying to make her pleasure part of him. His control slipped away. The warm ecstasy that was Aurora pulled him deeper, until with one final, desperate thrust, he exploded into her, releasing wave after wave of longing and need.

He slumped against her, his massive chest crushing her, making it difficult to breathe. But she didn't want him to move.

Wrapped in a warm, wonderful lethargy, Aurora cushioned his head on her breast, her fingers slowly stroking the soft hair away from his temples. His eyes were closed, his breathing ragged.

"I'm sorry," he muttered against her breast. "I was out of control."

Aurora smiled, her mind and her body deliciously drugged by the savage wonder of his lovemaking. "Don't be sorry," she murmured. "I'm not."

John raised his head, his body heavy with the aftermath of his violent release. He searched her face, his gaze hungry. She looked relaxed and smugly content. The blush of passion was still on her cheeks, and her lips were deliciously swollen.

Slowly his hand came up to trace the fullness of her lower lip. She smiled, her eyes half closed, her soft breath fanning his face.

"How do you feel?" he asked, holding his breath.

"I'm floating," she whispered, her feathery lashes raising and lowering in drowsy little movements that made him smile.

A primitive feeling of pride flooded through him. In this one way he could give his woman what she wanted. That was a start. He would build on that.

He bent forward and dropped a light kiss on her lips. "Sleep, my love," he whispered against her soft smile. She would never know of the fierce joy he felt just holding her close. Or of the deep longing he felt to love her.

A punishing pressure formed behind his eyes, and somewhere deep in his chest something moved as though it were trying to push through his skin. But the tightness inside him refused to release the pressure.

What was there—the feelings he had repressed, the love he had refused to feel—were still dammed inside him. Too many days of pain, too many dark nights of fear still kept them hidden from view. But Aurora was here now. In his bed. In his life. And he would fight like hell to break through that barrier.

Easing his weight to one side, he pulled her against him, careful to keep them from separating, even in sleep. For the time she would give him, she was his.

The pain in his shoulder woke John well before dawn. He bit off a groan and tried to ease the cramp knotting the heavy muscle of his upper arm.

But he couldn't seem to move.

His eyes snapped open, then warmed with the light of sudden remembering. Aurora was curled up next to him, her head pillowed on his shoulder, her hand loosely cupping his side. Her perfumed hair tickled his nose every time he breathed, and her soft breasts were pressed against his chest.

Sometime in the night her legs had gotten tangled with his, and one satin-smooth thigh lay over his, perilously close to his groin. He was so aroused he was afraid to move.

But he had to ease the knot in his muscles. Slowly, careful not to wake her, he moved until the pain in his shoulder eased.

She moved, mumbling in her sleep, and her hand dipped lower until her fingers curled into the thick hair below his navel.

The heat in his groin spread, making his skin feel too tight for his body. He wanted her again.

John closed his eyes and buried his face in her soft, clean-smelling hair. It felt so right to hold her like this. To sleep with her and wake with her and make love to her.

His chest swelled with a feeling he was afraid to call happiness, even though he knew that it must be. For so long he'd worked for the moment when Rory would begin to trust him again. He'd taken risks that had gone against his deeply ingrained sense of self-preservation, telling her things he himself could barely stand to remember.

Opening up to her had been the hardest thing he'd ever done. He still felt raw inside, as though a piece of him had been ripped away, leaving him terribly exposed and vulnerable. It would be a long time before he could talk about himself that way again. The old feelings were too volatile, too dangerous to share, even with her.

John tightened his hold on Aurora's soft body, willing the black memory to recede. He was no longer a skinny nine-year-old with a searing hatred burning a hole in his gut. He was no longer that poor little Indian beggar with the taste of tears stinging his throat, tears that he had refused to shed ever again.

He had made mistakes, a lot of them, but the Woman-of-Us-All had promised him another chance. And he was going to take it.

He would build a new life with Rory, in this place where he had come to belong. And the love would come. For both of them.

They had plenty of time, now that she was back where she belonged.

John inhaled slowly. The need to touch her was suddenly overwhelming, as powerful and demanding as the ache in his loins. Raising his left hand, he brushed his thumb gently over her lower lip and watched her mouth curve instantly into a smile.

"Come back to me, love," he whispered, his voice thick with a longing he couldn't hide. "Come love me again."

Aurora woke slowly, fighting her way up from the deepest sleep she'd ever had. She nuzzled the warm, smooth pillow with her cheek, stretching and pouting and muttering to herself.

"My little love. How you hate to wake up." John's deep voice was a rumble beneath her cheek, and she frowned. Was this another dream, the kind that left her empty and sad when she finally woke?

She whimpered in protest, squeezing her eyes shut, but the slow even pace of her breathing quickened, and her nipples began to pucker.

"Rory, baby. Wake up."

She moved with drowsy lethargy, not wanting to leave the wonderful dream. A warm hand began stroking her bare back, and a restless urgency began spreading inside her.

Her eyes fluttered open. The room was bathed in the hazy gray of the time between night and dawn. She was wrapped in John's arms, her head resting on his shoulder. A single sheet angled over her breasts and draped over his hard, flat midriff. Somehow her hand had found its way under the cover and her fingers had become tangled in the thick thatch of springy curls below his belly button. His arousal was hard and hot against her knuckles.

Heat rose in a rush to burn her cheeks, and she inched her hand upward to his chest. This wasn't a dream.

"Good morning, love." His statement carried a hint of amusement. The heat spread into her hairline.

"Morning," she murmured, her voice sleep husky. She moved her head until her gaze found his face. He was looking at her with such a tender expression her breath caught in her throat.

"Are you ready to get up?" His voice was a sensuous whisper that brushed her face like a caress, and his dark morning beard was delightfully rough against her brow where his cheek rested.

"No, I don't want to move," she murmured, her eyes still drowsy and her body aching in a special way.

He laughed. "Sounds fine with me. I'll forget about my hungry horses, and you forget about your students. We'll let the whole damn world do its thing without us today."

His hand covered hers, and he began to play with her fingers. She smiled, adapting her breathing to his as she lay curled against him, listening to his heartbeat. She rubbed her leg against his, and the beats came faster and faster.

"Your heart is racing," she said, flattening her hand against his chest.

"Always, when I'm with you."

When she began to move her hand lower, John inhaled sharply, his massive chest rising so fast her breasts tingled.

"Careful, love. You have one very aroused man in your bed here."

"I know," she whispered, trailing her nails down the center line of his chest. "I was hoping he would want to do something about that."

John growled deep in his throat and threw off the sheet. He captured her hand and then, with one powerful movement, rolled them over until he was on top of her, his chest pressing her into the mattress, his thighs straddling hers.

His arousal, swollen and ready, pressed the silky mound between her thighs. This time she was the one who inhaled sharply as he dipped into her, letting her feel his hardness.

She arched against him, and he groaned.

"Not yet, love," he said, withdrawing. He wanted her too much to have much control once he was inside that sweet, moist sheath.

With his left hand he pushed her hands over her head and bent to tease her nipple into a hard, throbbing peak with his tongue. When he was done with one brown bud, he moved to the next one, working the same sensuous magic.

Aurora moved restlessly, the urgency growing inside her. Her hands raked the shaggy hair at the nape of his strong neck, then moved to his shoulders. She tried to bring him closer.

His mouth took hers. His tongue thrust between her lips, doing what she wanted him to do with her body. He tasted her deeply, hotly, thoroughly, his free hand moving down her body to the delta of her thighs. With a light touch he stroked the tender flesh, finding the place where she was most sensitive.

She clung to him, mindless with the elemental desire he was building in her. With each thrust of his tongue, with each stroke of his fingers, she wanted him more, until she was beyond longing, beyond needing, beyond thinking.

Just when she knew she couldn't stand the ecstasy another instant, he pulled away. She whimpered at the loss of his touch and his kiss, even as she knew that he was keeping his promise to protect her.

"Rory, my Rory," he said, caressing her again, his need riding him like a jagged spur. "I've got to have you now."

His knee brushed her thigh and she opened herself for him, arching upward to envelope him. His hand moved to her buttocks, and he lifted her toward him until her body accepted all of him.

She was hot inside and melting smooth, and he groaned as the heat seared him. He was being pulled apart inside, savaged by his own need.

"Oh baby, I can't—"

He fought to hang on to his control long enough to satisfy her. His body shuddered with the effort.

Aurora moved against him, feeling his need as her own. She flexed her knees, trying to absorb him. He moved slowly, but when he felt her response, he loosed the rein on his control.

The wondrous pressure built inside her until it was unbearable. She moaned John's name and clutched his arms, trying to pull all of him inside. And then, as he thrust deep, the pressure was released and the world erupted in a shower of stars and sunshine.

"Yes, Rory, oh, yes." John watched a look of rapture cross her face, and he closed his eyes, taking that image with him when his body convulsed.

The first light of dawn was slipping into the room when they fell asleep, clutched in each other's arms.

## Chapter 12

John walked along the perimeter of the crumbling ruins, the exhilaration of his night with Aurora still inside him. Ahead of him the dawning sun was a fiery glow spreading above the horizon. Behind him, tethered to the wind-twisted trunk of a half-dead piñon, Cortes waited, eager to resume the gallop that had brought them to this place.

The morning air was as clear as the raindrops that had cleansed it, and smelled of damp sage. Beneath John's boots the ground was still wet in low-lying spots, but most of the moisture had already soaked through the sandy surface.

He walked slowly, trying to get things straight in his head. As always when he was troubled, he found himself heading for the sheltered spot where he and Aurora had first made love. When he came to the familiar place where the wall loomed tallest, he stopped.

With the scuffed toe of his boot he kicked aside a dried clump of fallen adobe, then rested his back against the sun-hardened wall and watched the sunrise.

For the first time in as long as he could remember he hadn't awakened with a nagging feeling of emptiness in his gut. For the first time in years he hadn't started his day wondering about Rory—what she was doing, whom she was with, if she had stopped hating him.

From the moment he had joined his body to hers, he had known he couldn't live without her again. Physically he would survive, but without her smile and laughter and warmth, his life would be as empty as the land stretching in front of him.

Months ago, here in this place, he had vowed to give her what she wanted most. Last night it had been pleasure. He knew enough about women to be certain of that. But what about today or tomorrow or the next day?

She didn't love him. He could accept that. He could even live with that, if he had to.

But what about her? Did she still want him to love her?

John heaved a deep sigh, then winced as the movement brought pain to his sore shoulder. Rory had never gotten around to rubbing the liniment into his aching muscles. Not that he cared. What she had given him had eased more than his physical pain. She had made him feel whole again.

John cast a glance at a lone hawk soaring overhead. Since Rory had left him, he'd been like that solitary bird, always alone.

Suddenly the hawk folded its wings and dove straight toward a small jackrabbit half hidden by a clump of sage. The doe stood frozen, her ears back. Acting on impulse, John snatched up the chunk of clay and flung it toward the paralyzed rabbit. The dirt clod hit inches from her nose, and she leaped sideways into the brush. With an angry screech, the hawk soared upward, its talons empty.

"Go find your babies, mama," John said, watching the rabbit lope away. When he could no longer see the little doe's white tail he shifted his gaze to the south, where Aurora was still tucked up in his bed, asleep. When he'd eased himself out of her embrace, she had murmured his name, and he'd had the devil's own time leaving her.

John pushed away from the wall and began walking again. Ten long strides took him to the place he sought, the place where he had knelt in front of the vision of Woman-of-Us-All on that last desperate dawn. He had been dying, at the end of his endurance.

At the time he hadn't even realized he had sought out the same spot where Rory had allowed him to make love to her for the first time. He knew now that he had wanted to be close to her in that final moment of the life he had used so badly. In his delirium he had wanted to carry her smile with him into the beyond.

John lowered his gaze to the rocky ground where the blood from his torn feet had dripped into the dirt. Inches away a cluster of fragile white flowers grew out of a crack in the rock, looking far too delicate to survive amid the prickly desert foliage.

John lowered himself to his haunches and reached out a finger to touch one of the petals. They were the sacred anthea blossoms, the physical embodiment of Woman-of-Us-All. Picking them was forbidden.

Straddling the fence between the white world and this one as he had, he knew that the spiritual teachings of his people were considered naive by even the most enlightened whites. He had thought so, too. Once.

But he didn't now.

Turning to the old ways, believing in the words Woman-of-Us-All had spoken had given him the strength to change day by day, week by week until he had found the courage to face Aurora again.

For some reason Rory had changed, too. This time she had made love to him without strings, without expectations. She hadn't asked him for his love. She had taken him as he was, without promises.

Maybe she didn't expect love, after all.

A tremendous feeling of relief flowed over him. For the first time since he could remember, he felt free, as though he had just been released from a dark pit.

John got quickly to his feet and walked with a fast stride toward the stallion. Gathering the reins, he vaulted into the saddle and kicked Cortes into a gallop. The eager horse shot forward, his long powerful strides eating up the distance between the ruins and the ranch house. They were going home.

Aurora bit her lip, her nerves strung tight. As she cinched the wide belt around her waist, her hands shook slightly. Morning-after jitters, she told herself as she took a last look at herself in the bathroom mirror.

Though she wore no lipstick, her mouth was rosy and slightly swollen into a sultry curve by John's kisses. Her cheeks still carried a faint bloom where his whiskers had rubbed in the early morning hours when they'd made love again. Beneath her drawn brows, her smoky eyes were soft and lustrous with a sensuous glow that hadn't been there yesterday. She looked well and truly loved by a man who knew how to take his time with a woman.

Using John's brush she made a quick swipe through her hair, then drew her belt one notch tighter. Beneath the pink dress her stomach began to flutter.

Aurora closed her eyes and listened to the silence trapped between the thick adobe walls. She needed to feel John's arms around her, holding her, comforting her. She needed to hear his voice telling her that he would keep the promise of love his kisses had made.

But John wasn't here. And he hadn't been beside her in bed when she woke again, just as he hadn't been there to give her the reassurance she had needed so desperately after Dawn's death.

She took a slow, deep breath, trying to fend off the anxious thoughts tumbling in her mind. She felt so alone.

The sound of iron hooves on the hard dirt cut through her thoughts. Apparently John had been riding.

Pushing back her shoulders, she left the bathroom and hurriedly began to make the bed. As she walked from one side to the other, a splash of color on the highboy in the corner caught her eye. Her breath caught in her throat, and her eyes widened in shock.

John had one of her pots.

"'Dream's End,'" she murmured, moving toward it like a woman walking in her sleep. She'd thrown that pot on the day she had decided to live instead of die. Her tears were trapped in the bright glaze, and her grief for her lost illusions was carved into the design.

She hadn't seen this pot in over a year, not since she had carried it to the gallery. Before that, it had been stored on the top shelf of her closet, out of sight. Because she had never wanted to see it again, she had instructed the owner to keep it until it was sold.

Slowly, knowing that she shouldn't, she raised her hand and traced the vivid red slash with her fingertip. As soon as she touched the clay, a rush of near physical pain assaulted her, ripping away a layer of scar tissue. Rage and anguish poured into her, as alive and vivid as the colors in front of her.

"No," she gasped, jerking her hand away.

After she had finished this pot, she had cried until she'd been empty, vowing on her knees never again to allow herself to love another man until she was certain he loved her.

Like a woman in a trance she stared at the bright wool rug beneath her feet. Like all of the weavers in the tribe, Morningstar had woven strands of many colors into a pattern that she'd held only in her head.

Had she, like Morningstar, been weaving John's words and actions into a preset pattern that she had created in her head? Was she trying to see things in John that weren't there because she still loved him?

Biting her lip, she raised her gaze to the rumpled sheets still bearing the imprint of their entwined bodies. John had joined his body to hers with an almost desperate passion, but he had said nothing of love.

Aurora stifled a tiny moan as the truth struck her. She had let the sexual attraction that still sparked between them cloud her vision until she truly thought they had a chance. Like the illusion of reality in the rug, she had created an illusion of love.

She'd been wrong when she told John she was no longer that naive twenty-year-old who had believed in him. This time she was thirty-three and she had still set herself up one more time.

Somewhere in the house a door slammed, and John called her name.

A chill began over her heart, spreading rapidly until she was cold through and through.

"Rise and shine, love. Coffee's ready and the sun's out."

John entered the bedroom and stopped in mid-stride, struck by the stunned look on Aurora's face. She was dressed in the clothes she'd worn yesterday and was standing in front of the highboy in the corner, staring at the pot he'd bought in Dallas.

It took him less than a second to realize that something was wrong, something that had taken the smile from her eyes and the glow from her cheeks.

"Why did you buy this?" she asked, her voice strangely flat. She kept her gaze fixed on the pot.

John took a slow breath. "Because it's a magnificent piece of work," he said, choosing his words carefully. "And because you made it."

Aurora turned to look at him. "How does it make you feel when you look at it?"

John's gaze narrowed, then shifted to the pot. She was pushing him into a corner, and he didn't know why. Or what he wanted him to say.

"What's wrong, love? Are you mad at me because I left? Cortes needed exercise—"

"No, I'm not mad. Just curious," she said in that same dead tone. "I need you to answer my question. How do you feel when you look at 'Dream's End'?"

John shoved his hands into his pockets to keep from reaching for her. "What do you want me to say, Rory? That I hurt inside every time I look at it? That I wish like hell I could give you back the magic in the clay?" He dropped his gaze to the scarred floor, then raised it again. "I bought the pot because I needed to remember what I did, so that I would never do it again."

Aurora nodded slowly. She believed that he was truly sorry and that he had tried to make it up to her in the best way he could. She also believed that he wanted her sexually. But his past had crippled him so terribly he couldn't love her, even if he wanted to. It wasn't his fault, but it was also a fact that wasn't ever going to change.

"Rory, what's wrong? Do you want me to put away the pot? Is that what this is all about?"

"We made a mistake."

"What are you talking about? What mistake?" His brow creased in a frown.

"Sleeping together. Having sex, whatever you want to call it. It was my mistake, I acknowledge that, but I—" She waved her hand toward the bed. "This never should have happened."

She started to move past him, but he caught her arm. "I thought last night was pretty damn wonderful. And this morning was off the scale." His mouth jerked. "I guess you didn't think so."

"I did, I *do* think so," she said, her voice catching. "But I need more than a...a roll in the hay. I told you when I...I left you that I needed you to love me. I still do." Aurora forced herself to look into his pain-filled dark eyes. "Do you love me, John?" she asked in a quiet small voice.

There was a long silence. Aurora heard her heart beating in time with the sharp ticking of the clock. Tell me that you love me, she begged silently, hoping that she was wrong about him.

When John finally spoke, he looked years older. "I want to love you more than anything I've ever wanted in my life." His voice was held under rigid control. Twin stains of dusky red blotched his cheekbones, and his jaw was tight.

"I...see," she said, fighting a terrible need to lay her head against his chest and sob. "In other words your answer is no." With a sinking heart she knew that she had guessed right. He couldn't say the words because he didn't feel them.

John saw the hope fade from her eyes. She was leaving him again before he even had a chance to convince her to stay forever.

His heart began to race, and his palms began to sweat. He couldn't let that happen.

He took a deep breath and reached down inside, forcing himself to share his deepest fear with her. "It's all mixed up inside me, Rory. The feelings I had for my mother, the feelings of helplessness, the hatred. I can't seem to . . . to separate them. And if I let out the love—" He lifted his massive shoulders in a stiff shrug.

"You're afraid the violence will come out as well," she finished for him.

He jammed his hands into his pockets as though he was afraid of what they might do. "If it does, I don't know if I can handle it."

He turned abruptly and walked to the window, looking out at the rain-drenched land. His old man was buried at the foot of Mesa Rojo. After the burying ritual John had never returned to the grave. He never would.

He dropped his gaze to the worn sill. Behind him he could feel Aurora's presence. Her warmth, her compassion, her radiant love of beauty.

Slowly he turned to face her. The pain in her eyes made him swear under his breath. "Rory, I came back to ask you to marry me again—"

Her soft cry stopped the words half spoken. "I can't," she whispered. "Please don't ask me."

"Why not?" The happiness inside him slipped into the black emptiness that was always waiting.

"If Dawn had lived, would you have loved her?"

John's eyelids flickered, the only sign of pain he allowed himself. "I would have tried."

Aurora felt the blood drain from her cheeks, and a sick feeling settled into the pit of her stomach. "But that's just the point," she said. "What if we had another child and you couldn't let yourself love her? I couldn't stand it if our child someday...felt the same about you, the way you feel about your father.''

He went white. "Are you saying I would use my fists on a child?"

"No, oh, *no*," she said, her voice shaking. "But a child should be loved by both parents. You of all people should know that."

John didn't hear the suffering in her voice or see the shine of tears in her eyes. All he heard were her words, which hit him with the force of a knockout punch.

Like a damn fool, he'd opened himself up to her so that she could understand why he'd made some bad mistakes with her, and now she was using his secrets against him, the way his father had used a young boy's love for his mother to wound so deeply.

The familiar throbbing started in his temple, and the adrenaline started to pump through his veins like red-hot lava.

"So you're not going to give me a chance, is that it?" he asked, his voice laced with the same barely contained fury she'd heard that first day out by the barn. "You give me your body, you let me think we can start over, and then just when I start to hope—" He made a chopping gesture with his big hand.

"Forget it, Rory. I get the message. No matter what I do for you it's not enough. No matter how many ways I say I'm sorry, or how hard I try to show you I care, it'll never be enough for you. I can't make myself perfect for you, like one of those damned pots you love so much."

John gritted his teeth against the vicious rush of blood that threatened to explode his veins. He fought for control, fought to keep his feelings dammed up inside where they couldn't hurt her. And then, with a violent oath, he picked up the pot from the dresser and crashed it against the wall.

Before she could do more than gasp, he crossed to the dresser and snatched the truck keys. "I'm leaving in ten minutes. If you don't want to walk, you'd better be ready."

"Feel good?" Alex bent over his wife and smoothed the cool lotion over Casey's belly.

Casey sighed blissfully. "Wonderful. Baby and I look forward to this every night."

Casey began to play with Alex's thick, black hair. Outside the bedroom window a light rain fell, but inside the stone house it was cozy and warm and soft music played. Alex finished, then dropped a kiss on the place where the baby's head pushed a small bulge into her swelling stomach. "Only two more weeks to go."

His slight accent was suddenly more pronounced, signaling the concern Casey knew he was trying to hide from her.

"Alex, I'm going to be fine."

Alex leaned back against the pillows and settled her bulky body against his broad chest. He rested one hand on her belly, the other cupped her heavy breast. Casey rested her hand over his, and enjoyed the feeling of contentment being in his arms always gave her.

"I'm going to cancel my trip—"

"Alex, we've been over this a dozen times. This is an important board meeting and the chairman should be there. It's only three days, Butch will take care of me while you're gone, and John is only a phone call away if I need him." She ran her hand down the corded arm resting on her belly. She loved it when he held her like this. After so many years of being apart, she never took his presence for granted.

Alex frowned. "That's not much of a selling point, *querida*. John can barely take care of himself these days."

Casey frowned. "He did look bad when he stopped by this morning, didn't he?"

"Bad, hell. The man looked worse than he did after he walked out of the damned hills and collapsed."

"Aurora doesn't look much better. Her clothes just hang on her, and she looks so lost. I tried to talk to her, but she claims there's nothing to talk about. Things just didn't work out between them, she says. I know she's hurting, but I don't know what else to do for her."

Alex rubbed his chin against her temple. "You can't make things better for everyone, Case," he said, his voice deepening with affection. He bent forward to kiss her bare shoulder. Desire shot through her, hot and insistent, just as it always did when Alex touched her.

"I know, but I like Aurora a lot. And I love John—" At Alex's muttered word of protest, she grinned. "Like a brother."

Alex kissed her, and she rested against him for a flurry of heartbeats. Pregnant as she was, his kisses still had the power to shake her to her toes. "He can't just let her go."

Alex rubbed his hand over her belly. "He can and he is. Her job is finished. There's no reason for her to stay."

"But Alex—"

"John knew the odds were against him, but he gave it his best shot, anyway. The lady has made it clear she doesn't want him. There's a fine line between fighting and groveling, *querida*. John would hate himself if he crossed it."

Casey nodded. "Do you think he loves her?" she asked.

Alex's arms tightened. "I think all those hormones racing around in your bloodstream are making you talkative as hell." He nipped her earlobe with his teeth. "And very sexy, *Señora* Torres."

Alex ran his hand down her belly to the warm nest of silky hair between her thighs. The doctor had said no more sex until the baby was born, but there were other ways of showing his woman how much he loved her.

A flow of heat enveloped her, heightening the sensitivity of her already sensitive skin. "Stop trying to change the subject," she ordered. Her words were punctuated by a small gasp as his fingers began caressing her. "Does...does John love Aurora?"

Alex slid his hand to her hip and turned her so that she fitted into his arm. He knew his adorable, compassionate wife. She wasn't going to let up on him until she had her answer.

"No, *mi amor*," he said on a sigh. "In a way he's a lot like me before you came back into my life. Until he can find a way to forgive himself for the things he did to drive her away from him five years ago, I don't think he will ever be able to love her.''

''Too bad Aurora doesn't love him enough for both of them,'' Casey said softly, touching the cougar tooth Alex wore on a heavy chain around his neck.

She gave him a tender smile that brought a fierce light to his black eyes. Alex had won his battle against the guilt that had driven them apart. John hadn't.

She felt terribly sad. For both of her friends.

John stared at the figures in front of him. No matter what he tried, no matter how he juggled the budget, he was still short a good fifteen thousand dollars. Unless he manufactured a miracle, he was going to have to stand up at the council meeting tomorrow morning and admit that he'd failed.

He was sure to be voted out of office, after that. Diego was already boasting that he intended to take over the lease on John's land. But the horses were still John's. As long as he had them, he had a future, even if he was banished from the pueblo.

He closed the ledger and swiveled his chair so that he could see the string of people walking toward the studio where Aurora was holding an informal graduation ceremony for her students.

She had done a hell of a job, he thought with a grim pride. No one could have done it better. Her students were thrilled at the progress they had made. Three dozen perfect replicas now sat on the shelves, waiting to be packed into cartons for shipping to their first eager customers.

Tomorrow she would be gone. Out of his life forever.

He missed her already. The past five weeks had been torture. After the first night without her again, he'd taken to sleeping on the sofa because he couldn't stand to sleep in the bed without her. Even the office seemed haunted by her.

He glanced around the office, remembering the day he'd brought her here. And kissed her.

John cursed aloud, then kicked away the chair she had used. He stood, his gaze lighting on the safe in the corner. He had promised his people decent medical care. He had promised Rory he wouldn't sell the Santa Ysabel.

Setting his jaw, he flipped open his address book and ran his hand down the list of names until he found the one he wanted. He picked up the phone and punched out Todd Gulbranson's home number. Even if he had to sell every one of his horses, the pueblo would have a doctor.

The studio was packed. All of the windows were open, and the sound of laughter from the children playing outside had punctuated the words of Aurora's students as one by one they'd stepped forward to say a few words.

As she listened Aurora studied the faces in front of her. So many were familiar—Casey, the families of her students, her neighbors—people who in eight short weeks had become dear friends. She was going to miss them.

Applause swelled through the room, then faded.

Aurora stepped forward again, this time to introduce Alice Comacho, the youngest of her students. As Alice began to speak, Aurora's gaze searched the faces in front of her one more time. John hadn't come.

Then, just as she gave up looking for him, he slipped into the studio to stand at the back by the window. He was dressed as she would remember him now, in worn jeans and a plain cotton shirt with the sleeves rolled up for comfort instead of show. He leaned his broad back against the wall and crossed his arms, acknowledging her startled glance with a curt nod.

He looked controlled and distant, the way he'd looked the day he'd left for San Sebastian without her. But there was a loneliness about him now, even in this crowded room, that hadn't been there then.

After they had retrieved her car, he had bidden her a terse goodbye and left. For three days no one, not even Alex and Casey, saw him.

When he reappeared, he was thinner, and his face bore new lines. Because she couldn't bear to be around him and not love him, she had stopped using the Santa Ysabel as a model.

In the past few weeks she had seen him infrequently and when they had happened to meet by accident, they hadn't exchanged more than a few words. She had never been more miserable.

Aurora swallowed the regret that stung her throat and made herself concentrate on the graduates.

Ralph Horse Herder was the last to speak, and as Aurora introduced him, she gave him a proud smile. None of her students, here or in Dallas, had ever shown the kind of promise that he had. She had been proud and pleased when she'd learned that he was to be in charge of the studio after she was gone.

Ralph waited for the room to quiet, then squared his shoulders and began to speak. "When I took art classes at boarding school in Albuquerque, I used only modern methods because I thought the old ways weren't any good. Even my teachers told me I wouldn't be successful as an artist if I was…contaminated by the crude techniques of the past. That's why I almost didn't volunteer when Mr. Olvera told me about this project."

A buzz of comment arose in the room, and heads turned until all eyes were on John. Including Aurora's.

John met her gaze steadily, his expression as blank as his years of practice could make it. In her eyes he read surprise and regret and a hint of an emotion he didn't understand before she jerked her gaze from him. Whatever it was, though, it no longer mattered. He had given her everything he had to give, and it hadn't been enough.

"Mr. Olvera told me that I could be Indian and successful at the same time," Ralph continued in a strong clear voice. "That I could walk in two worlds and take the best from both, and that if I tried to be something I'm not, I would regret it the way he had. He said that I would find my strength in the land of my people, in the traditions and in the customs and even in the beliefs that I thought were old-fashioned and silly." Ralph gave his father an apologetic look and accepted the old man's dignified nod with a brief smile.

"So I came back, not expecting a lot. But Mr. Olvera was right. Dr. Davenport made me feel the spirit of my people. She encouraged me to put the things I felt inside into my work. She made me believe in my own instincts."

He gave her a warm smile. "Because of her I understand how special we really are. And why we never need apologize for the color of our skin or the uniqueness of our beliefs. She made me proud to be an Indian."

Tears flooded Aurora's eyes, and she bit her lip. Through the buzz of the crowd, she sought out John's face. But there was only a blank wall where he had stood. He was gone.

# Chapter 13

The studio was silent. Outside dawn was breaking, sending streaks of yellow and orange across the sky. It was cool in the large room, and the air smelled of damp clay.

Aurora inhaled slowly, letting her lungs fill with the earthy scent she loved. She would miss this place.

She was leaving. Her work was over. Her suitcases were in the station wagon outside. Her apartment was clean, waiting the next occupant. She had said private good-byes to her students and neighbors. She and Casey had exchanged tearful promises to write. All that remained was this final farewell.

Eyes misted with tears, she walked slowly across the room, her gaze touching the familiar surroundings one last time. As soon as she reached the spot at the end of the table that had been hers, she stopped and turned slowly, letting her gaze trail along the shelves.

Each potter had put a piece of his or her soul in the clay, just as she had taught them to do, and the replicas were alive with fire and sensuality and rare beauty.

All but one, the one on the end, the one she had made. Over and over she had tried to recapture the magic. Late at night, early in the morning before the others arrived, time and time again she had tried until her fingers were raw, tried and failed. She knew now that she would always fail.

Grief shuddered through her. The magic was truly gone. Nothing would bring it back.

"I can still teach," she whispered, approaching the shelves with leaden steps. As soon as she got home, she would dismantle the studio in the spare bedroom and give away her equipment. Maybe then it wouldn't hurt so much.

She swiped the tears from her cheeks, then reached out to remove the flawed pot. Behind her the door opened with a force that drove it against the wall. Her hand jerked, sending the pot crashing to the floor.

Alarmed, she spun around to discover John standing just inside the door. "My God, John, you—"

"Casey's in labor," he interrupted, his face drawn and pale. "Alex isn't due back until tomorrow."

Aurora felt a flare of panic. "The midwife?"

"Is out on a call near Mesa Rojo. There are no phones out there. Casey wants me to drive her to the hospital in Gallup, and she wants you with her." He glanced over his shoulder toward her yellow station wagon. "It's a good thing I saw your car or I would have missed you."

Aurora swallowed the panic rising in her throat. "I'll get my purse."

Two minutes later, they took off in a shower of gravel.

The pockmarked road rocked the truck from side to side as John drove at a speed that had Aurora hanging on to the edge of the seat. His hands were white on the wheel, and his forearms bulged from the effort of keeping control of the wildly bucking vehicle.

His jaw was clenched, and his mouth was set in grim lines. Even the bones of his face radiated a brutal power barely held in check.

"Put on your seat belt," he ordered, sparing her a brief glance. "I don't intend to waste any time. Casey sounded damned scared."

Aurora nodded, a sick feeling spreading through her. This was all so familiar. Too familiar. Five years ago she had been the one who had been scared. For her baby and for herself.

They drove in tense silence. John kept his gaze on the road, and Aurora sat as far away from him as she could manage.

When they reached the intersection with the main road John shot a glance to the left, then skidded the truck into a screeching right turn. He increased speed until the scenery outside sped by in a brown blur.

Aurora tried to steady her breathing. Her hands and her face were clammy, and her heart jumped wildly in her chest. "Did she call Alex?"

"I didn't ask. I figured she'd tell us when we got there."

Recoiling from the impatience in his voice, she stared sightlessly at the road ahead. Snatches of memory came toward her like freeze-frame images—the breakneck ride to the hospital in the back of a state trooper's cruiser, the smell of sweat and blood clinging to her clothing, the sound of her moans, Morningstar's soothing words. The small body wrapped in one of Morningstar's towels.

"John...please..." She pressed her hand against her mouth, trying to contain the rising sickness.

"What's wr—damn."

Aurora closed her eyes, feeling the truck skid to the shoulder. Blindly she reached for the door handle, only to have the door open and strong arms reach for her.

John held her while she retched, then gently wiped her face with his handkerchief. He looked almost as sick as she felt.

"I'm all right," she said in a shaky voice. "We have to go. Casey shouldn't be alone."

John looked at her haunted eyes and her trembling mouth. For the first time he realized just how much she had suffered. The pit inside him yawned wider. No wonder she wouldn't allow herself to trust him again.

"Are you sure you're okay?" he asked helplessly. The things he wanted to tell her could never be said. He didn't have words strong enough to express his remorse and shame.

She nodded. "I'm fine, really. It...must have been something I ate."

He looked as though he were being pulled apart inside. Biting off a cry, she climbed into the truck and slammed the door. John jogged around the back and slid into the driver's seat.

"I'm sorry," he said stiffly before he reached for the key. Aurora knew that he was talking about his inability to love her. A terrible pain twisted inside her as she gave him a small smile.

"So am I."

They found Casey in bed. She was wearing a plain cotton nightshirt and was partially covered by a sheet. Her knees were raised, and she was panting loudly. Sweat beaded her forehead, and her cheeks were pale.

Butch sat on the floor by the bed, his green eye unblinking, his fur ruffled around his ears.

As they entered, Aurora in the lead, Casey looked up and managed a weak smile between breaths. "Sorry," she said when the contraction eased. "Baby seems to be in a hurry. I think it's too late to make the hospital."

John experienced a moment of raw terror. His hands began to shake, and he slid them into his back pockets before the women could notice.

"Sonofabitch," he muttered, staring at the ceiling.

Casey burst out laughing. "That's exactly what Alex would have said, except he would have said it in Spanish."

*"Ai, Dios mio!"* he added in honor of his friend.

"How far apart are the contractions?" Aurora asked quickly. "There might be time—"

"Five minutes."

Somehow Aurora managed a calm expression. "The midwife will probably be back in the pueblo in plenty of time," she told Casey.

Casey's gaze shifted to John, and he nodded. "I left her a note. No doubt she's on her way right now."

The contraction eased, and Casey collapsed, then muttered, "Thank God."

John turned to look at Aurora, and she saw the question in his dark solemn eyes. "We can handle things until the midwife arrives," she said, forcing a lilt of confidence into her voice. Inside she was shaking so badly she marveled that any sound had come out at all. "Can't we, Butch?" she said, sidestepping the cat on her way to Casey's bedside.

"Poor Butch," Casey said, bestowing a sympathetic glance on the cat she had once saved from a pair of hungry coyotes. "He hasn't been more than a few feet from me since Alex left."

Aurora plucked a tissue from the box by the bed and gently wiped Casey's brow.

"Thanks. I—oooh." Caught in the grip of another contraction, Casey leaned forward and began panting. Aurora supported Casey's back and talked to her in soothing tones. "Relax into it, go with the pain. Try not to fight."

Casey's laugh turned to a groan. "Relax," she managed, closing her eyes. "Easy for you to say."

John gripped the tall bedpost so tightly the tendons in his wrist stung. He hadn't felt this helpless since he had received the telegram from Rory's father.

"Tell me what to do," he told Aurora in a low voice. "This is a hell of a lot different from delivering a foal."

Aurora bit her lip, desperately trying to remember the things Morningstar had done for her when Dawn was born.

"We need newspapers, clean sheets and towels," she said, thinking aloud. "Some string, scissors, and, uh, boiling water to sterilize the scissors." Had she forgotten anything? It was so difficult to remember. So much that had happened during those long, agonizing hours was blurred by the pain and terror she'd felt.

"I'll see to it." John hesitated, then leaned over Casey and grasped her hand. "Hang in there, mama," he said, kissing her wet brow.

"You, too," she said, squeezing his hand.

"No problem." He scooped up Butch, who growled and tried to bite his hand. He grinned at Casey and left, taking the furious cat with him.

When he was gone, Casey let out a long sigh. "Alex is going to kill me," she said with a shaky laugh. "I gave him an ironclad guarantee nothing would happen while he was gone."

Aurora rubbed Casey's shoulders. "Is he on his way home?"

Casey nodded. "But even in the Jetstar it'll take him four hours or longer."

"Was he excited?"

"Was he ever! He was practically incoherent, getting his Spanish and English all mixed up." Casey beamed. "He ordered me to wait until he got here."

Aurora laughed, but inside she was raw. This was the way a baby should be welcomed, with excitement and joy and love.

"Can you hold the fort while I wash my hands?" she asked smoothing the pillow behind Casey's tousled head.

"Sure."

As Aurora stepped down the hall to the bathroom, she heard pots banging in the kitchen followed by the faint sound of running water. There was no sign of Butch, and she assumed John had locked the fiercely protective animal out of the house.

Seconds later, when she returned to the bedroom, Casey was panting through another contraction. When it eased, she sank back against the pillow. "They're getting worse," she murmured, closing her eyes. "The Lamaze teacher didn't say it would hurt so much."

"It'll be over soon," Aurora reassured her. "You're doing great."

Casey opened her eyes. "It really is going to be all right, isn't it, Rory? I mean, women have been having their babies at home for centuries, and...and the babies are fine. Ri-ight?"

Another contraction gripped her. Aurora took Casey's hand and talked her through it. "Don't worry. This is all normal. Perfectly normal."

But was it? Aurora couldn't help remembering her own labor. The minutes had seemed like hours; the hours, days. In the end the baby had died.

She bit her lip and tried to focus her attention on Casey.

Finally the contraction eased. "Whew, that was a rough one," Casey muttered as she rested against the pillow.

Aurora sneaked a look at her watch. It had been a little more than two minutes since the last contraction.

Casey closed her eyes, then stiffened. "Uh-oh, here comes another one."

"Relax, breathe, that's good. Very good, Casey. That's the way."

Three contractions later, John returned. He had rolled his sleeves above his elbows and smelled like the soap he'd used to wash his hands. Slung over his broad shoulder were two large white towels. In his arms he carried several folded sheets and a newspaper still wrapped in a brown mailing label.

"I put the string and scissors in the hot water," he said. "I figured we should leave them there until we...Susanna needs them."

Aurora nodded. "That's fine. I'm sure she'll be here soon." She knew her voice sounded strange. She hoped Casey hadn't noticed.

John dropped the sheets onto the mattress and stripped off the brown paper. "Hey, what do you know, the *Wall Street Journal*," he said with a grin, holding up the front page. "Hoss will be pleased that you're training this kid right."

Casey grinned, and Aurora gave John a grateful look. His air of calm filled the room, keeping her fears at bay.

"Put down the sheet first, under her hips, and then the paper," Aurora said as she eased the sheet from Casey's straining body. The contractions were coming faster and stronger.

Swiftly John did as he was told, the planes of his face stiff with concentration. As he bent forward, Aurora saw the sweat staining the back of his shirt between his shoulder blades. It wasn't hot in the stone house, far from it. Apparently, for all the calm he projected, John was as nervous as she was. He was simply better at masking his feelings.

Telling herself that she could do the same, she forced a light note into her voice. "It won't be long now."

Casey grinned through her pain. Her face was flushed, and her voice was weak. "Good, good."

But as the minutes stretched into an hour, into another, and then into three, Aurora began to realize that all was not well. There was scarcely any time between contractions now, and Casey was getting progressively weaker. Beneath her writhing body the sheets were drenched with sweat, and her hair was wet and plastered to her brow. Her eyes were tightly closed and she clung to John's hand. Her gasping breaths filled the room.

Aurora touched John's shoulder, then bent over to whisper, "Something's wrong. I can't see the baby's head."

His eyes grew dark, almost black. "Damn, that sounds like a breech, or at least that's what it's called in horses," he said in a low voice rife with worry. "If it is, the baby has to be turned."

"What's wrong?" Casey managed between pants. "Tell me, is something wrong?"

John bent low so that Casey could hear him. He hadn't been able to save Rory's child. He had to save this one. "Casey, can you hear me?" He fought to keep his voice steady.

At her weak nod, he said gently, "I'm going to turn the baby. I'll try not to hurt you, but I have to use my hands, find the baby's head. Don't push, okay?"

Another feeble nod. Her eyes were red-rimmed and smudged with dark circles. Her breathing was painful to hear.

"Promise me," she whispered, clinging to his arm.

John had trouble saying the words. He had made promises before and failed. But Casey had to believe in him, or her strength might flag. "I promise. Nothing's going to happen to this baby or you. Alex would beat me senseless if it did, and you know what a coward I am."

Casey's lips twitched. He kissed her damp cheek, then straightened and squared his shoulders.

"I have to wash my hands in alcohol," he told Aurora.

She glanced hurriedly at Casey, then clutched his arm and led him to the door. "Maybe you should call headquarters again. See if the midwife has returned."

He heard the whisper of terror in her voice, and his control faltered. He wanted to take her into his arms and keep her safe. And more than anything he wanted it to be his child he was bringing into the world. His and Rory's. But that would never happen, not now.

He forced a confident note into his answer. "We can't wait, Rory, but don't worry. Everything will be fine."

With the back of his fingers, he brushed the damp hair from her cheek. And then he turned and hurried out of the room.

Aurora took a deep breath and returned to Casey's bedside. The fear inside her felt alive, but she made herself ignore it. Casey needed her. Later, when this was over and the baby was safe, she would give in to the terror shaking her.

When John returned, she asked softly, "What can I do?"

He handed her a shallow pan holding the string and scissors. "Keep her calm, if you can." He rested his knee on the bed and leaned forward, then glanced up. "Pray for us."

Aurora could only nod as she placed the pan within reach.

"Casey, listen to me," he said, his voice filled with a sharp command. "I called the airport in Gallup. Alex's plane is due to land in ten minutes. I left a message for him to come straight here. The way he drives, he'll make it in less than an hour."

"An hour," Casey repeated through parched lips. "Alex."

Aurora riveted her gaze on Casey's face as she murmured quiet words of encouragement. Casey turned blindly toward the sound, and her hand crushed Aurora's with surprising strength.

John leaned over, his wide shoulders blocking his hands from Aurora's view. But she could see the ripple of muscle in his back as he worked desperately to turn the baby.

"Come on, little one, help me," John muttered, his voice ragged. Sweat trickled down his face and blotched his shirt. Casey cried out, twisting and turning until Aurora was forced to hold her down.

"Hurts so much," Casey grated. She rolled her head from side to side. "Alex...Alex...where are you?" Her voice was a thin thread.

John turned white, and his jaw clenched.

"Alex is coming," Aurora said over and over, somehow keeping her voice low and soothing. A buzzing began in her head, then grew louder. Her mouth went dry, and her throat tightened. The baby was going to die. Just like Dawn. She knew it.

"Finally," John muttered. His muscles bulged with strain, and his face was contorted with concentration as he drew the baby's head into the birth canal.

Casey screamed.

"Hang on," Aurora soothed. "It's almost over. I promise."

"Now, baby, come to me. That's right, move." Suddenly John grinned and withdrew his hands. "It worked, by God. It worked," he said, his voice exultant. "Push now, Casey. Push hard. Yeah, that's it. There's the head. All right. All *right*."

Aurora saw the naked relief in his face and knew then that he hadn't expected to succeed. But he hadn't given up. Not this man. He never gave up.

"C'mon Casey," he encouraged gently. "Let's get this baby born."

Casey's strident gasp mingled with John's cry of triumph as the child came into the world. As gently as he could he caught the slippery baby in his hands. For a moment, he couldn't speak.

Very carefully he turned the baby over. "You did it, Case," he managed finally. "A fantastic little girl."

In spite of her exhaustion, Casey struggled to sit up. Aurora rushed to support her.

"She's adorable," she told Casey. "With masses of black hair like her daddy. A perfect little girl."

"Alex has his daughter," Casey whispered in happy exhaustion. "Alexis Elena."

John rubbed the baby's back, and the tiny infant began to cry, loud lusty wails that made him laugh. "She's Alex's daughter, all right."

"Thank you. Both of you for saving my baby," Casey whispered, tears of joy running down her face. Aurora felt her own tears flow freely. Johns' eyes were dry as he gently laid the baby on Casey's stomach and took the scissors and string Aurora held out to him.

He cut the cord, then looked up. "Can you push again for me, Casey?"

Aurora's hands shook as she took the baby from Casey's stomach and wrapped her in one of the blankets she had found in the new nursery.

The baby was a warm, wonderful weight in her arms. A perfect little life only minutes old. And from the sounds of her squalls, she was very angry to have been taken from her dark, wet world into the bright cold.

The baby looked so much like Dawn it hurt. But strangely the terrible, wrenching sadness that usually accompanied thoughts of her daughter was gone.

Casey managed to do as John asked. When the afterbirth was delivered, he wrapped it and the newspapers in the sheet and threw the bundle into the corner.

Aurora leaned over and deposited the baby in Casey's arms. "She's beautiful," Casey murmured, her voice filled with awe. Slowly she unwrapped the blanket and looked at her daughter. "Look at those tiny feet. And that stubborn little chin." She looked up and laughed. "Just like her papa."

With a gentle finger Casey rubbed the soft cheek that was still wet with fluid. The baby mewed and turned her face, trying to suck.

Aurora felt a sudden fullness in her breasts. If things had been different, if John had been different, she might already be carrying another child.

Unable to watch the joy of the bonding between this mother and her daughter, she turned away. John was leaning with his back against the wall. He looked utterly drained.

John felt Aurora's gaze on his face. He raised his head and looked at her. An ashen weariness had replaced the natural bloom on her cheeks, and the mouth he longed to kiss was tight with tension. All during that hellish morning she had forced herself to be calm and supportive, holding Casey's hand until her own was red from Casey's frantic grip. For hours she had been living out her own nightmare, somehow making herself do things that had to be tearing her apart inside.

He wanted to hold her and comfort her the best way he knew how. But she didn't want him.

He had tried to tell himself he loved her. But he knew deep down he didn't, not in the way she defined love. He had failed.

"I'll check on Alex's plane," he said, and walked out.

"She really is a doll," Aurora told Casey as she finished bathing the baby in the large dishpan she'd brought into the bedroom because Casey couldn't bear to have her daughter out of her sight.

"Hm," Casey murmured drowsily. She was trying valiantly to stay awake until Alex arrived.

Aurora smiled as she diapered the baby and pulled a soft flannel shirt over the tiny sweet-smelling body. She gave Casey about five more minutes before the body's natural instinct for sleep took over.

"Are you sure Alex is coming?" Casey asked for the third time.

"You heard John. Alex's plane landed on time. He'll be here." Aurora wrapped the baby in a blanket and started to hand her to Casey, only to discover that Casey's eyes were closed. She was breathing heavily but evenly as though she had fallen into an exhausted sleep.

Aurora glanced at the rumpled, wet sheets and Casey's sprawled body, then shifted her gaze to the open door.

Making up her mind, she carried the baby into the living room. John was standing in front of the window, gazing out at the bright autumn afternoon, his hands stretching the tight pockets of his jeans. He seemed so lonely.

Pain clutched at her throat. She would be lonely, too, when she left here. She suspected that this time it would take her a very long time to stop loving him.

"Are you all right?" she asked softly.

John turned his head to look at her. "Fine," he answered curtly. "How's Casey?"

Aurora walked toward him, the baby's small head pressed into the curve of her neck. "She's sleeping. I'm going to straighten up before Alex gets here."

Her voice sounded stilted, but John's expression didn't change. "Should be soon."

She nodded, then glanced at the bundle in her arms. "Would you like to hold the baby? I hate to put her in that big crib all alone."

He look startled but pleased as he rubbed his hands over his hard flanks in an endearing gesture of masculine insecurity. "I've never held a baby before. What if I do something wrong?"

"You won't. Just make sure you support her head." She smiled at the awkwardness with which he held out his arms. When her fingers brushed his arm, a feeling of terrible sadness welled up inside her. When she had been pregnant, she had dreamed of the moment when she would hand John his child for the first time.

"She doesn't weigh anything," he said, his voice husky. He stared down at the small red face peeking out from the folds of the soft blanket.

The baby frowned, then began making sucking motions with her rosy mouth. John laughed as he rubbed his thumb over her cheek.

The pain inside Aurora was like an icy hand squeezing her heart. "I have to see to Casey," she said, her voice choked. She was nearly running when she reached the bedroom and closed the door.

Twenty minutes later, she returned.

John sat in the rocking chair by the window. The soft squeak of the old chair and the loud purring of the cat curled up at his feet were the only sounds in the cozy room.

His head was turned away from her and bowed slightly, his face in profile. She couldn't see his eyes, only the rise of his high cheekbone and the shiny black hair that brushed his ear.

She paused, struck by the poignant beauty of his scarred masculine arm cradling the tiny child against his wide, strong chest. One of the baby's small pink hands was wrapped around his forefinger, and she was staring up at him with deep blue eyes, her delicate features intense as only a baby's could be.

The baby whimpered, and John bent forward to kiss the top of her silky head.

Aurora stifled a sob, and he stiffened. As he turned to look at her, she took a step back as though warding off a physical blow. His dark eyes were filled with an anguish that made her cry out. Tears streamed unchecked over his hard cheeks.

"Oh, John," she whispered as she hurried to his side. She knelt by the chair and gripped his arm. "Casey's fine. The baby's fine. You saved her life. Everything's all right, now."

Slowly he shook his head. "It'll never be right, and it's my fault."

"No—"

"Yes." His voice carried a shudder of pain. "When I put off my trip home, I told myself that you were in good hands. You had your parents, the best doctor in El Paso. Nothing would go wrong, I thought. And what the hell, I would be there in plenty of time, wouldn't I? Sure I would. I had it all calculated, handled just the way I had handled every other damn thing in my life."

"You couldn't have known—"

"If I'd been in the States, you wouldn't have been here alone. Dawn..." He stopped, his face contorted by pain. Stunned, Aurora realized that this was the first time she had heard him mention the baby's name. And the first time he had cried.

She had been wrong to think that John couldn't feel pain. He was hurting, as much as she had hurt. Only his pain seemed raw and twisting where hers had dulled through the years to a constant ache.

He shifted his gaze to the tiny child in his arms. His voice shook as he continued. "I wanted our baby, Rory. And I miss her, even though I never saw her. She was a part of us, something so precious, I—" His voice broke, and he closed his eyes in a spasm of terrible pain. For the first time she had a glimpse of the depth of the emotion he had been trying so hard to keep from erupting.

John tugged his finger from the baby's tenacious grasp, then passed Alexis into Aurora's arms. He stood and, with a strong hand under Aurora's arm, helped her to her feet.

"You were right about me, Rory," he said in a ragged voice. "I can't love anyone. When I try, I only end up hurting them. I won't risk doing that again. Not ever."

John laid a hand against her cheek, needing her strength as much as she needed his. When she leaned into his palm, he felt as though he were dying inside. If he gave into the longing inside him, if he held her again, he knew that he wouldn't be able to stop himself from begging her for one more chance.

And that would kill him.

"Take care of yourself, my love. I'll always wish I could have loved you." He turned and walked out.

# Chapter 14

She smells so sweet." Casey pressed a soft kiss to her daughter's silky head.

Aurora managed a smile. Numb with exhaustion, she had curled up in the chair she'd dragged in from the living room. "I think she's going to be a good baby. She hasn't cried once since I finished bathing her."

Casey traced the baby's delicate black eyebrows with a gentle finger. "I know this was hard for you, Aurora," she said in a subdued tone. "If I had thought she was going to be born so quickly, I wouldn't have asked John to bring you." She raised her head to give Aurora an apologetic smile. "I'm so sorry things haven't worked out for you and John."

Aurora sighed. "Me, too," she said in a sad voice. "I love him so much. This time I'm not sure I'll ever be able to stop."

"John loves you, too. Maybe you can't see it, but I can. I saw the way he was before you came back. He was only half alive."

Aurora stared at the floor. Casey was wrong. "He told me he couldn't love anyone."

Casey used one hand to push herself higher on the pillows. "For a long time Alex denied that he loved me, too. It was his way of surviving the pain he felt inside."

Aurora shook her head. "John doesn't lie, not even to himself."

"I'm not saying he's lying. Maybe he really does believe he can't love." She took a shaky breath. "But look at the things he's done for you. John is a proud man, as proud as Alex, and just as driven to succeed. And yet, he sacrificed his career to come back here to fight for you. He risked losing everything, even his home because you asked him not to sell the Santa Ysabel. He even risked death to change the man who had hurt you. He did all those things because he loved you so much nothing else mattered. If that isn't love, I don't know what is."

Aurora stared at her friend, her mind replaying Casey's words. Casey was right. John *was* a private man with a lot of pride. It must have cost him dearly to tell her of the humiliation he had suffered at the hands of his father.

But he hadn't done it in a bid for sympathy. No, he had done it because he was fighting to win her back. Over and over he had taken risks, some that must have been intensely threatening to him, to prove to her that he was no longer the man who had hurt her so callously.

When they had made love, she had sensed that change with every kiss, every lingering caress. But like the magic in the clay, the meaning of that difference had eluded her, hovering just beyond her ability to find it.

But now she knew.

John loved as violently as he hated. He loved her with a depth that made her shake inside.

"I was afraid," she whispered, her voice splintered. "I love him, but I refused to trust him."

"You were hurt," Casey said gently. "You were protecting yourself. I know what that's like. I did it, too—until I realized it hurt more to live without Alex."

Aurora took a ragged breath. She had never been brave. She wasn't sure she was brave now. She only knew she loved John more than anything else in the world.

But what about him? He had given her everything he had to give, and she had told him it wasn't enough. No wonder he wasn't willing to risk his heart again.

*I didn't understand, my darling. I'm so sorry.*

Could she somehow convince him to try again? Could she convince him that his love wouldn't destroy her when he was so sure it would?

Maybe her words couldn't, just as his words hadn't convinced her to trust him again. But what about her actions? Maybe she could show him.

She bit her lip. How? she thought desperately. What could she possibly do?

Suddenly she remembered the pot he'd smashed against the wall. He had seen her anguish in that pot. He had understood, even if he hadn't been able to feel it.

She would make another pot, not a copy, but an original. She would put it all into the clay—her understanding, her forgiveness, her need, her love.

But what if she failed again? What if there was nothing there when she finished?

"I have to try," she whispered to herself. She glanced up to see tears glistening in Casey's warm gray eyes. "I won't let him go."

Casey's face split into a grin. "I'm so glad—"

Just then the front door banged open. "Casey? Are you all right?" Alex burst into the room, breathing hard as though he had run all the way from Gallup. "John's message said to come here and—"

He stopped abruptly, his piercing black gaze fixed on the baby. *"Ai, Dios mio,"* he said. "You really had a baby." He sounded stunned.

Casey laughed, her face radiant. "With a little help from my friends." She folded back the blanket, then touched the little girl's cheek. "Say hello to your papa, Alexis." The baby opened her eyes and blinked tiny black lashes in a drowsy greeting.

Alex swallowed hard. "A little girl." He approached slowly, a look of reverence on his face. "She's beautiful already, like her mama." He slipped an arm hand around Casey's shoulder and bent his head to give her a deep, loving kiss. When the kiss ended, he brushed a hand over his daughter's small head, then kissed her forehead and whispered softly, "_Te amo_, Alexis."

Casey touched his cheek, her fingers wiping away the tears as gently as he had kissed their daughter. "Thank you," he told his wife. "Now I have it all."

Feeling like an intruder, Aurora swallowed the tears clogging her throat. She wanted to have what Casey and Alex had. She wanted to hold John's baby in her arms. She wanted him to look at her in the same way that Alex looked at Casey. She wanted to give him the same kind of happiness she saw on Alex's face.

She stood, feeling as though she were drowning. "I, uh, it's time for me to leave you two alone." She edged toward the door, but Alex stopped her before she reached the end of the bed.

"Hey, don't go because of me," he said with a sheepish look as he pulled her into a rough hug. "Thank you for being here."

"Congratulations, Papa," she said, her voice breaking.

"I owe you," he told her when he released her. "Any time, any place."

Aurora shook her head. "John delivered the baby, Alex, not me. He's the one you owe."

She gave Casey a hug. "Can I borrow your car?"

"Of course. The keys are in it."

"Wish me luck."

"You know I do. I wish you both luck."

Aurora thanked her, then turned and hurried from the room.

Alex waited until the front door closed, then gave Casey a quizzical look. "What's going on?"

Casey beamed. "Aurora is going to fight for her man."

"Sounds like a hell of an idea to me. Whose was it, yours?"

"No, hers. I just pointed out a few similarities between you and John."

He circled the bed, kicked off his loafers and eased in next to her. With a gentleness he revealed only to Casey, he drew her against his chest. "Like what?"

She snuggled against him, her lashes fluttering as the day caught up to her. "Like the fact you're both stubborn and proud and absolutely wonderful."

Alex dropped a kiss on her shoulder. "I'm glad you fought for me, *querida*," he said in a ragged voice.

"So am I," Casey whispered as she smiled down at their daughter. "So am I."

Aurora snapped on the light in the studio. Night had fallen while she had been driving back to the pueblo. The room was cool and silent. She felt completely alone.

Something crunched under her feet, drawing her tired gaze. Shards of the pot she had broken that morning littered the floor, taunting her with her failure.

Fear seized her. Her hands began to shake uncontrollably. And then she remembered the band on John's wrist, the symbol of his willingness to risk humiliation and pain and even death to change. "Please help me," she prayed to the spirit he had called Woman-Of-Us-All. "Please let the magic be there for me one last time."

She took a deep breath, willing away her fear. This time she wasn't making a pot for herself. She was making one for John. Even if he rejected her, she wanted him to know how much she loved him.

Moving quickly, she assembled the things she would need, then shrugged into one of the smocks hanging from a peg on the wall. She pulled up a stool and reached for the clay.

It had been weeks since she had tried to work, and her hands were stiff as she lifted the damp cloth from the moist earth.

She filled her mind with thoughts of John, allowing her hands and fingers to find their own rhythm. Slowly she worked the smooth material until it felt alive.

The feeling crept up her hand, her wrist, her arm, reminding her of the warm resiliency of John's skin. His chest had been hard muscle and elastic sinew. His shoulders and arms had been firm, exciting her with the power she felt there, power that she sensed had been rigidly restrained because he didn't want to hurt her.

She shivered, but she didn't stop. She couldn't. Every movement she made was dictated by memories of John, of his rare slow smile that was like a fight he gave her, his gentle teasing that had made her laugh even when she'd felt like crying, his indomitable spirit that wouldn't let him give up, even when the odds were against him.

The first rays of the sun were lighting the horizon when she finished. Blinking her stinging eyes, she stared at the pot in the middle of the wheel. The clay was still damp and the surface unglazed, but the design stood out in stark relief on the smooth surface.

The shape was simple and clean. The complex pattern etched into the clay was bold without being arrogant. Great strength tempered with a hidden compassion was carved into every line. Immense power restrained by gentleness was reflected in the daring shape.

Carefully, reverently, she touched the noble curve of the lip. John's spirit, his fierce courage and his quiet pride called out to her.

"My darling John," she whispered, pain clutching her heart. "I'll always love you."

Tears filled her eyes and spilled over onto her cheeks. The pot was the best she had ever done.

Loving John had given her back the magic.

John leaned against the corner of his desk and closed his eyes. He sighed and rolled his head from side to side, trying to ease the painful kinks in his neck.

He was tired inside and out. His muscles burned from the endless bales of hay he'd bucked into the loft in an effort to drive Rory from his mind.

The dull drone of voices floated down the hall from the council chambers where several of his supporters were still celebrating his victory.

The recall vote had ended in a tie. In accordance with tribal law, the shaman had been obligated to cast the deciding vote. He would never forget the shock that had traveled through him when Grandfather Horse Herder had cast his vote in favor of retaining him as chairman. Grandfather had delivered his opinion with such eloquence and dignity that not even Diego had dared challenge the old man. Because John had brought his son back to him, John deserved to remain in office.

He had won, by God. So why wasn't he happy? Why wasn't he celebrating?

"Good morning."

John jerked his head toward the sound of Aurora's soft voice. She stood in the doorway dressed in white, a pot, newly made by the looks of it, in her hands.

But it was her face that riveted his gaze. The elegant lines of her fragile features seemed even more beautiful. His breath stopped. In the muted light she looked like a vision he'd seen in his delirium. The woman of his heart.

"I saw Ralph outside. He said you were reelected chairman."

"By one vote, but I'll take it."

Aurora wished that he would smile. Or hold her. Or kiss her. But he had withdrawn from her, protecting the soft part of himself from more pain. Somehow she had to push through the shell that he'd slowly been learning to shed.

"He also said you found the money for the doctor."

John took a careful breath. "So that's why you're here. To find out if I broke my word to you."

Aurora shook her head. "You would never do that."

John heard the ring of certainty in her voice, and it tore him to shreds inside. Two weeks ago he would have been the happiest man alive knowing that she believed in him. Now that particular truth only rubbed salt into the raw places that would take a long time to heal.

"If you came to say goodbye, consider it said. I hope you have a safe trip back to Dallas. And a successful year."

When would this biting need he had for her go away? he wondered as he braced his hands against the desk to keep from reaching for her.

She set the pot on the desk. "Actually, I came to give you this."

John stared at her gift. He had never seen anything more beautiful, not even "Dream's End." "I can't take this," he said in a choked voice. It would hurt too much to see it every day and know that he could never have the woman who made it.

"I made it for you," she said, making herself ignore his words. "To tell you I love you."

She saw shock come into his eyes, followed immediately by the wary look of a man used to protecting his heart. His lashes lowered until they made black shadows on his high cheekbones. He didn't believe her.

Tears stung her eyes. "No one is ever going to love you the way I love you." She took a deep breath. "I want your kind of love, John. Just the way you know how to give it, more than I've ever wanted anything in my life," she said fiercely, her voice strong.

"No, Rory. It would kill me to fail you again." Only his eyes moved as he watched her. She saw doubt and pain there and buried deep in the midnight depths an emotion that looked like the faint glimmer of hope.

"I'll have to go back to Dallas to tender my resignation and pack up my things," she told him softly, "and then I'll be back." Her voiced wobbled, and she lifted her chin.

"Don't," he said in a rough tone. "I'm still the same man you refused to marry—"

"If you won't let me live with you, I'll live in the apartment you fixed up for me. And if you kick me out of there, I'll... I'll build my own house like Alex did." She paused for breath.

"I really think you would," he muttered. He was terrified that if he moved, if he reached for her, she would drift away from him, like the woman in the vision.

Aurora moved closer until she could feel the tension surrounding him. "I was afraid five years ago. Afraid to face the empty nursery, afraid to have another child. I'm not afraid now."

"What about children, Rory? What if I can't give them what they need?"

She raised a hand to caress his cheek. He stiffened but didn't pull away. "I saw your face when you looked at Alexis, John. I saw your tears. You said you couldn't cry, but you cried for our baby. You cried because you loved her."

His gaze fell. For so long he had kept a part of himself locked away. He was afraid to let anyone get close enough to see the real man inside, the man who just wanted to know love.

"I'm not even sure what love is," he said, his voice deep and tortured. "I can't promise you I'll ever be able to say the words and be sure I mean them."

A smile curved her lips and warmed her eyes until they shimmered with emotion. "You don't have to say the words. Not for me, John. Not ever for me. I can feel how much you mean them."

She took his hand and pressed it against the clay. "Feel how much I need you, John. Feel how much I love you."

"Rory, I can't—"

"Yes, you can. The man who let himself cry will let himself feel."

John closed his eyes, desperately wanting to believe. At first he saw only darkness and felt the same biting regret that had been with him for days.

*Feel how much I love you.*

The pressure built inside until he had to struggle for each breath. In his heart and in his soul he longed for her love with a violence that nearly drove him to his knees.

But I don't know how to love you in return, he wanted to cry out to her.

In the black emptiness a light began to glimmer, growing brighter and brighter until it seemed to surround him. In the light he saw a woman's face, ethereal and wreathed with kindness. Woman-of-Us-All smiled at him, her eyes bathing him in gentleness.

*You have done well, Warrior Who Walks Alone. You have waged a fierce battle, offering yourself without asking anything in return, and you have won. The love you seek to give is like life itself to the woman of your heart. Deny it and you both perish.*

The woman faded, but the light remained.

Rory, he thought. My love. My dearest love. As long as she was with him, he would know love.

John began to shake. His control snapped, and he reached for her. His mouth found hers in a feverish kiss that gave as well as took. His arms tightened until he could feel all of her against him.

He tore his mouth from hers and buried his face against her neck. "Rory," he whispered, afraid to let her go. "Are you sure?"

"I love you, John," Aurora whispered, trembling with hope and dread. "I'm not leaving. I'm not ever leaving."

"You better mean it," he whispered hoarsely. "Because it would kill me to let you go again."

He didn't deserve her love, but he would take it because he was only half alive without it.

Aurora pressed her hands against his strong back, holding him tenderly as a hard shudder shook his powerful body. "I mean it," she said, tears of joy coursing down her cheeks. "I'll never leave you again."

* * * * *

 *Diamond Jubilee Collection*

## It's our 10th Anniversary...
## and *you* get a present!

This collection of early Silhouette
Romances features novels written
by three of your favorite authors:

**ANN MAJOR**—*Wild Lady*
**ANNETTE BROADRICK**—*Circumstantial Evidence*
**DIXIE BROWNING**—*Island on the Hill*

* These Silhouette Romance titles were first published in the early 1980s
  and have not been available since!

* Beautiful Collector's Edition bound in antique green simulated leather to
  last a lifetime!

* Embossed in gold on the cover and spine!

This special collection will not be sold in retail stores and is only available
through this exclusive offer.
Look for details in all Silhouette series published in June, July and August.

DJC-1

**Diana Palmer's fortieth story for Silhouette . . . chosen
as an Award of Excellence title!**

# CONNAL
## Diana Palmer

Next month, Diana Palmer's bestselling LONG, TALL
TEXANS series continues with CONNAL. The skies
get cloudy on C. C. Tremayne's home on the range
when Penelope Mathews decides to protect him—by
marrying him!

One specially selected title receives the Award of
Excellence every month. Look for CONNAL in August
at your favorite retail outlet . . . only from Silhouette
Romance.

CON-1

You'll flip . . . your pages won't!
Read paperbacks *hands-free* with

# Book Mate • I

**The perfect "mate" for all your romance paperbacks**
**Traveling • Vacationing • At Work • In Bed • Studying**
**• Cooking • Eating**

Perfect size for all standard paperbacks, this wonderful invention makes reading a pure pleasure! Ingenious design holds paperback books OPEN and FLAT so even wind can't ruffle pages – leaves your hands free to do other things. Reinforced, wipe-clean vinyl-covered holder flexes to let you turn pages without undoing the strap . . . supports paperbacks so well, they have the strength of hardcovers!

Pages turn WITHOUT opening the strap

SEE-THROUGH STRAP

Reinforced back stays flat

Built in bookmark

BOOK MARK

BACK COVER HOLDING STRIP

10 x 7¼ opened
Snaps closed for easy carrying, too